HOLY PARROT

HOLY PARROT

ANGEL A

ANGEL'S LEAP

Angel's Leap Pty Ltd

Contents

First published by Angel's Leap PTY LTD 2022

Copyright © 2022 by Angel's Leap Pty Ltd

This novel is entirely a work of fiction. The names, characters and incidents
portrayed in it are the work of the author's imagination. Any resemblance to
actual persons, living or dead, events or localities is entirely coincidental.

Angel A asserts the moral right to be identified as the author of this work.

First edition

Paperback ISBN: 978-0-9876222-5-9

EPub: ISBN: 978-0-9876222-6-6

Prologue

I wasn't there when it happened. Plenty of people in the village were witnesses, though. Their testimonies all led to the same likely conversation. They were speaking to each other in Spanish, the dominant language of Colombia, their country. Despite being a pleasant fishing village on the Caribbean coast, Buritaca gets only a spattering of visitors. So only a few people in the village speak English. Luckily, Palomino, thirty minutes down the coast, is more of a catchment for travellers with wanderlust in search of pristine beaches and a palm-studded horizon. Thirty minutes in the other direction is one of the best of the Colombian Caribbean gems. Cabo San Juan del Guía, in the heart of the Tayrona National Park, is the patch of paradise most dream of for their escape from more mundane realities.

I prefer a lack of distraction for my work. For a scientist who is studying provincial culture and its outstanding peculiarities, throngs of beach bums in thongs are just a nuisance. Despite Buritaca being somewhat hidden between the crowd-pleasers on either side, I sometimes think I spend more time being a translator for foreign visitors than doing my job. There have been a plethora of things to distract me from my job since this conversation occurred. So once again, I'll translate what was allegedly said on that inauspicious day as well as what transpired in its wake:

"Pablo, I'm pregnant. You have to marry me."

"You're pregnant? Marry you? But we're only sixteen."

"I don't care. Marry me, or my father is going to kill me. And I don't want to have this child alone. He needs a father."

"I'm sorry, Maria. I can't."

"But you have to!"

"No, I can't. I can't be part of this. I'm sorry. You're on your own."

Pablo then apparently ran away. Multiple witnesses reported what Maria then screamed at Pablo's fleeing heels.

"Pablo! Get back here! I'm going to kill you if you don't get back here!"

Chapter 1

Her name was Maria. I don't know if I adored her at the beginning, as I simply can't remember a time when I didn't. I had to leave the one person who had become the centre of my world, and I was not alone in that claim of interest. She had become transcendent in the eyes of millions.

We would never have met if not for my work at the Buritaca Facilidad de Ciencia Buritaca (the science facility of Buritaca). I was an undergraduate science student from Melbourne University on a study grant provided by Pravus, a well-funded pharmaceutical company. The Pravus directors had their eye on the prize to discover what made provinces around the world, like Magdalena, special. My specialty was genetics, which apparently made me perfect for the job. I was one of the "lucky" students nominated for a grant to study abroad. Their vision was to discover if there was a particular elixir that could account for the exceptional health outcomes of the residents, replicate it, and then sell it.

Buritaca itself was a small fishing village. Local fishermen had found a protected haven in which to moor their boats in the Buritaca River that bordered the village. My office overlooked the river to the sandbar that protected the village from the wilder waves that tore at the seashells and silica dunes in the monsoon seasons. Beyond that, the Caribbean dream stretched for as far as the eye could see, and the towering peaks of the Sierra Nevada mountain range served as the backdrop to the entire dreamscape. The palms along the coastline added a draped

fringe to the blanket of wild and lush growth woven over the steeply
elevating terrain.

I could have saved the Pravus shareholders all their money just by
showing them photos of the celestial surrounds. The little patch of
paradise was perfect in so many ways. I was about to meet an opposing
opinion.

Although my job was to discover something special in the region,
I wasn't expecting the person I stumbled across. To be clear, when we
met, it wasn't some out-of-the-blue version of Stendhal Syndrome, with
me overwhelmed and captivated by a vision of beauty that I spotted
gracing the beach of an exotic oasis. I actually thought she looked kind
of scruffy. She was wearing a light knee-length dress that had probably
started as white at the beginning of its life. Buritaca's unpaved roads
left us all lightly frosted in brown dust by the end of the day, and
it clung to our clothing in a brew of humidity and sweat. Her dress
had bright red butterflies, or maybe they were flowers, patterned haphazardly within the cotton weave. Dark brown curlicues extended well
below the shoulder strings of her dress and, thanks to the humidity,
hung like the tails of a damp mop that needed a good rinse.

I had stepped out of my office to have a smoke. The fact that I
was a scientist chosen by Pravus for being promising and bright made
this habit enough to cast doubt over their illusions of me. The office
was really just a glorified pressed-mud hut. It looked to be held together somehow with bamboo shards and spit. The roof was the same
as every other dwelling in the village—thatched straw or reeds—and I
never took the time to discover how rain didn't make its way through
the maze of prostrate vegetation. There was an embossed sign out front
declaring to everyone that it was a science facility despite the ram-
shackle construction.

She was standing in the middle of the street. It caught my eye because anyone or anything in the middle of the street was likely to get bowled over by a truck or a pack of wild-eyed kids on scooters. She was holding her belly, perhaps in the way that pregnant women often do, but her expression suggested hurt or confusion. I figured she wouldn't be there, in the middle of a road, unless a despondent moment had stopped her in her tracks. I walked toward her as I lit my cigarette. My Spanish was, and remains to this day, embarrassingly pathetic. My defence is that the grant application and implementation were only months apart. I didn't have time to do any lessons. So I had to learn the language on the fly.

"Would you like one?" I asked her in Spanish as I held out the packet of cigarettes. Perhaps the second indictment against any suggestion of intelligence on my part.

"I can't. I'm pregnant. Anyway, I'm only sixteen," she replied, also in Spanish. At least one of us had an inkling of smarts in the moment.

"Sorry. I didn't know."

"That I'm pregnant, or that I'm sixteen?"

"Either."

"Your Spanish is terrible," she said in English.

I guessed my lack of foreign language skills was hurting her ears. I followed her lead and continued in English. "We're off to a great start, aren't we? What's your name?"

"Maria."

Her face was pretty, but her eyes were the jewels that grabbed your attention. Just like her sun-kissed skin, they were brown, but with golden highlights like a tiger's eye crystal. I think I must have paused a little too long, resting in her charm, because she shifted uneasily.

"So you speak English?" I asked. It's all I could think of to say to break my awkward pause.

"A little. For the tourists. Are you a tourist?"

Now I felt as though I was being thoroughly assessed.

"Do I look like a tourist?"

"Everyone who isn't born here is a tourist. There's no reason to stay."

"Well, you're still here."

"I'm not planning to stay," she answered with a frank sense of certainty. She began rubbing her stomach anxiously.

"Do you need help?"

"Buy me something to eat," she said, with the conspicuous absence of a request in her tone.

"I did ask, I guess."

I escorted her to a small food stall typical of the region where deep-fried offerings displayed on racks behind glass accompanied packaged sweets and snacks dangling from strings on pegs. Maria started helping herself to some food and didn't seem to lose pace despite her hands being full.

"Are you gestating a footy team in there?"

"What?"

"That's a lot of food."

"My mother needs food too. I have to take care of her," she said without pausing her gathering efforts.

"Is there anyone else you would like me to feed?" I added, hoping she would notice my sarcasm.

"Well, I'd normally get food for Pablo, but right now, I want to choke him with something."

"Who's Pablo?"

"Nobody. Thanks for the food. What's your name?" she asked, her arms laden with supplies that I was about to pay for.

"Leonard, and you're welcome," I replied. I paid the vendor without protest, which was a sign of the influence this curious young lady already had over me.

"You talk funny," she pointed out with a candour that I was warming to.

"I'm Australian. Maybe that's why."

"So you come from a long way from here?"

"Yes."

"Maybe that's where I should go. Australia." Her disappointment with life in her village was now obvious. "Why're you here?"

"I'm a science student from Melbourne University." I could see the word *why* still lingering on her lips, so I continued. "I'm here to find out why you all live so long."

"We live long? Here?"

"Yes, you do," I said, but her expression reminded me that living any longer in the village was not in her game plan.

Although Buritaca clearly held no further interest for Maria, it was captivating for me. It's a village within the Magdalena Department. It was special because they had recently recognised it as one of the few "blue zones" in the world. Blue zones were regions where the resident population appeared to live long, healthy lives beyond the normal expectations of other world territories. Magdalena extends from the Caribbean Sea to La Guajira and Cesar to the north and east. It borders Bolivar and Atlantico to the west and the Cesar Department to the east.

Maria could have left with her bounty, but she seemed interested in discovering more. So I continued to justify my presence. "I'm here to find out why you all live so long so Pravus can bottle whatever it is."

"Who is Pravus?"

"A drug company."

"It's probably something in the water," she concluded.

"Then Pravus will soon sell bottled water."

"Thanks for the food, Leonard." She smiled for the first time and turned to leave.

"Again, you're welcome." It had been a brief but captivating moment and a minimal investment to be rewarded by that smile. "You know, you don't look very pregnant. Are you sure it's not just a big worm in there that's making you so hungry?"

"Of course I'm sure," she said, seeming unsure of herself for the first time in the conversation.

"So you did a pregnancy test already?"

"What's that?"

"A pregnancy test? The baby produces a hormone called HCG—Human Chorionic Gonadotropin. This hormone will be in your urine." Adding such inconsequential detail was the third stupid thing I did for the day. *Not everybody is interested in science*, I reminded myself.

"What?"

"It's a test—to confirm you're pregnant."

Either she wasn't interested, or I still hadn't explained it correctly because she spun on her heel again to leave. A few steps out, she called back over her shoulder, "Do you want to see the water?"

"What water?" I had to catch up that her mind was back on the discussion of why I was there.
"The water of longevity?"

"Yes. It's a secret, though."

"Secret water? I'm intrigued." I actually was.

"Do you want to see it or not?" she repeated, reminding me again that directness was her style.

"Yes, I want to see it," I blurted. Did I? Unlike her, I wasn't so sure of my choices that day.

"Then meet me here an hour before the sun rises tomorrow. And then after you do the pregnancy test for me," she said, again in a commanding tone.

"Seriously?"

And then she walked away.

Chapter 2

The science facility had a small kitchenette, shower, and toilet facilities. It was my fault that I didn't read the fine print in my contract regarding accommodations—I think it only stated "accommodations included"—so I had no one to blame. I wasn't exactly expecting a Shangri La franchise in a Colombian fishing village. It actually suited me to finish my work and just crash on the bed sometimes. It also allowed me quick and easy access to the lab when I wanted to check results that necessitated waiting. The lab room itself wasn't much. It had just enough space for my laptop, two microscopes perched on a foldaway table, a centrifuge, a ThermoFisher genetics analyser, a quantitative polymer chain reaction instrument, and a petri-dish fridge. The standout feature was the antiquated knee-high Fort Knox safe tucked under the foldaway for all my test results. Pravus was adamantly keen to hide these from its competitors. Its next home was surely going to be a museum.

That night, after meeting Maria, I hadn't slept well. My bedroom was a spare room in the science facility that was just big enough to be habitable. The bed was comfortable, although it couldn't have been a standard-sized mattress. Being six feet tall, I found sleeping diagonally was really the only way to stretch out. I had gone to bed with no intention of considering her peculiar invitation. I had awakened unexpectedly in the early hours of the morning with my heart racing. The moment was akin to waking startled just before you hit the ground in a dream involving falling. Although I woke with a start, it felt like my mind was returning from somewhere afar, and I had to wait to orientate myself. I'm usually not good at remembering dreams, but because I was so rattled, and the images experienced were so perplexing, I remembered the details vividly.

The dream possibly influenced my participation in the forthcoming events in Buritaca. It began inside a building in front of a mirrored elevator. The elevator opened, and I stepped in. I didn't know how tall the building was, but the number of buttons available to press seemed inordinate. I pressed the button for the top floor. My dream's lift was super-fast. The doors opened again almost immediately to the sound of a customary *ping* that signalled arrival, revealing a long, white-walled corridor. In fact, everything was white, and it was difficult to differentiate the walls from the floor or the ceiling. It was difficult to measure distance as well, because there was nothing outstanding to focus on. There was someone at the other end of the corridor, so I stepped out of the lift into the bleached nothingness. I somehow found myself at the other end of the corridor, again somewhat instantaneously. I recognised the person standing there. It was Maria. She was in a white long-sleeved shirt and skirt combination that was as pallid as the surroundings. Her shirt hung loosely over the skirt and splayed open at the bottom to allow for the overt pregnancy behind it to protrude. She smiled at me, her tiger's eye irises glistening brightly. She placed her hands on her rotund belly and then calmly opened her stomach as though it were a suitcase. Blinding light emanated from the opening she created. It filled the corridor and consumed everything, including me. That's when I woke up.

The hype of activity in my mind and the stampede of rapid heartbeats pounding in my chest had thwarted any hope I had for reasonable slumber. I turned on the light and checked the clock. My eyes reacted to the light of my bedside lamp, causing me to relive the fragment of the dream when Maria opened her belly, and I somehow groggily merged this with the recent memory of Maria's odd invitation to discover the water that was apparently special. It was just before dawn. Surely she hadn't been serious, and the dream was just my mind playing with recent events? I was awake enough that I got up to make myself a drink, hoping it might flush out the excess activity going on in my head.

I was a sucker for certainty. The pitfall of an academic mind. As I waited for the kettle to boil, I slipped on my shorts and shirt and opened the front door. In the minimal predawn light, I thought I could see the silhouette of someone standing on the road in the distance. I slipped on my sandals and headed out. I wanted to know for sure if Maria had been serious.

"You're late!" Maria called out as she paced toward me.

"I really didn't know if I was meant to take you seriously," I defended sheepishly.

"You'll be glad you did."

"Why so early?"

"Papa collects the coffee workers in his truck and takes them out to the plantation in the mountains now. I help him prepare the truck every morning," she explained as she took my arm and turned me around. "And it's only now you see that." She pointed to a solitary bright star that sat low on the horizon.

"What's that?"

"Where we're going," she replied as she pulled me by my arm in the star's direction. "We have to hurry. We're already late. The star disappears when the sun comes up, and I won't be able to show you how to get there."

Within minutes, we crossed the highway known locally as the Troncal del Caribe, which divided the coastline from the imposing Sierra Nevada, and entered up through the forest marge. I hadn't ventured into the mountains since I had arrived, so the idea of trekking through the jungle following a petite pregnant pilot to discover special water seemed reasonable and safe. My research had been leaning toward discovering a plant or particle that the locals were ingesting or imbibing anyway, so I decided not to protest the predawn adventure. The canopy wasn't as thick as I expected it to be, and we easily followed the solitary star as it flickered in and out of view through the lofty foliage. We continued across a ridge where no hint of a track seemed clear, with only our stellar guide to rely on. Ahead of me, Maria navigated a route with certainty, giving me an odd sense of confidence that she knew what she was doing. As the sun beckoned to illuminate our journey, our celestial guide faded.

Maria must have sensed my mounting concern because she turned to reassure me. "We're almost there." The star disappeared from view just as she surmounted a knoll that offered a view ahead. As I joined her, she pointed to a gulley between two mountain peaks. "There it is."

I didn't know exactly what she was pointing at, as I was expecting to see water.

"Great" was the only word I could puff out.

"It's about a two hours' walk from here," she declared enthusiastically.

"Two hours?"

The dawning sun flushed my face as I reflected we hadn't discussed how long this journey would take.

"I can't see a track."

Maria continued walking, declaring, "There isn't one. And I have to be home when Papa returns from the plantations."

Apparently, she was the only one who had responsibilities that day. I doubted my capacity to find my own way back, so I accepted the fact that my day would likely be consumed by this traipsing escapade. I hastened my pace to catch up.

Questions regarding the integrity of Maria's conviction filled my head. "How do you know how to find this place we're going to?"

"You wouldn't believe me if I told you," she replied, which wasn't particularly reassuring.

I had doubts that we would get back to Buritaca at a reasonable hour. "What time do you have to be back?"

"I need to look after Mama. And we usually unload the coffee that didn't sell to the buyers and then have dinner."

I stopped asking questions, as the answers were only creating more concerns about how long this was going to take. I trudged along the forest floor, taking in sights and sounds that were completely foreign to my urban upbringing.

Howler monkeys called to each other from clandestine perches. Bird nests hung from towering trees like gourds full of hidden delights. Fig trees with tangled vines draped over rocks and rotting logs. Ants scurried single-file along fallen trunks, bearing their leafy prizes aloft. The two hours easily drifted by as I became lost in my fascination with the calls and sights of the wild.

As promised, Maria led me from the maze of vegetation into an opening where a beautiful, clear pond was being fed by a waterfall that streamed over an embankment from a hidden source. Maria continued around the pond to a small cave, where she stripped off all her clothing. She piled her garments neatly in the cave's mouth and then gingerly tiptoed into the shallows of the little lagoon.

"Are you coming?" she beckoned as she plunged into the inviting water.

It was in that moment that my adoration became truly cemented in my mind. I was already in awe of the divine surrounds, but I had never before been so imbued with such a sublime image of perfection. Was it the oasis? The waterfall? Or the brazenly bare creature swimming so carefree in the sun and water, her skin shining like luminous amber?

She looked at me curiously. "Well?"

My blissful mirage shattered with cutting self-consciousness. I was a reasonably fit and healthy twenty-one-year-old nerd who usually found comfort by caressing a computer terminal. Swimming naked in a tropical garden may have been second nature for Maria, but it was a palpable stretch of my sense of comfort. However, I knew if I didn't, I would make her uncomfortable, and she may want to leave. I removed my sandals, shirt, and shorts. The mild eczema that clung to the creases of my pale Caucasian arms heightened my embarrassment. It was now in full view and a telling reminder that a cure for this itchy affliction was a mystery that was hiding from me. I'm usually self-conscious about people seeing my eczema, but Maria's unashamed innocence had a power over me. She swam toward the waterfall, so I took the opportunity of her distraction to remove my underwear and splash awkwardly into the pond. The chilly reprieve from the sticky heat washed away my thoughts of self-deprecation, and I swam to Maria.

"This is amazing! If we needed a star to find this place, how do we find our way back?"

"Good question," she replied as she duck-dived away from me in playful invitation.

We played in the pond like teenagers who had snuck into someone's backyard pool. We climbed the rocks behind the waterfall and clung to the slippery precipice where the tumbling water thundered past us, beckoning us to follow from our mossy holdings. The cascading waterfall splashed our faces as we swam under it. I quickly lost sight of my self-consciousness, comfortably enamoured by her beauty, intrigued by her boldness, and liberated by her freedom of spirit.

I don't know how long we enjoyed playing in our private garden. We dived into the inviting water from the surrounding ledges, ducking down to collect pebbles from the deepest parts of the pool, and lounged on the larger rocks around the pool to bake our dripping souls. I was sure more time passed than I cared for. Eventually, responding to some internal signal, Maria exited the pool, headed toward her clothes at the entrance of the cave, and started getting dressed. I should have looked away. A grown woman would have asked me to. But this girl looked back at me with the sweetest smile of unencumbered youth. My clothes were closer to the path, at the other end of the pool, so I headed toward them and started getting dressed. I continued to admire her for her trust, her playfulness, and her ability to liberate me so effortlessly. She walked toward me.

"You seem a lot happier than when I met you on the street yesterday," I commented as she approached.

"This is my happy place. I don't have a care in the world when I'm here."

"What was yesterday all about?"

"I don't want to talk about it. We should go."

"How do we navigate this?" I had to ask.

Maria pointed away from her secret oasis. "You can always see the way better from a higher perspective."

She was right. It was easy to see where the coastline was. Maria led the way, and we headed back toward Buritaca.

Chapter 3

The next day, I tried to make up for lost time in the lab. It was a chore to resume work. Images of Maria naked under the waterfall flashed wildly in my mind's eye every time I closed my eyes. I wanted to concentrate, but I dared not blink, for the flicker would only invite images of her. My work was important. I had found that a potential indicator of the blue-zone effect in Buritaca was telomere elongation amongst the villagers. Telomeres are like totem poles at the ends of our DNA. Essentially, long totem poles equal a long life. If I could find the cause of the telomere elongation, it would be like discovering the fountain of youth. I was testing collected herbal preparations and measuring their effect on in vitro DNA samples. It's a science much like creative cooking. You add an ingredient to a tissue sample in a petri dish and measure what happens. I had narrowed my findings to an alkaloid preparation that was showing early signs of causing long totem poles, so to speak.

I had been so distracted by a frolicking forest nymph that I forgot to take a sample of the water from the pond. Maria's concerns were also ruminating in my mind. I realised I knew very little about her. What had been bothering her that day on the road when I first met her? When we left the pool, I tried to get her to open up about her life, but she seemed adamant about finding distraction in the sights and sounds in the jungle of life around us.

My efforts to concentrate on my work were well and truly thwarted around midday when a loud and persistent knocking echoed from the lab's front door. I opened the door, and without invitation, Maria launched herself through the doorway into the room as though running from an impending threat. I was both surprised and happy to see her, but this was a different version of Maria than I had encountered so far. She was trembling inconsolably, her eyes swollen with tears that ran rivers down her face.

"Leo! I'm so glad I found you. You have to protect me. Papa's going to kill me!"

"What are you doing here? What's going on?"

"I told you already!"

"Why is he going to kill you?"

"I told him I'm pregnant."

"He didn't know?"

"Obviously!"

My mind was trying to catch up with everything she was telling me. "The other day, you wanted to choke someone called Pablo. Today, your father wants to kill you. Is Pablo the father?"

"No!" she answered incredulously.

"I don't get how you all live so long, all while threatening to kill each other."

"What?"

By this stage, I think we were both confused, so I pulled up a couple of chairs and asked her to sit down and take a few deep breaths. I closed the lab door, protecting her from whatever or whoever might come barging into the room next. She seemed to calm down.

I sat in the chair opposite her and took her hand to reassure her. "So what happened?"

She explained the events that had occurred in her house that morning in a frantic flurry of disjointed information in both Spanish and English. It likely took her longer to explain the events to me than they took to occur. As she bounced back and forth between the two languages, reliving moments of panic and confusion, she unveiled the most perplexing recollection of events I have ever heard. When she finished, I sat back in my chair and attempted to reconcile what I had just been told.

******

Maria had been feeding a large, majestic wild macaw in the yard behind her small thatch-roofed house. She rocked backward and forward while the parrot ate seed from her hand. There were no workers to transport and no coffee deliveries that day, so her father's delivery truck sat sentinel outside the house.

"Today will be a good day. Today will be a good day..." Maria mumbled to herself in Spanish. This was apparently her mantra for willing the universe to bestow good fortune on herself and her loved ones.

Once her delicate palms were devoid of edible offerings, Maria left the macaw and walked toward the house. Maria's father, Gustavo, portly and unkempt, sat at the dinner table as he usually did on his day off as her mother, Sylvia, a middle-aged and greying version of Maria, kept herself busy in the kitchen as was her corresponding habit. Maria entered the house as her mother brought food from the kitchen for her father. Seeing that her parents were in the same room, Maria wasted no time in sharing her news.

"Mama, Papa, I have something to tell you," she said in Spanish. Apparently, Gustavo and Sylvia's only language was Spanish. "I'm pregnant."

Her father leapt aggressively from his chair and blasted Maria in his native tongue.

"What?"

"I'm pregnant. I'm so sorry, Papa."

"You little slut! How could you?"

Sylvia tried to intervene with calming intention. "Gustavo, please, let her explain."

"Shut up, mother of a slut!" Gustavo roared at her.

Maria realised Gustavo was not about to be reasoned with. He was standing between her and her mother, and she had no protection from whatever punishment was heading her way.

"Papa, please" was all she could muster in defence through frightened gasping and tears.

Gustavo undid his belt and whipped the leather out in an ominous gesture of assault.

"Gustavo, no!" Sylvia protested, her eyes wide with trepidation as she stood frozen in fear across the room.

The macaw that Maria had been feeding then did the most unprecedented thing. It flew from its feeding perch in the yard to the windowsill of the room and squawked loudly as it flared its wings, commanding the attention of the family. Gustavo stepped back as he was nearest in the house to the cacophonous display. Maria saw that the bird's unusual behaviour was enough to distract her father from his aggressive stance, so she continued to explain herself.

"I didn't tell you earlier because I knew you wouldn't believe me. I didn't believe it myself. But now my body is changing."

Gustavo was still unsure of the bird and what it might do, so he snapped a reply to Maria whilst still keeping an eye on their avian visitor.

"Believe what?"

"It was Gabriel," Maria declared, pointing at the macaw on the sill that was now eyeing Gustavo warily, mirroring his own distrust. "He told me I was going to bear a child. *The* child. That I was to be the mother of the new Christ."

"What?" Gustavo finally turned to face Maria as the incredibility of her testimony now outweighed the surprise of the bird's presence. He raised his belt menacingly. "You lying little—"

Sylvia raced forward and put herself between Maria and her father to save Maria from her father's wrath.

"It's a miracle!" Sylvia declared with spontaneous reverence to Maria's claim.

****

I sat forward in my chair and looked at Maria, who was now sobbing in the chair in front of me. She appeared to be in the recovery phase of shock, her tiny frame jolting and twitching with each tender gulping breath.

"Who is Gabriel?" I asked, in an attempt to fill in the final gaps in my understanding of the morning's events.

"The parrot," she answered, as if everyone already knew this.

"Why is he called Gabriel?"

"Because he says, 'Today will be a good day.'"

"Why does he say that?"

"Because I say it," she replied, again with a tone of stating the obvious.

She looked up at me and realised that she would have to share this detail with me the same way some parents explain things to a dim-witted child.

"People joke that he is an angel from God with a message," she explained slowly. "It's good luck if you hear him say, 'Today will be a good day.'"

"And this parrot told you that you're pregnant?"

"Yes."

"With the new Christ."

"Yes," she declared defensively. "You don't believe me either, do you?"

I wanted to say no, but I took pity on her fragile state. "It's just a lot to take in. Has the parrot told you anything more?"

"No."

"So no divine instructions? You don't need to build an ark or any-thing?" I asked, perhaps to remind myself to not take the conversation too seriously.

"You're mocking me now," she retorted with anguish in her tone. "I can't go home. He'll kill me. You can protect me here."

"I can't do that," I quickly replied.

"Where do you sleep?"

I pointed to my room. "It's barely a bunk," I added, thinking it would discourage her current line of query.

"Fine," she said and got up from her chair and marched across the room.

She headed into the room and closed the door behind her. There was no indication that she wanted any company or further consoling. I eventually recovered from my silent protest, telling myself that she likely needed a quiet and safe place to calm down for a little while. I thought that rest and time alone would help her to come up with a more likely explanation for her pregnancy. She was quiet, and she didn't ask for anything, so I resumed the work that I was now even further behind on.

I delved into my work with the assumption that Maria's problems would eventually solve themselves, and I lost track of time. When I opened the front door to the science facility for a stretch and smoke break, I saw that the sun had already completed its cycle for the day, and the light was fading quickly. Knowing I had a problem awaiting me in my bedroom that I needed to sort out fairly quickly, I finished my cigarette in a hurry. I approached the closed door to my room and knocked gently.

"Maria?"

Silence. I knocked harder.

"Maria?"

"What?"

I wanted to reply, "You're in my room. Get out." But instead, I chose, "Can I come in?"

"Yes."

I entered my tiny bedroom. I didn't turn on the light because the moonlight was enough to illuminate the portable bed that Maria was curled up on under a blanket that I had left folded at the foot of the cot. She had her back to me. I looked at the small desk in the room's corner and my open rucksack lying limp on the floor where I had left it. Nothing appeared displaced. The obvious lack of movement around the room only cemented my pity for this poor frightened girl, who was clearly recovering from a traumatic experience. I shoved some of the clothing I had left dishevelled on the floor out of the way with my foot, likely a remnant behaviour of being told to clean my room for guests to see.

"Maria, you can't stay here."

"Just one night," she replied with quiet desperation, not turning to look at me.

"Maria, go home," I insisted.

Maria lifted the covers behind her.

"Just hold me."

"Maria..."

"Please, Leo."

I don't know how long I stood there, knowing the next move I made would either eliminate this distraction from my work or confound it exorbitantly. Softening, I pushed down Maria's hand, which was holding the blanket aloft, so that the blanket enveloped her. I kicked off my sandals and lay on the bed behind her. I could argue that I was trying to be polite or respectable by rejecting her offer of joining her under the bedcover, but to be honest, I had never slept with a blanket in the science facility as I had only been in Colombia for three weeks and was nowhere near acclimatised to the heat. It was usually too hot most nights for me to even consider a sheet. I was tired. There wasn't enough floor space, and I wasn't about to jump under a blanket with a life-sized pregnant heat generator. I figured I could allow this as a once-off to give her time to calm down, and I could get some rest. She was tangibly trembling. I put my arm around her, acting as the comforting blanket I assumed she was seeking. She pulled me closer as if pulling a shield across herself. Only heaven knew what this shattered girl was going through in her mind and heart.

Chapter 4

Maria woke and turned toward me. It must have been around dawn. Her mind was clearly catching up to the memory of her decision to seek safety in my room. She looked at me and around the space like a detective looking for clues.

"How did you sleep?" I enquired with a comforting tone. "Actually, I already know."

"What do you mean?" she asked with a groggy voice.

"You sleep like a wonky washing machine on a spin cycle that's all over the place. You talk in your sleep too."

"What did I say?"

"It wasn't clear. But I heard 'stop' repeatedly. And I think I heard 'don't hurt her.' What's that about?"

She glanced away like people do when trying to grasp an elusive thought.

"I don't know" was all she could offer regarding her restless dreams.

I regarded her petite, feminine face only inches from mine. I felt as though I needed to be a detective, wanting answers to all the mysteries that surrounded this intriguing girl. "You know I have to take you home."

Alarm replaced the repose in her pretty eyes. "I don't think that's a good idea. What if Papa thinks you're the father and—"

I cut her off before her mind could conjure any more distressing images regarding her father's reaction. "I'm prepared to take the risk." She looked as though she was still building fortresses in her mind, so I added, "And don't worry. I'll take care of you. He won't hurt you."

I rolled out of bed, still fully dressed from the day before. I pointed out the shower and bathroom facilities to Maria and put on the kettle. She promptly headed in to wash away some of the stale fear and the dust and dirt that clung to her skin from the day before. It gave me a moment to gather my thoughts and review my apparent ease in accepting this girl at her word and offering to be her champion in any upcoming confrontation with her father. He was a man I had not met, and I knew nothing about him. What was I getting myself into? While Maria bathed, I popped out quickly to get some food. I was already familiar with her appetite, and I was becoming fond of the warm corn-meal arepas served by the street vendors.

Maria was finishing up in the bathroom as I returned. Perhaps she had gotten a whiff of the tasty offerings approaching because she did not hesitate in meeting me at the door to accept the feed. It was again rewarding to see her smile. We sat quietly together in my lab, which doubled as my dining room. A plastic bottle on the bench caught my eye. I grabbed the bottle and handed it to her.

"I need a urine sample—for the pregnancy test."

"You want me to pee into this?"

"Yes."

"How do I do that?"

"Carefully."

I could see that she was no closer to understanding what to do. "You can use the plastic tub in the bathroom and then transfer the liquid to the bottle afterward if you like."

"But I've already been to the toilet," she retorted with innocent concern.

"No worries. Take the bottle with you and get a sample back to me when you can."

I continued on to the shower with a fresh set of clothes as Maria polished off the last of the arepas. I had promised her that I would escort her back home. It was likely going to be a day of distraction again as I was undeniably curious to discover if the events of the preceding day and everything about her pregnancy, allegedly prophesied by a parrot called Gabriel, were actually as she had described. The trained logic of my brain determined that they simply couldn't be.

We walked together along the gritty Via Buritaca out of the main village and veered left onto a smaller dirt road with no name that appeared to flank the Buritaca River. As we walked, I thought perhaps I should have asked how long the walk was going to be. The last time I hadn't asked had cornered me to commit to an entire day.

Before I could form the query on my lips, Maria turned to me with a smile. "It's just up the road a little more."

We arrived at Maria's tiny family home. It was a lovingly decorated version of the thatch-roofed dwellings scattered throughout the village. There was a front porch that gave the house a bungalow appearance. A post and wire fence surrounded the rear garden, and I imagined the Buritaca River drifted peacefully not too far behind the property. My most significant observation was the copious amount of fruit and vegetables specially arranged on mats and in baskets outside the front of the house. The display reminded me of the offerings that regularly adorn shrines. A woman dressed in a traditional colourful cotton dress opened the front door and walked onto the porch. Based on Maria's description, she had to be Maria's mother, Sylvia.

"Mama!" Maria called in order to gain her mother's attention.

"Angelica?" Sylvia hailed in exuberant response.

Sylvia gusted toward Maria to embrace her eagerly. I recollected that Maria's parents spoke only Spanish. They conversed with rapid eagerness in their native tongue.

"Thank God!" Sylvia exclaimed.

"Mama, I'd like to introduce you to Leonard. You can call him Leo. He's a scientist from Melbourne, Australia."

Apparently, it was okay for people to call me Leo. I didn't know this. Her Spanish accent made my name sound like "Layo." Sylvia looked at me with undisguised alarm.

Maria deciphered her mother's expression. "No, he's not the father."

I held out my hand to Sylvia and greeted her in Spanish. "Pleased to meet you, Mrs...."

"Santos. Sylvia Santos," she replied politely. "Pleased to meet you too."

I thought it best not to waste time and get straight to the point about why I was there. "Mrs. Santos, Maria is terrified and confused. She believes your husband may harm her based on her current situation."

Sylvia shot an undisguised glare at Maria.

Maria looked to the ground and quickly changed the topic. "What's with all the fruit, Mama?"

"Offerings from the people of the village. Blessings for you, child," Sylvia replied, softening with the change of focus.

"How do they know?" Maria queried.

"Well..."

"Mama, how could you?"

"It's a miracle, Angelica."

A couple of local villagers arrived with young children in tow as we were speaking together. Amidst a great deal of bowing and muttering of prayers, they offered Maria gifts of fruit. The women kissed her forehead, and one of the little boys touched her abdomen in awe. I could appreciate the villagers referring to a speaking parrot as a messenger from God. Colombians can be conspicuously superstitious. But to believe so quickly that Maria had a divinely implanted pregnancy seemed presumptuous.

Maria looked at her mother emphatically. "Mama?"

Sylvia avoided her daughter's consternation and invited me into the house with Maria. Clearly, Maria's mother had been effectively convincing when sharing Maria's tale. She was wonderfully hospitable. She gestured for me to enter and make myself comfortable by taking a seat in the living room. As I passed her, she turned to the boy, who must have been about six years old. She reached into her bra and pulled out some pesos.

"Ve a buscar un poco de pandebono. Rápidamente," she ordered as she waved the cash before the boy.

The boy looked at his mother for approval. When she nodded, he snatched up the money in his little hand and ran toward the village.

Sylvia walked past me to the kitchen, which was behind the living room that immediately joined the front door. Maria thanked the ladies for their blessings and gifts and joined me at the table. I could see that Sylvia was making us aguapanela as she retrieved a block of guandolo from the fridge. It was a popular iced water drink made with unrefined sugar cane and lemon juice. I knew it well, as it saved me most days from passing out from dehydration. As Sylvia busied herself in the kitchen, I took advantage of the opportunity to ask more questions. "Your mother called you Angelica at the door?"

"Yes, it's my middle name. I answer to both Maria and Angelica."

"So your full name is Maria Angelica Santos?" Which I translated in my head to be Maria Angel Saint.

"Yes."

"Could you be any more Catholic?"

Maria laughed and spontaneously held her abdomen.

"And birthing the new Christ is your commitment to Christianity?"

"I didn't ask for this," she defended abruptly.

"Does your mother understand any English?"

"No."

"Okay, then tell me—how did the parrot tell you about the pregnancy?"

"Gabriel speaks to me in my dreams."

"Do any other parrots or animals speak to you in your dreams?"

"Leo! How do you think I found the secret cave and swimming hole in the forest? Gabriel told me in my dreams where to find it."

"Okay. So what exactly did he say?"

"He came to me in my dreams many times. Perhaps because I wouldn't believe him. He speaks mainly in whispers and images. Light surrounds him when he comes to me, and he shows me things. I saw myself pregnant. I saw the child. And I remember one word: 'Christos.'"

"Christ?"

"Yes."

"Does he announce himself using the name Gabriel?"

"No, but I know it's him."

"I have to ask, is there a chance that anyone else could be the father? Have you—"

Maria shook her head earnestly. "No. Never."

"Are you saying that you're a virgin?"

"Yes. We keep ourselves for our marriage. It's very important to my family. Papa would kill me if I was having sex with a boy."

That comment had me stumped. She seemed genuinely flabbergasted by the thought of betraying her family's trust. I didn't know whether I was exposing a parody or exploring a phenomenon. I pressed on with my questions.

"What does he sound like in your head? Like a bird?"

"No, like a person. You don't believe me, do you?"

The little boy returned, huffing and puffing from his eager running. He presented himself at the front door entrance, proudly displaying a filled paper bag whilst sporting a very enthusiastic smile. Sylvia placed a glass of her aguapanela in front of me and another in front of Maria and met the boy at the door. She stroked his hair graciously as she took the bag.

"Gracias, Antonio."

"De nada," the young boy replied as he spun around to run back toward the village. He had to dodge past a man approaching on the porch, who I assumed to be Gustavo, Maria's father. He entered the room like a thundering bull. His bulbous nose and thick, singular brow made his face appear almost a caricature of himself.

"Where is the little slut? Is she home yet?" he roared in Spanish.

Maria dived behind me. I spontaneously sprung to my feet with a more protective posture than I was likely prepared to act on.

"Who's this?" Gustavo challenged with a threatening gusto.

I quickly spoke up for myself in their language. "Mi nombre es Leonard. Yo no soy el padre. Estoy aquí para ayudar." I desperately hoped that my translation of *I'm not the father* was correct, and I added an assurance that I was just trying to help.

I didn't know what was going to happen next, but I felt I needed to prepare for just about anything. Gustavo was larger than I was and likely twenty years my senior. I could possibly whip around him on a fitness scale, but his forearms, forged from years of heavy work, were like the ropes that secure ships to ports. No doubt he could pack a punch if he wanted to.

"What's with all the fruit?" was Gustavo's choice of reply.

Sylvia distracted him by opening her paper bag virtually under his nose. The inviting smell of the pandebono, a freshly cooked mixture of cheese and pastry, wafted up from the bag to Gustavo's nostrils. It did the trick. He launched his hand into the bag to retrieve one of the tasty temptations, and it quickly disappeared into his mouth.

As he munched on the offered morsel, Sylvia replied, "It's all from the villagers. They wish to pay their respects to Maria and her child, the Chr..."

"The Christ, Mama. You can say it."

Gustavo warmed appreciably to the idea. "So, people are bringing us food? Are they bringing money?"

"They probably will," Sylvia replied encouragingly, holding up the bag again as though calming a ferocious beast with its favourite treat.

"This food—what can we sell?"

"You'll have to look, dear," Sylvia continued as she emptied the last of the pandebono onto a plastic plate that sat in the middle of the table.

Maria eagerly helped herself to the puffed biscuit-sized treats, which didn't surprise me. I held back as it still wasn't clear what Gustavo was going to do next. He turned his attention back to me.

"So you—how are you going to help us?"

Sylvia must have also sensed that the tensions were still high. She scurried past Gustavo and out the front door as he awaited my reply.

"I am a scientist, Mr. Santos, and a geneticist. I will assist you in discovering the truth about Maria's pregnancy."

Sylvia walked back into the room, her arms laden with gifted fruit and vegetables.

"It's clearly a miracle," he challenged menacingly.

"Clearly, sir," I replied stoically.

Chapter 5

Maria woke and turned toward me. It must have been around dawn. Her mind was clearly catching up to the memory of her decision to seek safety in my room. She looked at me and around the space like a detective looking for clues.

"How did you sleep?" I enquired with a comforting tone. "Actually, I already know."

"What do you mean?" she asked with a groggy voice.

"You sleep like a wonky washing machine on a spin cycle that's all over the place. You talk in your sleep too."

"What did I say?"

"It wasn't clear. But I heard 'stop' repeatedly. And I think I heard 'don't hurt her.' What's that about?"

She glanced away like people do when trying to grasp an elusive thought.

"I don't know" was all she could offer regarding her restless dreams.

I regarded her petite, feminine face only inches from mine. I felt as though I needed to be a detective, wanting answers to all the mysteries that surrounded this intriguing girl. "You know I have to take you home."

Alarm replaced the repose in her pretty eyes. "I don't think that's a good idea. What if Papa thinks you're the father and—"

I cut her off before her mind could conjure any more distressing images regarding her father's reaction. "I'm prepared to take the risk." She looked as though she was still building fortresses in her mind, so I added, "And don't worry. I'll take care of you. He won't hurt you."

I rolled out of bed, still fully dressed from the day before. I pointed out the shower and bathroom facilities to Maria and put on the kettle. She promptly headed in to wash away some of the stale fear and the dust and dirt that clung to her skin from the day before. It gave me a moment to gather my thoughts and review my apparent ease in accepting this girl at her word and offering to be her champion in any upcoming confrontation with her father. He was a man I had not met, and I knew nothing about him. What was I getting myself into? While Maria bathed, I popped out quickly to get some food. I was already familiar with her appetite, and I was becoming fond of the warm corn-meal arepas served by the street vendors.

Maria was finishing up in the bathroom as I returned. Perhaps she had gotten a whiff of the tasty offerings approaching because she did not hesitate in meeting me at the door to accept the feed. It was again rewarding to see her smile. We sat quietly together in my lab, which doubled as my dining room. A plastic bottle on the bench caught my eye. I grabbed the bottle and handed it to her.

"I need a urine sample—for the pregnancy test."

"You want me to pee into this?"

"Yes."

"How do I do that?"

"Carefully."

I could see that she was no closer to understanding what to do. "You can use the plastic tub in the bathroom and then transfer the liquid to the bottle afterward if you like."

"But I've already been to the toilet," she retorted with innocent concern.

"No worries. Take the bottle with you and get a sample back to me when you can."

I continued on to the shower with a fresh set of clothes as Maria polished off the last of the arepas. I had promised her that I would escort her back home. It was likely going to be a day of distraction again as I was undeniably curious to discover if the events of the preceding day and everything about her pregnancy, allegedly prophesied by a parrot called Gabriel, were actually as she had described. The trained logic of my brain determined that they simply couldn't be.

We walked together along the gritty Via Buritaca out of the main village and veered left onto a smaller dirt road with no name that appeared to flank the Buritaca River. As we walked, I thought perhaps I should have asked how long the walk was going to be. The last time I hadn't asked had cornered me to commit to an entire day.

Before I could form the query on my lips, Maria turned to me with a smile. "It's just up the road a little more."

We arrived at Maria's tiny family home. It was a lovingly decorated version of the thatch-roofed dwellings scattered throughout the village. There was a front porch that gave the house a bungalow appearance. A post and wire fence surrounded the rear garden, and I imagined the Buritaca River drifted peacefully not too far behind the property. My most significant observation was the copious amount of fruit and vegetables specially arranged on mats and in baskets outside the front of the house. The display reminded me of the offerings that regularly adorn shrines. A woman dressed in a traditional colourful cotton dress opened the front door and walked onto the porch. Based on Maria's description, she had to be Maria's mother, Sylvia.

"Mama!" Maria called in order to gain her mother's attention.

"Angelica?" Sylvia hailed in exuberant response.

Sylvia gusted toward Maria to embrace her eagerly. I recollected that Maria's parents spoke only Spanish. They conversed with rapid eagerness in their native tongue.

"Thank God!" Sylvia exclaimed.

"Mama, I'd like to introduce you to Leonard. You can call him Leo. He's a scientist from Melbourne, Australia."

Apparently, it was okay for people to call me Leo. I didn't know this. Her Spanish accent made my name sound like "Layo." Sylvia looked at me with undisguised alarm.

Maria deciphered her mother's expression. "No, he's not the father."

I held out my hand to Sylvia and greeted her in Spanish. "Pleased to meet you, Mrs...."

"Santos. Sylvia Santos," she replied politely. "Pleased to meet you too."

I thought it best not to waste time and get straight to the point about why I was there. "Mrs. Santos, Maria is terrified and confused. She believes your husband may harm her based on her current situation."

Sylvia shot an undisguised glare at Maria.

Maria looked to the ground and quickly changed the topic. "What's with all the fruit, Mama?"

"Offerings from the people of the village. Blessings for you, child," Sylvia replied, softening with the change of focus.

"How do they know?" Maria queried.

"Well..."

"Mama, how could you?"

"It's a miracle, Angelica."

A couple of local villagers arrived with young children in tow as we were speaking together. Amidst a great deal of bowing and muttering of prayers, they offered Maria gifts of fruit. The women kissed her forehead, and one of the little boys touched her abdomen in awe. I could appreciate the villagers referring to a speaking parrot as a messenger from God. Colombians can be conspicuously superstitious. But to believe so quickly that Maria had a divinely implanted pregnancy seemed presumptuous.

Maria looked at her mother emphatically. "Mama?"

Sylvia avoided her daughter's consternation and invited me into the house with Maria. Clearly, Maria's mother had been effectively convincing when sharing Maria's tale. She was wonderfully hospitable. She gestured for me to enter and make myself comfortable by taking a seat in the living room. As I passed her, she turned to the boy, who must have been about six years old. She reached into her bra and pulled out some pesos.

"Ve a buscar un poco de pandebono. Rápidamente," she ordered as she waved the cash before the boy.

The boy looked at his mother for approval. When she nodded, he snatched up the money in his little hand and ran toward the village.

Sylvia walked past me to the kitchen, which was behind the living room that immediately joined the front door. Maria thanked the ladies for their blessings and gifts and joined me at the table. I could see that Sylvia was making us aguapanela as she retrieved a block of guandolo from the fridge. It was a popular iced water drink made with unrefined sugar cane and lemon juice. I knew it well, as it saved me most days from passing out from dehydration. As Sylvia busied herself in the kitchen, I took advantage of the opportunity to ask more questions. "Your mother called you Angelica at the door?"

"Yes, it's my middle name. I answer to both Maria and Angelica."

"So your full name is Maria Angelica Santos?" Which I translated in my head to be Maria Angel Saint.

"Yes."

"Could you be any more Catholic?"

Maria laughed and spontaneously held her abdomen.

"And birthing the new Christ is your commitment to Christianity?"

"I didn't ask for this," she defended abruptly.

"Does your mother understand any English?"

"No."

"Okay, then tell me—how did the parrot tell you about the pregnancy?"

"Gabriel speaks to me in my dreams."

"Do any other parrots or animals speak to you in your dreams?"

"Leo! How do you think I found the secret cave and swimming hole in the forest? Gabriel told me in my dreams where to find it."

"Okay. So what exactly did he say?"

"He came to me in my dreams many times. Perhaps because I wouldn't believe him. He speaks mainly in whispers and images. Light surrounds him when he comes to me, and he shows me things. I saw myself pregnant. I saw the child. And I remember one word: 'Christos.'"

"Christ?"

"Yes."

"Does he announce himself using the name Gabriel?"

"No, but I know it's him."

"I have to ask, is there a chance that anyone else could be the father? Have you—"

Maria shook her head earnestly. "No. Never."

"Are you saying that you're a virgin?"

"Yes. We keep ourselves for our marriage. It's very important to my family. Papa would kill me if I was having sex with a boy."

That comment had me stumped. She seemed genuinely flabbergasted by the thought of betraying her family's trust. I didn't know whether I was exposing a parody or exploring a phenomenon. I pressed on with my questions.

"What does he sound like in your head? Like a bird?"

"No, like a person. You don't believe me, do you?"

The little boy returned, huffing and puffing from his eager running. He presented himself at the front door entrance, proudly displaying a filled paper bag whilst sporting a very enthusiastic smile. Sylvia placed a glass of her aguapanela in front of me and another in front of Maria and met the boy at the door. She stroked his hair graciously as she took the bag.

"Gracias, Antonio."

"De nada," the young boy replied as he spun around to run back toward the village. He had to dodge past a man approaching on the porch, who I assumed to be Gustavo, Maria's father. He entered the room like a thundering bull. His bulbous nose and thick, singular brow made his face appear almost a caricature of himself.

"Where is the little slut? Is she home yet?" he roared in Spanish.

Maria dived behind me. I spontaneously sprung to my feet with a more protective posture than I was likely prepared to act on.

"Who's this?" Gustavo challenged with a threatening gusto.

I quickly spoke up for myself in their language. "Mi nombre es Leonard. Yo no soy el padre. Estoy aquí para ayudar." I desperately hoped that my translation of *I'm not the father* was correct, and I added an assurance that I was just trying to help.

I didn't know what was going to happen next, but I felt I needed to prepare for just about anything. Gustavo was larger than I was and likely twenty years my senior. I could possibly whip around him on a fitness scale, but his forearms, forged from years of heavy work, were like the ropes that secure ships to ports. No doubt he could pack a punch if he wanted to.

"What's with all the fruit?" was Gustavo's choice of reply.

Sylvia distracted him by opening her paper bag virtually under his nose. The inviting smell of the pandebono, a freshly cooked mixture of cheese and pastry, wafted up from the bag to Gustavo's nostrils. It did the trick. He launched his hand into the bag to retrieve one of the tasty temptations, and it quickly disappeared into his mouth.

As he munched on the offered morsel, Sylvia replied, "It's all from the villagers. They wish to pay their respects to Maria and her child, the Chr..."

"The Christ, Mama. You can say it."

Gustavo warmed appreciably to the idea. "So, people are bringing us food? Are they bringing money?"

"They probably will," Sylvia replied encouragingly, holding up the bag again as though calming a ferocious beast with its favourite treat.

"This food—what can we sell?"

"You'll have to look, dear," Sylvia continued as she emptied the last of the pandebono onto a plastic plate that sat in the middle of the table.

Maria eagerly helped herself to the puffed biscuit-sized treats, which didn't surprise me. I held back as it still wasn't clear what Gustavo was going to do next. He turned his attention back to me.

"So you—how are you going to help us?"

Sylvia must have also sensed that the tensions were still high. She scurried past Gustavo and out the front door as he awaited my reply.

"I am a scientist, Mr. Santos, and a geneticist. I will assist you in discovering the truth about Maria's pregnancy."

Sylvia walked back into the room, her arms laden with gifted fruit and vegetables.

"It's clearly a miracle," he challenged menacingly.

"Clearly, sir," I replied stoically.

Chapter 6

The advantage of Buritaca's newfound fame was that Pravus, the pharmaceutical company that sponsored me, accelerated my research by allocating me an assistant. Perhaps they worried that someone else was going to discover the elixir of life that was keeping the Magdalena district residents young and beautiful and beat them to the patent. Or perhaps they just liked the botanical hypothesis I had offered them that had grown from my description of my forest adventures. I had left out telling them about the part about swimming naked with Maria. I didn't think that detail supported the impression of vigilance directed to the assigned task I was hoping to inspire. My new assistant's name was Carlos. I guessed he was around twenty-five when we first met, but he may have been younger and just sporting more mature facial features. I had clearly watched too many drug-lord movies and tele-series because a Colombian named Carlos showing up at my door wearing mirrored sunglasses and a loose-fitting Hawaiian shirt had me on edge at first. Perhaps it was the way he rolled the "r" in his name, as though its sound should have impressed me as much as it did him. When I discovered he was a highly qualified botanist from the Universidad de Medellín, it became cemented in my mind that he would one day become the perfect drug lord. Who better to run a cartel than a Colombian botanist named Carlos? I asked him where his family was from, and he had replied "around," and that's about as far as our introductions went. I had introduced myself as Leo. Maria's influence over me now included me shortening my name per her preference.

"I'm told you need plants?" Carlos asked in a way that had me expecting the word *plants* was code for something narcotic.

I assumed that Pravus had arranged specific instructions for Carlos regarding his role to source botanicals relevant to my research project. Their communication with me was terrible, so I had to run with the confident Latino's understanding of his employment. His English was good. His accent had the thickness of a Colombian cigar. Part of me wanted to ask, "What do you mean by plants?" But I was happy to just appear stupid and not open my mouth to incriminate myself as dull. He took my silence as a yes and disappeared for a moment to go to his car. When he returned, he was carrying a load of native plants, herbs, and flowers that were clustered in the fold of a burlap coffee sack. He walked past me and dumped the floral load on the desk near my laptop.

"These are from high in the Sierra Nevada. Are they what you want?" he asked.

I looked through the plants he had laid out on the bench. "Yes, I think they are. I will need to know the botanical name of each plant for referencing."

"Of course."

I picked up a long stalk headed by pretty yellow flowers that were opened upward like tiny petalled cups. There were at least twenty flowers on each stem. It was an opportunity to discover the knowledge of my new assistant. "Like this, for example."

"That, my friend, is a Lupinus arbustus, the crest lupine. It is common in the Sierra Nevada above 6000 feet. It grows in fields and alongside rivers, which could work well for a 'something in the water' theory."

Did everyone believe it was something in the water, or had he been talking to someone about my work and my theories? Pravus had employed him directly, so I had to assume he had read my reports.

I dismissed my concerns and focused on the work at hand. "Let me show you how I prepare the samples."

I used the crest lupine as the introductory specimen and prepared it by macerating it and centrifuging the pulp in an aqueous alcohol solvent I had mixed earlier. The contents needed to settle, and then, using a pipette, I siphoned the pale yellow-tinged liquid that had separated from the pulp and added drops to agar plates of cell cultures I had stacked in the atmospherically controlled samples fridge. I wrote the plant name on a label and affixed it to the sample lid.

I turned to Carlos, who had been watching my procedures with interest. "That's pretty much it, for starters. I'll test the tissue samples using the qPCR every twenty-four hours to look for telomere influence."

"Got it."

"Do you want to give it a go?"

"Sure," he replied nonchalantly as he grabbed another plant sample and duplicated my procedure perfectly. He really was going to be an excellent drug lord one day.

"The Wayuu people are taking me deeper into the Sierra Nevada tomorrow," Carlos added as he placed the label on the sample he had created. "They say they know a village of the Tayrona that may have a traditional drink with the properties you seek. If we find them, I can ask what plants they're using."

The Wayuu people were the indigenous folk of the region, remnants of the large tribes decimated by the Spanish Conquistadors in the Caribbean. I easily identified them by their simple one-piece white cotton attire that was likely a sheet of fabric with a hole cut out for the head to pass through. They gathered the draped material with a waistband. Shoes or sandals were a rare accompaniment. Their local village was in the heart of the Tayrona National Park on the coast. Visiting their home was off-limits to tourists and Spanish descendant locals. I assume this was out of respect for them to continue their hunter-gatherer lifestyle without interference from curious spectators. I had heard that the Tayrona people suffered massive losses from battles with arriving Spaniards and had retreated deep into the mountains of the Sierra Nevada. Carlos was evidently referring to one of these villages. I didn't ask about his permission for such an expedition, as his apparent familiarity with the Wayuu people had me convinced that what he was up to was kosher.

"Sure, that sounds good," I said, betraying nothing of the questions that were bubbling up regarding my new assistant and his contacts.

We completed the first round of plant sampling together in about an hour. I actually appreciated the help and the likelihood that I would have access to samples from a much wider catchment than I could achieve myself. When we finished, Carlos excused himself and promised that he would return with new and exciting botanicals from the Tayrona village in about a week. I didn't know how far he was planning to venture into the Sierra Nevada jungle, so I was happy to accept that I would just see him when I saw him.

That left me free of work for the afternoon. Working on the supplied benches always left me aching across my shoulders, as their height was better suited to someone much shorter. I went for a walk to stretch out the tension knots that had taken residence across my back and soon found myself on the road to Maria's house.

It had been three days since I had last seen Maria and her holy parrot. The crowd surrounding the property had grown and now had a distinctly more international feel. Robin was sitting with some devotees. He spotted me, rose, and rushed toward me.

"Can you believe this?" he asked, forgetting that a greeting may have been a consideration.

"Hi, Robin. Who are all these people?"

"You've seen the Virgin Mary carvings being sold here, right? One would expect a comparison of Maria to the Christian virgin story."

"Yeah, so?"

Robin gestured for me to follow him. "Here, look at this."

He pointed to a symbol of a hand that was posted on a tree. Below the tree were Middle-Eastern-looking devotees. The women were wearing loosely fitted hijabs, and the men wore bright white kaftans with matching habits on their heads.

"Do you recognise this?" Robin asked as he diverted my eyes with his pointed finger.

"No," I replied, looking at what was clearly a symbol of a hand where the outer two digits were symmetrical and pointed outwards.

The three middle fingers pointed skyward over an eye that adorned the palm. He fossicked through the religious symbols that dangled from his wrist and isolated a tiny silver pendant that looked the same.

"That, my dear sir, is the hamsa. Otherwise known as the Hand of Mary. It's also known as the Hand of Fatima."

"Why's that important?"

"Fatima was the daughter of Mohamed. The princess of Islam. She was al-Zhara, the 'shining one.' These devotees are Muslim. They are calling Maria 'Maria Zhara'—'Shining Maria.' Can you believe it?"

"I'm not sure how that's important," I replied, not sharing any of Robin's excitement.

"Come over here." He beckoned again. "See these people?" he asked as he pointed to a bejewelled group wearing brightly coloured saris that flowed onto just as ornately patterned mats. "They're from India. They are calling Maria 'Matangi' because of Gabriel."

"I don't see a parrot pendant on your wrist or around your neck. You seem to have everything else, though."

"Give me time. I'm just looking for the right one."

Robin smiled as he approached the ensemble, who clearly recognised him as a friendly associate.

"Look at these images," he continued as he pointed to paintings of what was likely the Hindu Goddess Matangi and her green parrot poised with the goddess in various versions of relief.

"So?"

"Matangi is an incarnation of Parvati—a heavy-duty goddess of Hinduism. Matangi had a parrot, just like Maria. These devotees believe Maria is a reincarnation of Parvati. That's huge!"

"I don't get the significance. They're all just myths. These people can believe what they want."

"You really don't get it, do you?" Robin exclaimed with exasperation. "This could escalate in to the largest event of religious syncretism in modern history. There's two billion Christians in the world, another two billion Muslims, and almost two billion Hindus. They've all found reason to come here together to venerate and adore Maria in ways that suit their own religions."

"Holy shit."

"No. Holy Parrot!"

Chapter 7

I approached the house that was now hidden under swaths of tapestries, flags, and posters depicting a plethora of religious motifs. The house was transforming into a shine, venerating anything and everything linked in any way to the great mystery of Maria and her parrot. Thanks to Robin, I recognised the image of Matangi with her parrot, the one-eyed gilded hamsa, and the shrouded Mary of biblical stories. The strings of flags that draped from the roofline were likely Buddhist, with prayers intended to be lifted from the colourful material in the prevailing wind. Gustavo was standing guard at his usual spot on the porch. The money he was making from his admission fees kept him gleefully enthused. He had moved the burgeoning galley of gifts to a more secure location behind the house. I continued through the house into the yard. They had draped the surrounding trees with a myriad of religious iconography. Maria was sitting with her back to an audience of dozens of devotees. She was facing the perch that was overtly devoid of any parrot presence. Despite Gabriel's absence, I could see that she was rocking back and forth, perhaps reciting her chant "today will be a good day" to herself. "Loro Santo, Loro Santo" poured rhythmically from prayerful mouths around her. I weaved my way through the crowd toward Maria, trying to avoid stepping on the minefield of mats, rugs, and sarongs strewn in a semicircle around her.

"Maria!"

My voice was like a siren in a sea of whispers. Maria sprang to life in response to my familiar accent. She ran toward me, bowling through her followers and their belongings, and hugged me intensely.

"I don't know what to do. Who are all these people? Please help me," Maria pleaded.

I wrapped my arm around her and guided her through the outer crowd toward the house. Once inside, I closed all the doors.

"Maria, this has to stop. Just tell them the truth, and it will all go away."

"I am telling the truth! Make them go away!"

"I can't—unless you tell me who the father of this child is."

"I've already told you. Don't you believe me?"

"It's a little tough for me to get my head around the idea that a parrot told you that your unborn child is Jesus. Where is the bird, anyway?"

"He won't come back because of all the people in the yard. Get them out!"

"Okay. We can at least sort that out."

I reopened the front door, where Gustavo looked at me with a puzzled expression that betrayed his likely thought, *Why was I closed out of my house just now?* I called him inside. Robin approached the porch, so I invited him in, too, as I was never too sure how Gustavo would react to my recommendations under his own roof. I took a moment to translate a sentence in my head to Spanish for Gustavo.

"Gustavo, Maria is frightened because of all the people. She says

Gabriel, the bird, won't return because of the crowds. Make them go away."

"But they pay good money to see Maria and the parrot," he fired back in predictable protest. Maria ran to her room and slammed the door shut behind her in her own version of a protest to her father's obstinance.

"Soon, media will arrive, and they can be like wild dogs circling their prey, all hoping for a bite. You'll need to be prepared for this. If Maria is scared now, what will happen when the media arrives?"

"Mi familia lo es todo para mi," he grumbled to remind me of his devotion to his family.

"I have given you a solution. Get rid of all the people in the yard," I offered in the softest tone I could muster to soothe Gustavo, "and then maybe both Maria and Gabriel will return."

With a gush of frustrated breath, he pushed open the door to the yard and stormed out.

"¡Todos, salgan!"

Even those who didn't speak Spanish would have understood his combative command to leave. Maria, aware that her father was now outside as he bellowed his instructions, briefly reemerged from her room to pour herself a glass of water in the kitchen. She spun on her heel, holding the glass to her chin with both hands. She turned to me at the door of her room.

"Gabriel never said it was Jesus. He just said my child would be the new Christ!" she blurted with fragile tenacity.

She slammed the bedroom door again to barricade herself within.

Robin looked at me with bubbling zeal. "Do you realise what this means?"

"Yes. All these people will not piss off any time soon."

Robin paced the room, clearly attempting to run with the wild horses that were galloping in his head.

"Of course," he declared. "Jesus is only one version of the Christ."

I stood silently, as I knew nothing I could say would halt his dissertation.

"Jehovah is a tribal God who is to send his son as a leader to defeat enemies. That's why they're not here!"

"Who's not here?"

"The Zionists! I didn't realise until Maria just pointed out that Gabriel didn't say the name Jesus to her. That's the one 'Christ' we can rule out here."

"Why?"

"Because Maria is Colombian. The mother of their Messiah needs to be Jewish."

"How many Christs are there?"

"Where do I start? For the Egyptians, there was Osiris—the original living, dying, and then resurrecting deity. For the Greeks, there's

Dionysus. Asia Minor had Attis. Adonis in Syria. Persia had Mithras. The Italians, before Jesus, had Bacchus. And they're just the main ones."

"What are you saying?"

"Any culture can lay claim to this child as being their Christ. The only way I can see through this is to get a name. The name of the child will guide us to the origins of his or her divine identity."

"Assuming Maria's story is true."

"Of course. This is huge."

"It's the headache I'm getting that's huge."

"We have to ask Maria if Gabriel has given the child a name," Robin conjectured to satisfy his deductions. "It's essential."

Gustavo returned from the yard.

"Where's Maria?" he asked me. "I've moved the people away from the yard. She needs to call her bird."

"What did he say?" Robin asked, betraying his language limitations.

"He thinks Maria can summon the bird," I interpreted.

I approached Maria's door and knocked. Nothing. I turned to Gustavo and shrugged, looking as hapless as I could for his benefit. Gustavo glanced at Robin and then perhaps decided that yelling down the house with us present would not fare well. He paced to the front door and headed off to his truck.

I knocked on Maria's bedroom door again.

"Vete!" she yelled, confident that whoever was knocking would understand *go away* in Spanish.

"Maria, it's me, Leonard. Your father has left."

She opened the door, dragged me inside her room by the scruff of my shirt, and slammed the door behind me. She hugged me and cried with the desperation of a scared girl caught in a hurricane of events she could not fathom or control. I guided her to sit and just held her until her anxious sobbing eased to a calmer breathing.

They say time passes quickly when sitting with a pretty girl. Enough must have passed, as a loud squawk announcing Gabriel's return to the yard jolted us out of the fragment of bliss that our silent moment had offered. Maria was clearly elated to hear the calling of her companion, and she jumped to her feet. I followed her out of the room just as Gustavo returned through the front door carrying a long braided chain. Sylvia was right behind him, looking distraught. We had clearly missed a conversation between the two that wasn't going well. Gustavo held out the chain toward Maria, who froze in response to the gesture.

"It's to protect him," he declared as he pointed the clinking shackles in his hand in Gabriel's direction.

"How does chaining him protect him?" Maria protested.

"What if someone tries to shoot him or capture him for their own gain? It is best."

"I won't!" Maria declared, lifting her tiny torso as high as she could in a futile effort to match Gustavo's bulky presence. Gustavo moved forward to Maria, making it clear he would win this face-off.

"You will!" he said with a sneer and shoved the leg irons into Maria's hands. She ran outside into the yard, the metal loops trailing noisily across the floorboards, perhaps just as much to escape Gustavo's intimidation as to see Gabriel.

Chapter 8

The chanting of "Loro Santo, Loro Santo" began almost as soon as Maria became visible to the throngs of onlookers who were now barricaded at a distance from Gabriel's favourite perch. I watched Maria through the dining-room window. The whispers of veneration crescendoed with every step she took toward Gabriel. Maria sat on her haunches before Gabriel and started rocking backward and forward. Gabriel acknowledged her presence by spreading his wings in a grand gesture, accompanied by a loud shriek.

I couldn't hear her, but I could see the words in Spanish forming on her lips. "Today will be a good day. Today will be a good day."

She reached into her dress pocket and then held out her hand, filled with seeds, for Gabriel. He flew down from the elevated branch and landed on the wooden perch that had been constructed for his feeding at a convenient height for Maria's limited reach. Gabriel dipped his head and ate the seed in Maria's hand. Gustavo had moved to the door leading to the yard. Maria glanced over her shoulder at him. He was a man who had perfected the art of intimidation using nothing more than a stance. She turned back to Gabriel, and her rocking action quickened to keep pace with her anxiety. She lifted the chain and quickly clipped the latch over Gabriel's slender leg, just above the claws grasping the perch. Gabriel reacted with instant alarm, and his wing-span dwarfed Maria as he launched from the perch to escape. The chain slipped through Maria's hands in her recalcitrant effort to restrain

Gabriel. Gustavo rushed out and took the chain from Maria, carelessly pushing her off to the side. Maria collapsed to the ground, crying uncontrollably. She curled up in a protective foetal position around her pregnant belly that now protruded from her like a soccer ball. Gustavo struggled to restrain the protesting bird that was flapping furiously at the end of the chain barely two metres above him. Gabriel was no match for Gustavo's might as he edged backward toward a wooden post and rail that served as a stand for draping used coffee bean bags that were to be refilled. He threw the loose end of the chain around the post so that it coiled upon itself. Then he grabbed the tail of chain and tied it off. He let go of the length that had Gabriel fighting furiously at the other end and stood back. Gabriel continued to strain against his shackles and then had to concede, in likely exhaustion, by landing on the rail beside the coffee bean bags. He continued to scream his protest as he flicked his head frantically about, trying to understand and remove the restraint on his leg. Maria pulled herself to her feet. As Gustavo wrestled with detaining Gabriel, she ran past him into the house and straight into her bedroom. The bedroom door slammed once again behind her, signalling her need for sanctuary.

Robin and I looked at each other with the same what-do-we-do-now expressions. Sylvia was clearly accustomed to dealing with fractious events in her household, and she quickly ushered us toward the front door.

"Don't worry—everything will be okay," she assured us in Spanish. Perhaps she was seeking to reassure herself?

Once outside, the chanting of the onlookers was conspicuously absent. There was a stunned silence as the devotees watched Gustavo the demagogue tame their prized demigod. Perhaps they didn't know whether to protest Gustavo's cruelty or celebrate the new guarantee of access to Gabriel. I had an overwhelming sense that it was time for me to disentangle myself from these events that were spiralling toward an ill-fated outcome, so I hurried away from the tumultuous scene. I didn't bother explaining myself to Robin, as I wasn't in the mood for his exuberance, temporarily muted by Gustavo's feud with Gabriel. A blue feather tumbled in the breeze across the road in front of me. It was as long as my forearm and reminded me of the quills used to ink manuscripts in previous eras. The bright hue with the distinctively black edge told me it had previously belonged to Gabriel. The tussle had clearly damaged his plumage. I picked up the feather without breaking stride and continued toward the lab.

That night, an incessant knocking on my bedroom window woke me. As I clawed back to consciousness, my eyes adjusted to the light enough to identify the figure silhouetted in the moonlight on the other side of the window. I opened the research facility door.

"Maria?"

"Can I come in?"

"Of course."

Maria slid past me into my bedroom and hopped into my bed. She pulled the covers over herself and disappeared completely under the thin cotton veneer.

I called, "Maria! What are you doing?" As if it wasn't obvious.

"I can't take it anymore. I feel safe with you."

"You can't stay here."

"Okay, then take me away with you. Anywhere."

"Maria," I protested as I approached the bed.

"Hold me," she pleaded as she lifted the sheets to reveal her weary eyes and tear-smeared face.

I didn't know what time of night it was, but she had clearly been bawling out her terrors from the moment I had left her house.

I stood there a moment with a sleepy intent of offering an effective rebuttal. But with a sigh, I climbed into the little bunk beside her. She clung to me as though cruel winds of fate were about to blow her out of the bed. She buried her face in the shelter of my chest.

"Do you love me?" she asked softly.

"Why are you asking me that?"

"I need you to protect me."

"Is my love a condition for that?"

"What?"

"I'll protect you."

The tension fell away from her grasp of my frame, and her body relaxed. She fell asleep in our embrace and sealed the contract of her safekeeping in my arms. Despite my exhaustion, I lay awake and contemplated the consequence of the apparent allegiance I had just declared to her.

When she eventually woke in response to the dawn light, I was already awake, or maybe I hadn't quite made it to complete slumber. Her back was to me. I couldn't remember her moving, so maybe I got some rest.

"You can't keep inviting yourself into my bed. If this is something you do with other men, it might explain your pregnancy."

Maria jabbed her elbow into my ribs.

"I've never slept with a man."

"Well, everyone will think I'm the father if you stay here—and your father will want to kill me."

"Oh, my father. I hate him. He made me capture Gabriel. I didn't want to."

"I know."

Maria turned to face me. "You know, he bought himself a new truck with the admission fees he's charging."

"Really?"

"And the tax people came saying he had to declare the money as income."

"I bet he liked that."

"He told them that the money was donated. They disagreed."

"And?"

"Papa told them the money was for the church. So the tax people asked at the church. The priest said he had seen no money coming from Papa."

I chuckled, as I could imagine Gustavo desperately seeking ways not to part with any of his newfound loot.

"So they returned," she continued. "Papa told them he meant the new church. The Church of Gabriel."

"Your father has declared a new religion?"

"I think so. He said the money is to build a new hall, one that can hold hundreds of people. He said he will put Gabriel in there and hire people to collect money to see Gabriel."

I couldn't help thinking to myself that the word "hire" was a euphemism for "volunteer" under the circumstances. There was a knock at the door, so I rose to respond. It was Carlos, who had returned from his Sierra Nevada expedition. He looked at me in my boxer shorts and tee, then to Maria in my bed. I sighed, not bothering with a lame "it's not what it looks like" commentary.

Carlos had his arms full of plant specimens wrapped in bundles of damp coffee sacks. He nodded to me as he walked inside in the way that men do when they're acknowledging a conquest that has earned their unspoken approval and need for discretion.

"We didn't find the Tayrona village," he declared as he dumped the botanical load on the sorting bench. "The Wayuu people tell me the Tayrona don't appreciate being disturbed, anyway. We are nothing more than the offspring of the Spanish invasion to them."

Fair enough, I thought to myself. It *was* an invasion that almost wiped them out. I looked at the plants on the bench and drew attention to them. "If we discover a plant in those mountains that can extend telomeres directly associated with living longer, the Spanish invasion will have been nothing compared to the industrial invasion seeking to harvest the plant."

"Is that a good thing?" Carlos asked.

"It would likely begin in the name of science but end in the name of profit."

"That's not good."

Maria rose from my bed just as Robin's head peered through the doorway.

"I guess you've heard?"

Carlos looked at Robin and then at me for clarification. I introduced them.

"The Church of the Holy Parrot? Yes, I heard."

Robin looked at Maria, who was clearly just getting out of my bed, with the same incriminating expression as Carlos. I didn't bother addressing his "please explain" countenance, either.

"Can you look after Maria for a while?" I asked him, choosing a call-to-action to break the awkward silence. "I have to check the tissue samples that are soaking in the botanical fluids."

"Sure," he replied.

"By the way, I tested a tissue sample from one of Gabriel's feathers."

"Why?" Robin queried.

"I guess I wanted to see if there was anything unique that I could measure."

"And?"

"It's definitely a bird, and a macaw. One thing though. He's actually a she."

"Gabriel is a girl?"

"Gabriella?" I offered without hiding my amusement.

Maria seemed unperturbed by the announcement. "I'm hungry" was the only utterance she offered.

Part of me had hoped that I had exposed a lie that would rattle Maria. But her indifference only added to the doubts of my understanding. The parrot had never declared itself to be Gabriel. It was a name attributed to it.

Carlos rubbed his chin as though contemplating a deep thought. "Perhaps she is a female parrot that identifies as a male parrot who is regarded by others as a messenger from God?" He looked around the room for approval of his theory.

Robin, as expected, offered a more mythological interpretation of the gender issue. "If it helps at all, there's been debate whether the historical notion of the Holy Spirit was male or female. The dove has often been the symbol of this spirit, sharing messages from God. Ancient religions always portrayed the dove, in this ethereal role, as female. In this context, a female parrot is perhaps more apt."

So it seemed that the gender revelation wasn't relevant to the messages and images Maria received in her mind. I glanced across to the fridge that contained the tissue samples that I was meant to be more concerned with in the moment.

"I've got this," Robin said as he gestured for Maria to join him on a scout for food in the village.

Chapter 9

Three hours had passed. It was plenty of time for me to prepare the new plants for testing. Carlos was proving his worth both in collecting samples and assisting me in the lab. The room was more like a greenhouse than a science lab, filled with the vibrant colours of mountain flowers and exotic fragrances. Closing my eyes was the worst distraction—the sea of scents had me swimming naked again with Maria in her secret oasis. It was the one time I had truly felt free from most of the burdens that plagued my mind daily. Once you've tasted sweet freedom from the prison of your own mind, it's difficult to admit who it is that's guarding the gate.

The work allowed me to reconcile an uneasy feeling that had been welling within me. I was less concerned about the mythology surrounding Maria than I was about her effect on me and my work. I either had to draw a line in the sand to declare no more distraction from her turbulent world or accept that I was working in a foreign environment and that a cultural experience was part of the reason we took these positions. Plenty of scientists and business travellers attended local festivities and enjoyed cultural immersion alongside their commitments. As long as I could reasonably fulfil my obligations, my experience was only as colourful as the bouquets on my bench. I nodded appreciatively to Carlos for his contribution, picked up my cigarettes, and headed out the door. The cacophony on the street was leagues away from the quiet little coastal community I had first experienced. I lit my cigarette and inhaled a breath of its familiar flavour. Included was the ambient aroma of fried street food and incense that was the new normal on the dusty road leading to Maria's house. It was time to immerse myself once again in this extraordinary community event that had besieged Buritaca.

The movement of people reminded me of the ebb and flow of a tide. Previously, the flow was distinctly toward Maria's home. But a new energy had emerged in the brief period I had hidden in the lab. From the junction of the tiny track that led from my door to the Via Buritaca, the momentum of activity of food and craft peddlers, labourers carrying their loads, and even meandering tourists was in the opposite direction, toward where the river meets the open sea. It was my favourite part of the village, as it overlooked the tranquil waters of the river to the waves that were rushing the shoreline on the other side of the sandbar. I merged with the flow and ambled along while enjoying the last of my cigarette.

It was only a small village, and the cause of new attention was apparent within a stone's throw of the lab. There was a great hive of activity in and around what I remembered to be a carpark that bordered the sandbanks that led to the final shallows of the river. It was now the makings of a small stage where, previously, dilapidated cars and motorbikes would have converged. A stadium was being built by a multitude of locals and imports using upside-down coffee crates. Each crate consisted of slats of wood nailed to a support frame, and these were being bound together with twine. Woven grass mats were then layered over the arranged crates to create a platform. The periphery of the crates was being solidly reinforced with cemented Besser Blocks that rose high above the stage to shield it from the wind. The bricks were being rendered as fast as they were being laid. A pile of beams that were likely going to form the roof arrived on the stout, sweaty shoulders of builders. I couldn't see any plan or drawing being referenced, or any foreman directing construction in the dust storm of activity. One person would just yell the necessary instructions at another when required. The stadium faced the open sand dunes, which allowed for a vast open space before the river that served as an outer boundary.

The familiar chanting of "Loro Santo, Loro Santo" from the back of the stadium drew my attention. Maria and Robin were being followed by a festival procession of hundreds. They adorned Maria with garlands of bright flower heads in full bloom. Burgeons of beads with tassels and colourful jewellery hung in loops from her forearms. They had pinned even more flowers to her hair and clothing, making her look like a mobile floral arrangement. Even at a distance, I could see the familiar anxiety in Maria's eyes, like a deer sharing a path with hungry carnivores, all wanting a taste of her. She graciously accepted the gifts and garlands being offered as Robin instructed her with words that seemed to calm her apprehension from all the attention.

"Say something to the people," I overheard Robin saying to Maria as they moved closer.

"But I don't know what to say."

"Don't worry—I'll guide you. I've been to hundreds of events like these."

"Events?" Maria asked, clearly puzzled by the use of the word.

"More like greeting the people," he reassured her.

Pablo suddenly appeared through a gap in the adoring crowd. He shoved a piece of paper in Maria's hand and then ran past me up the road, away from all the commotion.

"Open the paper," she said to Robin, as she would not have been able to lift her heavily bejewelled arms.

Robin took the paper out of her hand and opened it. He noticed I had appeared, so he passed the paper across to me for translation. It had a hastily scribed single sentence that was almost illegible on the scrap. It said, in Spanish, "MEET ME AT THE ESTACION DE CABALLOS (horse station) TOMORROW AT NOON, OR I EXPOSE YOU AS A FRAUD." I read the translation aloud for Robin's benefit.

"Who was he? What does he want?" Robin asked the both of us.

"He's a liar and a thief," Maria responded angrily. "Don't worry. I'll deal with him."

The rumbling clatter of a diesel truck engine behind us left the matter of Pablo and his threatening remarks in Robin's pocket, where he shoved the paper. I gathered the shiny black pickup was Gustavo's new ride as he pulled it to a stop directly behind the stage. A flurry of activity poured from the vehicle as workers leapt from the tray. They slid bags of cement and planks of wood out into the arms of the labourers who had dropped their tools in anticipation of the new building materials. A squealing sound erupted from a gathering of the coffee pickers that had just alighted from the utility after the engine cut.

"Maria!" called a feminine voice that had hailed the squeal.

"Daniela!" Maria shrieked delightedly at the sight of her friend.

Maria could barely walk with all the trinkets and blooms adorning her, so she just held her arms out wide for the embrace that Daniela rushed into. The two of them reacquainted in bubbly, rapid Spanish.

"What are you doing here?" Maria asked excitedly.

"Your father offered me work here, for you!" Daniela replied with theatrical gestures. "I collect money from people who want to see your parrot."

"That's fantastic!"

"It's better than harvesting coffee beans all day. It's so busy. This is crazy! I can't wait to tell the other girls how popular you are. You're like a superstar."

"It's so good to see you."

Gustavo was now out of the truck and couldn't help but smirk when he saw his daughter looking like a decorated religious idol laden in jewels and gifts. His delight quickly transformed into a commanding tone.

"Danny, get back to work!"

"Yes, Mr. Santos," Daniela responded meekly.

Maria turned to her father. "Her name is—"

Daniela quickly grabbed Maria's arm to halt her defiant act. "It's okay. He'll never accept my choice."

Maria took Daniela's hand and led her in the opposite direction of her father's instruction. As they walked together, I realised what I had just learned. Daniela was likely previously known as Daniel. I had heard about the boys who worked the coffee fields who dressed as girls. They were called travesti and were remarkably popular in the otherwise conservative Catholic communities. The farmers got hard workers who were strong as young men, and the shopkeepers got pretty ladies who spent their earnings on anything that sparkled. Daniela wore a bright green polka dot dress with a matching bow tied in her hair that was as practical to hold her long, dark, curly locks away from her face as it was pretty. Her overtly effeminate gesturing offered a hint of her choice to explore a trans-dressing identity. Gustavo's condescending tone and insistence on not acknowledging her choice also helped me understand what was going on. I looked across to the group that Daniela had burst out of, and they, too, appeared to be travesti in skirts and crop tops or colourful cotton dresses matched with hair ties and twinkling jewellery.

Robin approached me, likely spotting the bewilderment in my expression. Admittedly, I was curious for an explanation of what had happened in the brief time I had left him alone with Maria.

"They just started following us," Robin offered with a shrug. "We were just walking, intending to buy a few empanadas to satisfy Maria's appetite. Do you know how much that girl can eat?"

"Yes, I'm aware," I replied with fond memories of Maria chomping through mountains of food.

"I was about to pay for the snacks, and they wouldn't let me. Then the idea seemed to catch on, and everyone wanted to offer her something. The offerings kept coming, and the people wanted to walk with us. It's not like we were going anywhere—it's a small village. I think we did three laps. And she ended up looking like a decorated doll."

Maria spotted Robin pointing at her as he talked with me. She took it as a signal to return to our company.

Gustavo called out to Daniela, "Oye, Daniel, ve y únete a las otras señoritas chicos."

I interpreted the phrase *señoritas chicos* as "lady boys," and Daniela took off to do whatever Gustavo had asked of her. The faithful continued to follow Maria's every step, chanting "Loro Santo, Loro Santo."

"You know she has great faith in you," Robin whispered to me so that Maria would not hear. "Perhaps it would be a good idea if you stood by the stage where she can see you, particularly considering what's about to happen."

"What's about to happen?" I asked, with a hint of apprehension.

"You'll see." Robin turned to Maria with a comforting smile. "Are you ready?"

Maria shot me a nervous look and then turned to Robin. "Really, I don't know what you want me to do or say to these people."

Robin nodded assuringly as he guided her toward the stage. "I understand."

I followed them toward the steps that led to the podium. They had been constructed and attached only moments earlier. The workers silently dropped their tools and stepped back in recognition of Maria's presence. A loud squawk heralded Buritaca's other celebrity. The grand macaw was clinging to a perch they had chained him to in the middle of the mostly completed dais. Remembering that the bird was actually female, I made a silent note in my head to refer to *her* as Gabrielle from now on. One of Daniela's travesti friends walked toward Gabrielle with a cane chair and placed it beside her. She then jumped down from the platform and joined Daniela and other travesti who had lined themselves across the face of the stage as sentinel security guards in flamboyant frocks.

Robin guided Maria forward to take a seat in the wicker chair beside Gabrielle. She was visibly trembling. I clutched at the eczema in the crook of my elbow, a nervous behaviour I was developing in response to all the obscure proceedings.

Robin crouched down beside Maria. I wasn't close enough to hear him, but he was facing me, so I'm fairly confident he said, "Now listen carefully. I'm going to teach you how to deal with this."

Hundreds of people merged into the space in front of the stage from all directions, like theatre folk choosing their seats over the sandy dune. With all the people descending into one place, I could no longer make out what Robin was saying to Maria. Eventually, he stepped away from her and moved toward the side of the stage.

He stopped on the edge of the platform and called to her, "You can do this!"

Maria started rocking backward and forward, muttering to herself. It was a behaviour with which I was familiar by now.

"Today will be a good day. Today will be a good day," Maria recited to herself, over and over.

Robin called to Maria again from the periphery. "Maria! Do as I taught you."

What had he taught her? They had only spent the morning together. Maria shot Robin a quick glance as more and more people gathered in the sandy space before her. She continued her rocking, but then suddenly changed her words.

"Loro Santo. Loro Santo. Loro Santo," she voiced, more and more confidently as the words became comfortable on her lips.

She closed her eyes and continued rocking and chanting her new phrase. "Loro Santo, Loro Santo."

What had Robin taught her? Why was it important for her to change her phrase?

"Maria. Focus!" Robin bellowed.

Maria's voice intensified. "Loro Santo, Loro Santo, Loro Santo." It was as if she was searching for something in the words.

The crowd, hearing her words, began to copy her.

"Loro Santo, Loro Santo, Loro Santo" poured from hundreds of mouths, and the chant rapidly crescendoed.

The power of the collective voices reverberated against my chest. Maria stopped her rocking, and a sudden calmness overcame her. Gabrielle, previously silent through the chanting ritual, screeched on her perch so loudly that the crowd responded with stunned silence. Maria opened her eyes and then said words I will never forget for as long as I live.

In a voice that was deep and calm, Maria declared, "Soy mensajero de Dios. Mi nombre es Gabrielle."

I couldn't suppress the thought. *That's not Maria speaking.* The pitch, the tone, and the pace of the words spoken were a stark contrast to her usual vibrant, anxious, and hasty delivery.

"I am a messenger from God. My name is Gabrielle" was the literal translation of her words. Robin was clearly beside himself with overt glee. He clutched at his chest and sighed deeply, like a proud parent does as their child performs on stage. I had no idea what was going on.

Chapter 10

I walked back to the lab in stunned silence after what was possibly the most bizarre presentation I had ever witnessed. Maria addressed the crowd for over an hour, offering thoughts, guidance, and philosophies that I would never have imagined would be uttered from a mind usually focused on life's simple pleasures and concerns. The voice that entranced the audience sounded peculiar compared to the pitch and tone of Maria's voice. Like most of the locals, she usually spoke in a frenetic flurry of Spanish, her words squeezed together tighter than a coffee press. It had made translation a nightmare for me, being a novice to the language.

Yet Maria had spoken precise and articulate Spanish in a calm and comforting tone. The pitch of this voice was lower and much slower than usual, and there was no faltering, no misplaced words, no searching for expressions. As she cradled her pregnant loins, she shared some amazing revelations, including the dawn of a new age and a new Christ, which her followers were likely expecting. She said that she needed to prepare us for the new Christ. Otherwise, people's fear would blind them. She explained God's purpose in creating diversity and how we must embrace an understanding of this. Perhaps what surprised me the most was her assertion that all the major religious faiths had an important role in the evolution of humanity. She described a divine triunity of value where Hinduism was the father, Christianity the Son, and Islam the Holy Spirit. She reminded us that, like any family, they may bicker regarding issues of identity and purpose, but they are still family. How did a village girl from Buritaca know about Islam and Hinduism? Perhaps she had learned of religious diversity from her followers? I expected a riot in response, where jealous religious zealots would demand acknowledgement of the superiority of their faith over others. But not here. There was only cheering and applause. How had she become so worldly, so instantaneously?

I think she was discouraging virtue, signalling with simple phrases. "Do not seek to be liked or to be like others. Your individuality is how you shine. It is a blessing for you and for others," she declared with the authority of a sage. Within her lengthy oration, she shared philosophical challenges. "Disease is dis-ease, or a lack of ease. Spiritual dis-ease is sin. Sin is not about seeking approval from a disapproving God. It is 'missing the mark' in your own potential that is in harmony with God's gifts to you." She described three divine gifts—love, life, and light—with precise certainty on the subject. Cryptic lessons for how to improve ourselves rolled effortlessly from her tongue. "Allow love into your life. Embrace life as you love, and be the light you wish to see in the world for the sake of love and life."

Outside of these events, I had never heard a peep from her about anything virtuous or spiritual. I found it confronting that her explanations were so effortlessly delivered, understandable, and relatable, even for an atheist scientist like me. The idea of an underlying order in all things past and present seemed unquestionably obvious from her words. I couldn't help but challenge the nature of my own values against her assertion that they should embody love, light, and life. I had never thought to filter my words and actions with universal values. My job was to study the nature of things, and I could never have expressed myself so eloquently about my career. All this insightful wisdom flowed effortlessly from a mouth that I had previously thought was mostly just an eager receptacle for street food.

I had to snap out of my contemplative daze as I had a row of eight Wayuu people sitting on cane chairs outside the science facility. Thanks to Carlos, we had arranged for the indigenous group to help us with our research by offering genetic tissue samples. The cells inside the mouth are multilayered and reproduce themselves rapidly, making them perfect for collecting genetic material without adversely affecting the test subject. Carlos and I had been wiping cotton swabs along the inside of the cheeks of the volunteers. We would then run genetic assays to evaluate the telomere strength of the test group. The next step was to grow the cellular samples in controlled conditions and monitor the effect of our plant extracts on the telomeres, looking for enhancement or delay of decay. Carlos was at the door, showing out one of the tested subjects, an elderly gentleman who cheerfully cradled his gift of a bag of roasted coffee against his chest.

"So you do still work here," Carlos teased as I walked past him into the facility.

"Thanks for starting without me."

I didn't want to explain where I'd been or what had transpired, nor was I ready to articulate what I had witnessed. There were far too many questions that I needed to get my head around. I pulled out a fresh pair of surgical gloves from the box in the supplies cabinet and headed back outside to invite the next volunteer in to be tested. I could hear a cacophony of chanting in the distance as the stage wasn't too far from the science building. The mob of cheerful devotees appeared on the road as I introduced myself to an elderly Wayuu lady who was waiting patiently for her turn to offer a genetic sample and receive her gift. The Wayuu people had their own Arawakan language, but there simply wasn't time to learn what they called Guajiro and Spanish in a matter of weeks. Some volunteers were completely silent despite their willingness to take part. Thankfully, most were happy to converse with me in Spanish, and they were often very curious about who I was, where I was from, and why I was there. I think I had explained myself and my work in Spanish so many times that it was becoming an art to find the shortest description to satisfy the curiosity of the locals supporting the research. We both turned to watch the spirited parade of colour float our way on the carpet of dust scuffed up by all the jumping and dancing. The tiny figure of Maria, flanked by Robin, was easily distinguishable at the front of the crowd. All the jewellery and garlands that had been given to her had been removed. She was pacing down the road at a rate that suggested a desire to escape her exhilarated fanfare. When she saw me standing with the Wayuu lady, she hastened her pace. Without acknowledging my presence, she ducked through the front door of the science facility, and then I heard my bedroom door slam shut. I sighed as I helped the Wayuu lady up from her chair. We walked together into the building, which was probably the best thing to do to avoid the crowd that had just descended upon us. At the door, I glanced at Robin, who was standing with his arms extended in a gesture to restrain the followers, who would have probably eagerly followed Maria into the lab.

"That was amazing," Robin declared eagerly as he caught my eye.

"What the hell was all that about?" I snapped back, concerned for Maria's wellbeing.

"I wish I'd taped it. I can't believe she spoke for over an hour," he continued, completely missing my tone of concern.

"Come in and close the door behind you. You need to tell me what just happened."

Robin followed us into the lab, shutting the door behind him as instructed, sealing us away from the hungry eyes outside. I guided the Wayuu lady to a chair and gave her the latest rendition of who I was, what I was doing, and how she was helping science. She smiled at me with kind eyes and nodded her approval. I figured I could continue my work while listening to Robin, hoping he would demystify the bizarre event I had just witnessed.

"It's called channeling."

"What is?"

"What you just saw and heard."

"What on earth are you talking about?"

"It's possibly not very earthly, to be honest."

I could tell that a straight answer wasn't likely to be forthcoming soon. The Wayuu lady opened her mouth, and I gently wiped the inside of her mouth with a swab stick. I then smeared the stick across the orange jelly-like gel in the petri dish I had opened.

"I'll try my best to explain. Essentially, Gabrielle was speaking through Maria. It's a spiritual technique that's been practiced for millennia. It's like tuning into another frequency on a radio other than your own."

"Really?" I challenged incredulously.

"Yes, really."

"So you're saying that Maria *tuned in* to Gabrielle like listening to a radio?"

"Somewhat, yes."

I wasn't sure what explanation I had been expecting, but this wasn't it. I sighed again. "Holy—"

"Parrot," Robin concluded for me.

"So you're suggesting it's a holy parrot that can articulate a thought? Where did it learn Spanish? It only says things like 'today will be a good day' as sounds, with no understanding of the phrase. Your suggestion is absurd."

"I understand it's an odd concept to grasp. It's not really Gabrielle that's speaking. Perhaps it's best to explain that Gabrielle's role for Maria is as a conduit to a mind that she usually would not identify with."

"Whose mind?"

"I can only offer you theories on that."

"I don't think I'm ready for those theories."

I thanked the Wayuu volunteer I had just been working with and helped her to stand. I gave her a bag of coffee and showed her to the door. The crowd of believers was still outside, but they had settled down. Many were sitting, perhaps awaiting a signal or direction from Maria. As I guided the Wayuu lady past the eager faces, I felt a strong pulling sensation at the level of my stomach that I would normally suggest was indigestion. But I was thinking about Maria and dreading what all this was doing to her. How was this sudden rise to fame and accessing this other "mind" affecting her? I closed the door behind the old lady and headed straight across the lab to my room and gently tapped on the door.

"Maria?"

I didn't hear any movement, so I opened the door. Maria was curled up under the cotton sheet, fast asleep. I closed the door again and looked at Robin.

"Why am I stuck in the middle of this?"

Robin just shrugged.

"I don't think I want anything from Maria, but I think she needs something from me. I get it. She needs a port in a storm. She tried to get Pablo to man up and marry her. That would have appeased her parents. When that failed, I was the next guy in her line of sight."

"She's terrified. She definitely values your protection."

"I had a strange dream about Maria when I first met her. I haven't worked it out yet. But it made me feel there's something important about her I shouldn't ignore."

"It seems you allowed her into your life—and your bed—with particular ease."

His tone wasn't judgemental. He just wanted to know more.

"My little sister, Leila, used to jump into my bed when our parents were out. She hated storms. All the noise and flashing light terrified her. I tried reason, coercion, and even bribery, but she wouldn't budge. So I accepted that her need for a sense of safety was more important to her than anything else I could offer her to leave me alone."

"So now you've got Maria helping herself to your bed for protection from her storm?"

"I guess so. When she told me her story, I didn't believe her, and I imagined her parents wouldn't either. It's bizarre how it's all turned out.

I wouldn't have predicted that. In the Bible, what did Mary's parents think of her divine delivery?"

"I don't know," Robin replied flatly.

"I thought you were the expert on these things."

"No one knows."

"Seriously? A girl births the saviour of the new world, and everyone forgot to tell the parents?"

"Perhaps an oversight." He shrugged without undue concern.

"Did Mary have a brother?"

"Don't know."

"Are you kidding?"

"Nope. We don't even know how old she was. There's speculation that she would have been around fifteen or sixteen, as the life expectancy back then was much shorter, and the girls were married off very young."

"I don't even know if that's legal in my country."

"Her fiancé, Joseph—"

"She wasn't married either?"

"No. And theologians suggest Joseph was older than Mary."

"Do you think Maria wants me to be her Joseph?"

"It's possible. But it sounds like she was hoping Pablo would fulfil that role." He paused momentarily, and I could tell that he was choosing how to express his next thought. "Speaking of roles, I am curious. Why are you here?"

I thought the answer was obvious. "For the research project."

"Yes, I'm aware of that. But why you? Why did you put your hand up for this?"

I felt my face flush instantly in response to the directness of his question. "I just thought, why not?"

"Really?"

I wasn't ready to share my life story with Robin and started to feel agitated.

"Could you please tell Maria's mother, Sylvia, that Maria is resting here," I said, "so that she might come and collect her later?"

"Sure," he replied as he headed for the door.

"And see if you can get the crowd to disperse. I think she's had enough attention for one day."

"Absolutely," he said as he headed outside, closing the door behind him.

I turned my attention to the task at hand. We had a quota of tissue samples that we were aiming to have available for the research. I invited the next volunteer into the lab, but my mind constantly drifted, wondering what was going on with Maria. What had she gotten herself into? How would she explain, in her words, how she could speak so confidently and insightfully to a crowd of hundreds?

Carlos didn't ask questions about the commotion outside or why Maria was back in my bed. I could only assume that he presumed she was there waiting for me to join her as her lover and the likely father of her child. Her affinity for helping herself to my bedroom might lead Gustavo to the same conclusion. That situation was becoming more precarious as he now vehemently defended Maria's assertion of a "holy" conception. My close association with Maria would have him perplexed.

The hours passed. Carlos and I collected thirty-four tissue samples from the local population, which was a mix of indigenous, Spanish, and African heritage. We were ahead of our estimated quota. I realised the sudden influx of population could be used to our advantage by asking some visitors for genetic samples to use as a control population to compare to the telomere health of the locals. Perhaps the local gene pool would react differently to the collected plant extracts because of tolerance or heightened biological responsiveness achieved through repeated exposure?

A heavy knocking on the front door of the lab abruptly interrupted my train of thought. I knew of one particularly hefty-limbed person who could wield such a thump. I responded quickly to save my door from damage. When I opened the door, Gustavo's ungainly form in the doorway choked away most of the light from outside. Sylvia pushed him aside before he accused me of anything that his expression suggested he was about to do.

"Is Maria here?" she asked in Spanish.

"Yes," I answered in kind.

The next part, explaining that she was in my bed, was going to be difficult in Gustavo's presence.

"After her presentation—" I didn't know what to call what she had done "—she ran into that room."

I pointed to the door in a way that sheepishly implied that I had no association with the bedroom.

"I've been working with Carlos all day."

I looked at Carlos for reassurance. His amused grin wasn't helping. Sylvia moved past Gustavo, and I stepped out of her way as she headed to the bedroom door. She knocked rapidly on the flimsy panels.

"Maria? Are you in there?"

"Go away!" was the immediate reply. At least Maria had returned to her usual candour.

Sylvia threw open the door and stepped inside. After a brief exchange of conflicting preferences, Maria emerged from the room under her mother's wing. As they walked out of the science facility, Gustavo glared at me but said nothing. I closed the door.

"That went well!" Carlos declared in a fit of laughter.

Not knowing exactly what Gustavo and Sylvia thought of finding their sixteen-year-old pregnant daughter asleep in my bed, I kept my distance over the next few days. I didn't ask Maria about her "channeling" experience, but I heard that her ritualised events had become a daily occurrence. Maria would walk from her house, guarded protectively by her travesti security entourage and guided by Robin. During her tour of the village, on the way to the stage, her devotees lovingly layered gifts and garlands on and around her. The gift-giving was often implied permission for the devotees to move closer to Maria. Many appeared genuinely in awe of her. They clutched at her palms and politely requested to touch her pregnant belly that was large enough now to push her dress away from her pelvis and thighs. Her appearance gave the impression that she was gliding or hovering along the road, as we could not see the movement of her little legs below the billowing cotton drape. She would then join Gabrielle on the stage and begin rocking backward and forward, chanting "loro santo" repeatedly until the moment when she would hear from Gabrielle in her mind. I looked up channeling to get a meagre grasp of what was going on. It turned out that Robin was right in that it was actually quite a well-known practice in more spiritually inclined circles. The channeler is akin to a language translator or an interpreter who can communicate with angelic beings, nature spirits, non-physical entities, and animals. In Maria's case, her nonverbal communication with a macaw, Gabrielle, was likely for her to interpret and share in her own voice.

The knocking of knuckles on my front door once again ripped me away from the daydream I seemed to escape to whenever Maria's name was on my lips. I could now identify Maria and Gustavo simply by the way they assaulted my door, so I knew it was someone different. I opened the door and was greeted by Robin's concerned face. He cut to the chase.

"I think you should come," he said.

I wondered whether it was just him or if it was an American thing to skip greetings.

"What's going on?"

"The police are questioning Maria about the disappearance of a village boy called Pablo."

"The boy she's been angry with?"

"Yes, the one who put that note in her hand threatening to expose her."

The squeezing feeling in my stomach returned instantly. I asked no more questions. I was going to have to deal with Gustavo and Sylvia's prejudices regarding my presence. We headed to the house together. The road leading to Maria's home looked like the circus had come to town. Squatters entertaining themselves with activities like juggling, dancing, and yoga-inspired acrobatics occupied every inch of land. Or they lounged in small groups on rugs and sarongs strewn haphazardly in small circles. Local vendors tiptoed around the maze of mats offering food, beverages, and memorabilia to the faithful gatherings.

The front door was open, and two policemen flanked the entrance. They looked at us curiously as we walked past them into the house. We had no reason to explain ourselves to them. I was eager to see Maria and ensure her safety. Inside, two more policemen were standing in the centre of the room before Maria, who was sitting on a kitchen chair. Across the room, Sylvia's attention was on Gustavo, who was clearly irate in response to the police presence in his house. I gathered she was trying to prevent Gustavo from launching himself across the room at the police, which would be his way of offering protection for his daughter. Maria spotted me between the gun halters of the policemen and launched up from her chair in my direction, inadvertently shoving the policemen out of her way. She threw her arms around me and pressed her face against my chest in an eager embrace.

"I didn't do anything. They won't believe me."

I lifted her chin to look at her properly. I thought I had glimpsed something odd on her face in her brief flight path across the room toward. A distinct bruise adorned her left cheek. The raised welt of red and blue choked alarm in my throat. I looked at the policemen as I mused over the Spanish translation of what I wanted to ask.

"What happened here?" I finally blurted out.

The policemen barely reacted to my query.

"It's nothing, really," Maria assured me.

"Nothing? The side of your face looks like a football! Did you do this?" I challenged the policemen with exasperation. Although I didn't know what I could have done if the answer was yes.

Neither of them reacted defensively. They both looked at Maria's bruised face with salient disinterest, and one just said, "No."

I tried to gather my thoughts.

"Did you meet with Pablo? Did he do this?"

"No! I swear! I was going to meet with him. But I didn't."

Unconvinced, I pressed further. "Did you fight with him?"

"No! The baby makes me clumsy. I slipped and hit a post." She turned to look at the policemen. "They think I have something to do with Pablo's disappearance. I swear I don't know where he is."

I grasped Maria's shoulders and looked at her earnestly. "Maria, I know about the note. Did you tell the police that Pablo has been threatening you with extortion?"

"No."

"Maria, you need to. Lying or concealing this will only get you in trouble."

"Okay, I'll tell them."

Robin stepped forward and pulled Pablo's note from his pocket. He handed it to Maria.

"I kept it. I thought it was possibly going to present itself as a problem at some stage."

"I will tell them everything. I have nothing to hide," Maria assured me as she turned to the police and handed them the note.

She explained the details of the extortion attempt to them, which was in line with my understanding of events.

"It's a missing person case. He could be anywhere," Robin mused as we listened to Maria's explanation of her relationship with Pablo to the police. "They can't charge her with anything if there's no known crime."

The police asked Maria a few more questions and then thanked Gustavo for his cooperation. I think it was their way of saying thank you to Sylvia for stopping Gustavo from starting a fistfight. As they left, Maria breathed a deep sigh of relief. The ordeal had clearly rattled her. She followed the police to the door in order to close it behind them. As they stepped down from the porch, a portly, middle-aged woman stepped up and walked determinedly forward. She faced off with Maria, who was holding the door on the other side of the opening. Without a word, she spat on Maria's face, turned on her heel, and marched away. Maria closed the door. She sighed again as she regarded the stunned expressions branded across everyone's faces in the room.

"That was Pablo's mother," she offered as she wiped the spit away from the bridge of her nose with her sleeve.

Chapter 11

The episode with the police left me rattled. Did Maria have something to do with Pablo's disappearance? Perhaps he was just away? If so, where? How did she really get that bruise on her cheek? If she had met with Pablo, it could have gone terribly wrong, as the conversations I had witnessed between them had only been hostile accusations. If Pablo really was the father of the child, then how far would Maria be willing to go to maintain her story of inception via divine grace? I wasn't ready to discuss all these concerns with Robin, as he seemed enthusiastic about embracing Maria's newfound fame, no matter how frantically the events escalated. I wasn't totally sure what his motivations were. What was he actually teaching Maria? When he instructed her to "do as I taught you" when she started channeling Gabrielle, had he taught her a trick? I scratched at the eczema in the crook of my elbow that flared and itched as I worried about the meaning of things.

We hadn't stayed long at Maria's house. The emotional tensions in the family were too high for me to sit quietly with Maria to ask her any of the gazillion questions I had regarding her channeling of Gabrielle, Pablo's disappearance, or her plans for the instantly popular Church of Gabrielle. Was channeling parrots going to be her ongoing career?

By the time Robin and I made it back to the science facility, the first busload of people arriving in Buritaca pulled up in front of Maria's oration stage, which now had its thatched roof secured. I had never seen a bus in Buritaca. Usually, the buses would just pull over on the highway, and the smattering of folks arriving would just walk the easy two kilo-metres into town. Otherwise, they could risk life and limb with one of the many teenage boys offering moto taxi motorbike rides who mainly targeted high-paying tourists eager to meet Gabrielle and Maria.

"This will not end soon, will it?" I sighed, hoping Robin would reassure me otherwise.

"Perhaps when the baby is born," he replied. "Although that could make it worse. I know you have your work to do, but could I ask you to accompany Maria to her next oration tomorrow? They're scheduled now."

"Scheduled orations? She's sixteen! You can see she's terrified."

"I think she's becoming as fascinated as the rest of us. She is present while she channels Gabrielle. So she learns from her too."

My mind boggled at the notion of learning from a parrot.

"What do I do?" I asked, stupidly, instead of protesting about the entire scenario being scheduled.

"You pretty much just stand there. If something goes wrong, fix it. I have to go to Santa Marta to collect the Manichaean."

"What's that?"

"Not what, but who. He's here from China. Apparently, he hasn't uttered a word for thirty years."

"How does he communicate?"

"I'm not sure, but we're about to find out. Historians link the

Manichaeans to the Gnostics, who had their origins in Egypt. The Gnostics were part of the shift from paganism to Christianity. It's so exciting!"

"Why are you so excited?" I asked, even though I knew it took very little to get Robin buzzing.

"Because there are no Manichaeans. The faith died out in the four-teenth century. So who's this guy?"

"Yes, that's a really significant question." I realised my query was actually greater than the context of the Manichaean. "I meant, why are you so excited about religion and faith?"

I felt I needed to understand Robin more, as he had just materialised in the middle of Maria's existential crisis and none of us really knew anything about him. I suggested he take a seat in one of the wicker chairs used by the volunteers along the front wall of the science facility. We sat together and watched the craziness of Buritaca stream by as he related to me the events that had shaped his life.

Robin took me back to his childhood memories of when he was a five-year-old living with his parents on an acreage near the lush estu-aries of the Louisiana delta. Alligators and religion were staples in the bayou, and his father was a pillar of strict Presbyterian values. Whereas he described his mother as a gentle and kind woman whose traditional beliefs were anathema to his father's faith.

"My father is Christian, and my mother was best described as Louisiana Voodoo."

"That's an interesting mix."

He continued to describe a particular memory of sitting on the weathered planks of the front porch during another Sunday of oppressive heat, slapping mosquitos and catching insects as they crawled up through the gaps of the aged and buckling timber. His mother appeared around the side of the house from the chicken pen that caged a regular supply of Sunday dinners. She held a flapping chicken upside down by the legs in one hand and a large carving knife in her other hand. He recalled that his mother was an excellent cook, offering delicious servings of gumbo, crawfish boil, and his favourite, shrimp and grits. She would prepare all her meals from scratch, to the extent of catching her own supply. He reminisced about accompanying his mother on long walks through the steamy delta that flourished with all types of flying and crawling life. At the water's edge, she would continue in, knee-deep in mud and slush, with the tails of her dress in one hand and a crawfish pot in the other.

On the particular morning that he was describing, he believed his mother assumed that her husband was still away on church duties. He usually was at that time of day as an avid participant in the recruitment door-knocking. But he had returned early that day to prepare a scripture reading that the minister had asked him to contribute to the service later that day. Robin clearly enjoyed remembering the image of his mother beginning her usual routine of culling a bird for their supper. His father had insisted she convert to Christianity. Which she did. But she still had voodoo ties. She would dance and sing as she traipsed her way across the lawn. Her light, melodic voice was like an angel whispering happy delights into his young ears. At the chopping block, in the tradition of her beliefs, she would chant a voodoo ritual for the life and spirit of the chicken that was about to be cleaned. The purpose of the behaviour, he later discovered, was a gesture of gratitude for the sacrifice the bird was making in order for their family to eat. She did this with all food, but never in front of her husband. Perhaps the ritual attempted to reconcile the fact that life needs to take life to sustain itself. On this occasion, Robin's father walked right into the ecstatic knife-wielding dance with his Bible clutched tightly against his chest.

"My father feared evil spirits had possessed her," Robin lamented. "He yelled out, 'Begone evil spirits' as he lunged at her, tackling her to the ground."

His father attempted to wrestle out the demons he assumed were possessing his wife. Robin detailed how his mother fell backwards right in front of him. Her skull cracked open like a ripe coconut on the edge of a rock that was jutting out of the ground behind her. He had killed her only metres away from the distraught five-year-old.

"That's terrible. So, is your dad in prison now?"

"No. He never actually served any sentence. He pleaded self-defence in court, and the Christian jury let him go."

"And where is he now?"

"Who knows? I left home when I was sixteen and haven't seen or spoken to him since."

"That'd make me hate religion," I said, as a presumption of Robin's likely response.

Robin contemplated my words and then looked at me with the most soulful expression.

"Before I left, I had ten years of my father telling me he did my mom a favour. He really believed that demons possessed her, and she was better off dead."

He diverted his gaze to the dusty ground before him and dug lines in the rust-coloured sand with his toe. I think he was trying to calm the emotion welling within him.

"Religion is like a gun. If you put it in the hands of someone full of fear, it's a dangerous weapon."

I wondered if he did, in fact, despise religion as a consequence of his father's actions.

But then he continued. "Also, like guns, religion is for protection and to defend the weak. It was my father, full of fear about voodoo, that killed my mother. Not his religion."

He gathered his thoughts.

"So I figured, if there are going to be fools who misuse religion as a fear-filled weapon of ignorance, my job should be to protect people like my mother by sharing the wisdom of all faiths."

His comment weighed heavy in the air for me, like the oppressive humidity that wicked sweat up through my pores. Robin had obviously deeply contemplated the harrowing events surrounding his mother's death, which had whittled him into a spear of destiny to address fear expressed as self-righteousness.

"That's a big job," I said and then thought about my vocation. "How about no religion if that's what divides people? Science is peaceful."

"Religion was once one of the greatest causes of genocide in the world. But now it's science—with its bombs and drugs."

"Science has offered a lot more than bombs and drugs. It has helped to save lives."

"So has religion. And science is unfortunately even more political than religion, and it's blatantly corrupted by profiteers."

"That's true."

"So I believe we need to help people find a universal faith. One that discourages division and encourages unity for the good of everyone."

I appreciated his trust in me to share such a sad and disturbing memory.

"That sounds like the ultimate science project, too."

"So, are you ready to tell me?"

"What?"

"Why you're here?"

"I told you already," I chided defensively.

"Okay," he replied softly.

I jumped up from my chair and headed toward the lab door, telling myself that I surely needed to be somewhere else, then stopped and took a deep breath.

"I was a father once."

Chapter 12

"Once? Aren't you in your early twenties?" Robin asked, baffled by my admission of parenthood.

"Yes. I got to hold her one time only, but the child died."

"Oh, I'm terribly sorry. We don't need to talk about it."

"I haven't. With anyone. Perhaps I should?" I asked as my chest tightened and the eczema on my arm itched as though on cue.

"It's up to you."

"The mother, Ruby, had an undiagnosed weak heart. It was a congenital heart defect, atrial septal defect." I could hear the quiver in my voice and took another deep breath to calm my nerves. I didn't know if I was going to be able to manage saying much more. "Ruby is from here. Well, near here. We had always planned to visit her parents. They live in San Basilio de Palenque."

"I know that village. It's about half an hour out of Cartagena, right? Is Ruby a Palanquera?"

"Yes."

"Her history is akin to my own. Palenque was the first free town of the Americas. Runaway African slaves established it."

"Sixteen ninety-one. She told me. The year the Spanish granted them independence from the colonial powers."

"How did you meet?"

"She was in Australia on a student scholarship. Still is. She was interested in genetics because, like you, she doesn't know her heritage beyond the country that they introduced her ancestors to as slaves."

"That's extraordinary."

"She was my girlfriend at college. She got pregnant. It was an accident." I sighed. I was beginning to relax again. It wasn't as challenging to share as I first thought. I wondered if it may even be helpful.

"I don't understand."

"What? Why did the child die? It was a malnourishment issue. She was born prematurely and simply failed to thrive."

"Not that. Why isn't Ruby here with you?"

"My mother hadn't exactly accepted my relationship with Ruby to begin with." I shifted uneasily and looked at the dirt that I began scuffing up with my sandal. "When we announced the pregnancy, and that we intended to keep the child, she reacted poorly and told us both that it would interfere with our studies and, perhaps, our careers. My mother is a magistrate, and she values academia above, well, probably everything else."

"And that upset Ruby?" Robin queried, eager to understand.

"That was just the warm-up round." I felt the quiver return to my throat. It was going to be difficult to continue, but I had forged a path that needed a destination. "When the child passed, Ruby overheard my mother express her relief."

"What did she say?"

I took a deep breath, but that couldn't defer the tears that welled. "Thank God for that."

"Oh, dear."

"That's one way of putting it. Ruby stormed out of the house and hasn't spoken to me since."

"But you're not responsible for what your mother says."

"She said it to me, and I didn't react. I think I was too numb. The loss had already shocked me. Ruby used my lack of outrage to fuel hers."

"I see."

I laughed as I wiped away my tears. "Imagine telling my parents about this sixteen-year-old girl in my bed, who is also Colombian, who is also pregnant, but with someone else's child, perhaps God's. What could go wrong?"

Robin laughed out loud as he stood and put his arms around me to hug my broken spirit.

"When this research opportunity came up, I think I applied out of spite." I hadn't considered my motivation until this point.

"Can I ask you something?" he asked across my shoulder. He took my silence as permission to proceed. "Is it important for you to impress your parents?"

"To be honest, probably."

"Imagine being free of that burden."

"Easy for you to say. You don't even talk to your father."

"You're right. I have my own cross to bear." He dropped his arms away and stepped back.

I continued to smear tears across my cheeks with grubby palms. "I assume that's a biblical reference? Jesus and the cross?"

"Yes, my friend. Some people interpret that life is destined to be a struggle. Others say that Jesus's suffering proves that love can overcome every hardship. He continued to love no matter what cruelty they subjected him to."

"Well, which one is it?" I asked, genuinely curious.

"I guess you have to choose," he said. "Now that I understand you better, how do you feel about your association with this young pregnant Colombian girl, considering what you've been through?"

I was feeling dizzy from the hyperventilating that had accompanied my tears. "I feel like I'm being challenged to pay attention to something I've been running away from."

"That's very honest and insightful. But may I ask you, who is offering you that challenge?"

"Bugger, you've got me there." I smiled. "I'm supposed to say God, right?"

"Say what you believe is true."

I think he was capitalising on my vulnerable state. "Do you really think there's someone or something out there, pulling strings?"

"I wouldn't say pulling strings. I'd say providing opportunities for growth. Otherwise, it's a pure coincidence that you and I are in Colombia with a girl who helps herself to your bed for protection from her storm, just as your younger sister did when you were a child, who is also pregnant, just like your ex-girlfriend, who has a history of slavery in her family, just as mine did."

"Enough! I get it." I didn't get it at all.

"And we will visit her village together, for our own reasons."

I laughed again despite being emotionally drained. "Will we?"

"Absolutely," he assured me with a beaming smile that reminded me of the picture on his credentials card. "You know the concept of God doesn't have to only be the image of an old man sitting on a cloud talking down to us. That's called literalism, when people believe creational concepts or metaphors to be literally true. Perhaps it was necessary to create a literal image of God to appeal to the masses? Now that they're curious, they're ready to graduate to the next level of understanding?"

"And what's that?"

"Interpreting the divine in terms of consciousness. A consciousness that is part of us, that we can interact with as a wave-force, or a point of focus. Modern science says that consciousness evolved from matter. Spirituality says matter is a dream of consciousness."

I raised my hands defensively. "I'm too tired for this now." I rummaged in my pockets for a packet of cigarettes. Once I found my prize, the familiar aroma calmed my mind from the whirlwind of emotions, like breathing in the stillness of a misty morning.

"Have you been to Palomino yet?" I asked, as a change of pace seemed enticing.

"No, I haven't," he said and smiled. He knew an invitation was brewing.

I took a few steps toward the Via Buritaca so that I could see if there were any moto taxis down the road. A couple of local lads with their bikes were hanging about outside the Cabañas Casa Nevada, waiting for their next transport assignment. I waved them over. They hitched us up behind them on their scooters, and we were on our way to Palomino. I tried to finish my cigarette as we virtually flew onto the Troncal del Caribe, but I gave up as the fresh air rushing against my face became far more appealing and invigorating.

It normally takes thirty minutes to get to Palomino, but I think we made it in twenty. I handed back to my pilot the helmet he had loaned me and filled his palm with enough pesos to buy him and his friend a party at one of the local licorerías.

The vibe of Palomino was distinctly different from Buritaca, despite the close locality. Whereas Buritaca is a fishing village inhabited mostly by locals, Palomino emerged more recently as a tourist hub, mainly attracting surfers and backpackers seeking a remote Caribbean coastal community. The main drag, known only as Carrera Seis, or street number six, had wall-to-wall rickety tiendas selling beads and bangles, artwork and organics, all tailored to the visiting hordes.

The moment I stepped off the scooter, the phone in my back pocket pinged the familiar sound of a message having been received. We were back in a cellular coverage area. I looked to see the first message with the three letters "WTF" emblazoned across the screen from my sister Leila to get my attention. I tapped in my code and read the reason for her acronym use: *Saw you on social media standing on a stage next to a parrot and a kid dressed like a piñata. Explain?* Robin walked toward me, and I showed him the message.

"What do you say we get a drink first and then deal with our publicity problems?"

I had every intention of ignoring any publicity, including my little sister's curiosities, allowing them to find their natural course without my intervention. I hadn't used social media since I left Australia, mainly because I wasn't particularly interested in seeing images or footage of my ex enjoying her life without me. It had been quite pleasant to disappear in the short period I had been in Colombia, but life catches up with every escape plan. As we walked together towards Rene's Bar, where I knew we would be rewarded with a refreshing cold brew, I amused myself by wondering how my sister would react if I texted back: *The parrot is Gabrielle, a messenger from God. The colourfully dressed kid is Maria. She's the mother of the new Christ. All going well. Miss you. x* I stopped myself from sharing any of this with her.

The slogan on the circular pink sign dangling from a beam caught my eye. Rene's Bar: Surrealismo Mágico. I couldn't have imagined a more appropriate watering hole to match the magical surrealism that was swamping my life. We settled in on the wooden bench seats below the painted image on the wall of two swirling carp in a pond that were chasing each other's tails to form a shape akin to the Yin and Yang symbol. Robin noticed how the myriad of painted motifs around us caught my attention.

"Please, God, show me a sign!" he said playfully, his hands raised in a theatrical gesture.

I laughed out loud, which really helped me to relax. We settled into a light discussion of favourite experiences in Colombia over a round of Cerveza Poker, a brew made in Bogotá. I chose the cooler rainforests around Minca, high in the Sierra Nevada, whereas Robin preferred the tropical paradise of Cabo San Juan del Guía, where the lush growth of the Tayrona National Park met idyllic beach coves shielded by reefs from the open Caribbean Sea. We shared enough beers that night to convince ourselves that we could achieve anything. This included a pact to drive five hours to visit the oldest free settlement of Africans in the Americas, and to make it back by sunset.

Chapter 13

Despite the intensity of my headache and the inescapable nausea that accompanied my hangover, when I arose the following day, I immediately remembered that we had agreed to hire a car and drive to San Basilio de Palenque. We allowed for two hours in the town and meals in Barranquilla along the way. It was going to be at least a thirteen-hour journey, but it was important enough for both of us to go. One message I had received in Palomino was from my supervisor. He was being pressured by Pravus executives to show results, so he dumped their expectations onto me. I had been in Buritaca for two months at this stage and had barely scratched the surface of collecting data and analysing it. If they wanted a miracle, they should have hired Maria or her parrot. It was tempting to write to Professor Jonas to offer this solution to Pravus, but I thought better of it. I texted my sister to tell her that what she had seen on social media was me taking part in a local festival. It was enough information, considering that I didn't really know what was going on, anyway.

I wondered if the best way to deal with my hangover was to walk it off, so I lit a cigarette and headed down the road toward Maria's house. From a distance, it looked more like an ornately decorated shrine than a home. Maria was in the backyard with a lady that looked very similar to her mother. They were mending coffee bags together. When I called out to her, Maria threw the bag she had laid across her lap to the ground and waddled across the yard to greet me. Her pregnancy didn't seem to know a limit to growth, as her belly now resembled a basketball.

She hugged me enthusiastically as usual and pulled on my hand to lead me back to where she had been working to introduce me to her aunt Felicia. Felicia stood in expectation of a formal introduction. Maria rushed her way through an explanation of who I was in Spanish.

"Aunty Felicia, this is the man I have been telling you about. My lion. He's a scientist. He's been helping me. You can call him Leo."

"Mucho gusto, Señor Leo," she replied with the same gracious smile that Maria's mother would often share.

Maria's aunt also pronounced my name as "layo." It was becoming a familiar sound. Maria explained she was teaching her aunt how to repair and recycle the damaged coffee sacks to be ready for use.

"Papa says I won't have time to do my work for the coffee company anymore, so I have to teach my aunty what I do. He is teaching aunty Felicia's husband, Enrique, his truck route. He wants to spend more time running the church."

Her aunt smiled at me the way people do when they don't understand a conversation but wish to appear supportive. It crossed my mind that it was clearly more profitable for Gustavo to focus greater attention on church responsibilities, which required Maria as the centrepiece.

"What about your schooling?" I asked, assuming that education was a part of Maria's routine.

"What schooling? I finished school last year."

Gustavo would have been keen to get Maria working for him as soon as possible, as opposed to offering support for her continuing education. I didn't ask whether he paid her for her work or whether the deal was food and lodging. Maria never carried money. I was starting to wonder whether Gustavo's often repeated assertion that he would do anything for his family was a diversion from his true intention to make his family do anything for him. Did my role as her "lion" include offering her financial guidance? Perhaps that was one of Robin's roles as he seemed to embrace a teacher relationship with Maria. I shelved the thought for a discussion on another day and told Maria that Robin and I were planning to make a return trip out to San Basilio de Palenque. The plan was to return the same evening so that she would know where we were and why we were away.

"I'll come," she blurted out.

"I don't think..." was all I could get out before she continued to cement her inclusion.

"I can be your interpreter! Your Spanish is still terrible."

Before I could consider a counter-argument, she pushed past me to go into the house.

"Which day?" she queried as she reached the door.

"I don't know. We hadn't decided yet."

"Okay, tomorrow then," she said as she disappeared inside the house.

I followed her inside to witness the response Sylvia was going to give. She passed the responsibility of deciding across to Gustavo, who would be home in the afternoon. Maria seemed confident that she could convince her father that she should join the road trip.

"I will meet you on the road outside your lab in the morning. If I'm not there, go without me."

"What time?" I asked, wondering why I was asking her and not the other way around.

"How far is it?"

"About five hours."

"Then I'll see you at seven. I've never been further than Santa Marta. It's going to be so exciting!"

I had no reason not to include Maria. If it suited Robin, then my task for the day was to arrange car hire. Sylvia took a packet of ponqué tradicional from the kitchen cupboard and began slicing it up. I recognised the familiar blue packaging of the local version of pound cake that was sold in most tiendas that offered food. She placed the sliced cake on the dining table and then began preparing us some fresh agua panela. Maria sat down and dug into the cake voraciously. I took a seat and listened to Maria list all the things she felt were going to be necessary for our journey.

Everything seemed to fall into place. I could borrow a car from another of Maria's relatives. Robin was happy to continue with the plan, and Maria was standing on the road outside my lab at seven o'clock in the morning. I swung my rucksack into the boot of the car, and Maria approached with her small bag of supplies.

"How did you convince your father to get a day off?" I had to ask.

"I told him that if he didn't let me go, I would never be involved in his church again."

She had found a leverage point with Gustavo by threatening his new income supply. Robin wandered casually toward us from the Hostal Alfon, his new Colombian abode. He added his bag to the load, and we headed out onto the highway in an old red Mazda that may not have been completely roadworthy. I became accustomed to the large crack right in front of the driver's side windscreen as much as I did the constant rattle that emanated from somewhere within the door beside me. Between us, we had enough food that we didn't need to pull into Baranquilla for supplies. This allowed us to make up time by bypassing the sprawling city. We stopped at roadside tiendas for regular toilet breaks. Maria's bladder was obviously struggling with the jolting vibrations that had me questioning the integrity of the car's shock absorbers. Outside of Barranquilla, we followed the Magdalena River much of the way to Palenque. It was a pretty drive as the sprawling river was often visible, and the small villages lining its banks all had their own rustic charm. The meandering journey offered plenty of time for Maria to ask me a myriad of questions regarding my past association with Ruby, the associated events, and the point of my interest in visiting her hometown. She took in all the information with keen interest without prying too much into the unfortunate circumstances that led to my eagerness to leave Australia.

We arrived where the San Cayetano road intersected with the dirt road leading into San Basilio de Palenque right on schedule. Young boys sat under the shade of the trees with their scooters near the bus stop on the side of the road opposite the junction. I figured they were waiting there to offer moto taxi rides into town for tourists who had taken the public bus from Cartagena. We drove slowly along the dusty road that offered many surprise potholes and ridges. The five-hour journey had given me time to think about what I was going to say to Ruby's parents, Julia and Moe. I hadn't known how to contact them. I just knew that they worked in a hardware store near a statue in town based on what Ruby had described to me previously. It was a weekday, so I banked on them being at work. If they weren't there, at least I would feel satisfied that I'd tried to contact them.

As we neared the town, we passed small, brightly painted houses

made of concrete blocks with corrugated tin roofs that were in a hap-
hazard assortment of well-maintained and dilapidated. Young boys on
small horses waved cheerfully to us as we passed. We all waved back as
I wondered what the large white woven plastic sacks that were slung
over the flanks of their horses contained.

We arrived at the imposing Casa de la Cultura Graciela Salgado
Valdez before its dark blue lattice gate and burgundy tin roof. The
tourist office in Cartagena had instructed Robin that this was where
we were to meet our guide. The custom was for tourists to enter the
town with a guide so that we could visit the highlights of the town
whilst respecting the privacy of the residents. Sure enough, standing
right at the gate was a fit-looking young man wearing a loose linen
shirt. He wore a lanyard around his neck that we soon discovered identified him as Mateo, our official guide. We parked the car and alighted
to be greeted by the warm smile of Mateo, who introduced himself in
Spanish. He then explained that he had been born and bred in San
Basilio de Palenque, so he could answer any of our questions. He didn't
speak English, which inspired Maria to fulfil her role as our interpreter.
She quickly explained that, beyond our curiosity to discover the highlights of the town, I was particularly interested in meeting Moe and
Julia Reyes for personal reasons. Mateo didn't ask what those personal
reasons were. He simply whistled a shrill pitch to capture the attention
of a young boy who was crossing the street about a block away. The boy
ran toward us, and Mateo whispered instructions in his ear.

"Can I ask your name?" he queried of me in Spanish.

"Leonard Lumière," I replied in kind. "They will know my name."

The boy nodded and took off at a sprint to disappear around the
corner of the building.

"Let me show you our beautiful and historic town," Mateo invited in Spanish as he pointed toward the centre of town.

We wandered through the town together at a leisurely pace, passing many locals who were simply relaxing on their front porches or passing us in the street, often carrying goods destined for domestic duties like washing or cooking. The houses were mostly small, single-fronted dwellings that were a brightly painted blend of concrete and brick with shingled or steel roofs. I appreciated that just about everyone waved to us and called out, "Hola!" as we passed. It caught my eye that there was a lack of fences dividing properties and that gated yards were few. It gave the distinct impression that we were visiting a highly connected community and not just a town of disjointed neighbours. Mateo explained to us that the town originated as a community called a palenque, which can be used as a term for a home or shelter. It was founded as a refuge for runaway slaves in the seventeenth century. The enclave is listed as Intangible Cultural Heritage by UNESCO. They had their own Palenquero language, which was a creole mix of Spanish and Bantu. He confirmed my observation that the town had a tradition of connection for the residents, called ma kuagro, where the community arranged itself into family networks and age groups. Membership in these groups came with social responsibilities, rights, and duties that encouraged a strong sense of internal solidarity and fraternity.

We paused in front of a green oxidised copper statue of a gloved boxer sporting a victory stance on a pedestal. I looked for a hardware store nearby, but I could see none. Mateo drew my attention to the name on the plaque that adorned the pale, puckered sandstone wall framing the statue. The plaque read, "Antonio Cervantes Reyes—Kid Pambele. Campeón mundial." Mateo pointed out that this world champion boxer was the uncle of Ruby's father. The accolade impressed both Maria and Robin. I wanted to be impressed, but I considered the need for boxing gloves in case anyone in Ruby's family was to react to my presence with hostility.

The boy that Mateo had sent off on an errand rushed up to his side. Mateo leaned down low enough so the boy could whisper in his ear. Mateo glanced at me as the boy filled his ear with information.

"Hm" was the only utterance he offered to signal the outcome of the errand. "Please, let us proceed this way," he said with a directional gesture.

We followed Mateo along the intertwining roads that were noticeably not paved. I had seen no bitumen since we left the highway, which reminded me of Buritaca. We passed small domestic blocks that were teeming with fruit trees and banana palms that often included meandering pigs and fossicking chickens. This, too, reminded me of Buritaca. The difference was apparent in the ethnicity of the inhabitants. Every smiling face that greeted us as we wended our way through the town was clearly of African descent. Buritaca was a fusion of indigenous, Hispanic, and African heritage. The lack of fishing boats and fishing nets sprawled out over pylons was another distinguishing factor that came as no surprise. Mateo continued to explain how the town had very complex cultural rituals and medical practices that were framed by a distinct spiritual belief system. I think Maria was enjoying the cultural exposé as much as Robin and I were. I was enjoying the time with Robin and Maria without the hordes of people eager to touch, speak to, or interact with Maria on some level. Maria translated Mateo's explanations to Robin, probably not because she had faith in my capacity to understand Spanish, but because she knew the information had Robin enthralled.

"Can we meet a local medicine man?" Robin queried.

Maria translated the request, and Mateo's reply—"That's possibly an excellent idea before we visit the Reyes family"—seemed strangely layered with innuendo.

We stopped before what appeared to be a bar or a music venue that was heavily decorated with paintings and posters depicting dancing and singing over a milieu of colourful graffiti on white- and orange-rendered walls. A small drinks cabinet that didn't look refrigerated was so heavily adorned with a random assortment of stickers on the glass that the contents on the shelves within were barely visible. There were drums with stretched animal skins stacked against the wall next to bamboo xylophones and painted metal boxes that looked like home-made plucking instruments.

"Please wait here," Mateo requested and then disappeared inside, pushing past the intricately patterned hanging cloth strips that shielded the entrance as a deterrent to flies and insects.

He returned to us in a matter of moments and invited us inside. The interior was distinctly different, most notably from the lack of graffiti. Cane furniture and handwoven rugs gave a far more domestic impression. We continued down a hallway to a grassed courtyard that had strips of thin bamboo suspended overhead on trusses to offer shade to the plastic table and chairs set below.

An old man followed us into the courtyard carrying an open cardboard box that appeared to contain an assortment of herbs, roots, and flowers and small green glass bottles decorated in woven wicker.

He placed the box on the table and extended his hand in warm welcome. "Hola. Mi nombre es Juan."

Robin reached forward eagerly to shake his hand as he worked it out that he was greeting a local medicine man. "Hola. Mi nombre es Robin." He laboured slowly through the words.

I introduced myself, and he took a particular interest in meeting

Maria. "I know who you are," he offered politely in Spanish. "Welcome."
He didn't elaborate, and Maria just smiled courteously.

"Come sit," he said as he headed toward rolls of rugs that lay against
the wall. He gestured for Mateo to move the table and chairs out of the
way as he laid the rugs out on the ground and topped them with an
assortment of cushions. The patterns on the rugs and cushions were a
mix of African animal designs, curvaceous women in traditional dress,
and colourful geometric patterns. He retrieved his cardboard box of
items and placed it on the ground before him. Mateo excused himself
from what was about to occur, assuring us he would wait for us outside.
I helped Maria lower herself to the ground so she could prop herself up
on cushions. We sat in a circle on the mats, and I wondered whether
I should mention the chairs as an option for Maria, at least. However,
she seemed quite happy to sit cross-legged on a cushion with her belly
nestled on another cushion over her crossed thighs. Juan opened one of
the green bottles and poured some of the clear contents into the cap of
the bottle. He offered the capful to me.

"Tónico." He smiled.

I took the cap and looked for Mateo, seeking some kind of assurance.
But he had already left us. Juan explained that the drink was an alcohol
base, usually rum, with a herbal infusion. I threw my head back and
tipped the concoction down my throat. It actually tasted really fresh
and slightly bitter from the herbs. He offered Robin the same, and he
eagerly imbibed. My research popped into my head, and I wondered
if a sample of the herbal tincture would be an option. Juan looked at
Maria and then gently shook his head as he rubbed his own belly. It was
a gentle way to make it clear to her that her pregnancy and the fireball
remedy were probably not a good mix.

Maria seemed keen to converse with the medicine man. "You said
you know who I am. How?"

"The wind brings whispers of your calling. The whole town knows who you are. We instructed them not to bother you."

Robin and I looked at each other with the same surprise painted on our faces.

"Robin is here as my river guide. He will guide me across the spiritual river. Leo is my lion. He protects me," she explained to Juan. "What can you do for me?"

Juan did not react to the directness of her question. Perhaps he was already contemplating the answer?

"It is good that you surround yourself with people who care about you. They are your kuagro."

We had just had the meaning and responsibility of this term explained to us. I realised Maria was not acting selfishly by asking her question. She was recruiting for her kuagro.

He glanced at Robin and me in a way that was only to confirm what he was about to say. "Your companions must heal emotional trauma regarding death to be stronger for you."

What did he mean by that? Robin saw my expression and asked, "What did he say?"

Maria translated, and Robin stared at the patterned rug he sat on, either to avoid eye contact with anyone or to contemplate the statement without distraction.

"Could you please explain?" I asked Juan in Spanish, despite being wary of the topic.

Juan paused and drew breath a few times in a way that looked like he was deciding how to deliver when dealing with a sensitive subject. "May I show you?" he asked.

Robin understood enough to reply, "Sí, por favor."

"Then please, close your eyes," he instructed.

Maria translated for Robin as I wondered how we were about to be shown something with our eyes closed.

"Relax your minds and breathe deep into your belly." He repeated this instruction for a few minutes, which is a long time for a hectic mind such as mine to focus only on breathing. "See the river before you as it flows past you. It is a large river that could be an ocean, as you cannot see the shore on the other side," he said. "Observe the many thousands of lights in the river that slowly float along with the current."

Maria continued to translate for Robin, and I could see, in my mind's eye, what Juan was asking us to visualise. I wondered if the drink he had offered us was to prepare for this process?

"Wade into the river. You are safe to do so. You do not need to swim. Use your mind to move."

The experience reminded me of the dream I had about Maria and the elevator. Like this, it had been vivid, and movement was an act of conscious attention alone.

"The lights you see in the river are souls. Find your kuagro in the river."

The question "How?" leapt into my mind.

"Feel for your kuagro. You will find them," he said in reply to the question he clearly expected. He gave us time to wade through the waters of our minds. "Once you have found your kuagro, collect them in your embrace. Do not allow them to float away from you."

I could see my arms embracing a source of indiscriminate light that was about the size of a medicine ball semi-submerged in a river.

"Take your kuagro across the river to the other side," he continued. "You will see the other side as you move through the water. It is la fuente de luz, just like the kuagro in your arms. It will become dazzling as you approach. Do not be afraid."

Maria stammered in interpreting "la fuente de luz" for Robin.

"Source light," I whispered for both to hear. The sound of words from my throat was a distraction from Juan's guided meditation. The suggestion of images from Juan had been transferring to me so seamlessly. I saw everything without a hint of challenge or confusion. It was as though he was expertly directing a dream. I remained silent from then on so as not to interfere with the process. The light had no distinguishing features, but I knew who the energy was that I was holding in my arms. I felt confident about who Robin was holding as well.

"Once you reach the bank, release your kuagro so that it may unite with the source light. See that they are safe and that they are peacefully at one with the light," Juan instructed.

The bundle of luminescence I had been cradling merged with the light as I opened my arms to allow the movement. Outside the dream, I felt that my arms resting on my thighs wanted to lift and open. Perhaps they already had?

"Now turn around and head back through the river to the bank on the other side." This was Juan's final dream instruction. He allowed us time to complete the task and then repeated the ritual that led us into the dream to return us to our real world. "When you are ready, open your eyes."

I wasn't in a hurry, but I slowly opened my eyes and looked across at Robin. His eyes were open, and tears were streaming down his face. The experience had clearly been vivid for him too. I looked at Maria, whose eyes were also sympathetically filling with tears as she watched Robin emerge from his experience.

"Gracias," Robin uttered through a deep sigh.

"Sí, gracias, Juan," Maria repeated. "¿Somos kuagro?" she asked of him directly.

"Sí," he replied with a smile. I could see that this made Maria particularly happy. She was keen for his support.

Robin looked at me for translation. "We're all family" was the best interpretation I could offer.

I wondered if this moment defined for me why we have funerals. Do we symbolically guide our departed back to their origins as we experience a step toward effective closure by participating in the delivery?

"Mateo is waiting for you outside," Juan said, signalling the end of our meeting.

As I helped Maria to her feet, Robin offered some pesos to Juan, who accepted them graciously. We headed out to the front, where Mateo was patiently waiting for us.

"How was it?" he asked enthusiastically.

I didn't know what to say, and Robin probably didn't understand the question.

"Let's go," Maria said cheerfully in Spanish.

As we headed up the road, I couldn't help but ask Robin, "So, who was your kuagro?"

"My mother." He shrugged. I expected that.

We wandered alongside the walls of the largest building I had seen in the town so far. It was completely white with a three-story tower, possibly the tallest structure in town, that was surmounted by a large Christian cross. It stood at one end of a large, red-brick paved square lined by palm trees.

"So do you think that's our role, to assist our loved ones in finding the light?"

Before the church was another large sandstone pedestal featuring a bronzed statue. This statue was clearly an artistic representation of a slave from a bygone era. He appeared to be emerging from the sandstone, reaching for liberty with one hand bearing a broken shackle, the other clutching the chains of his oppression.

"Possibly. But I'm pretty sure Juan said that you and I had to reconcile death and not that we needed to assist the departed. What we just experienced was likely to assist us in letting go of our deceased kuagro. Who did you see?"

"My daughter."

Behind the statue was a small, brightly painted pink brick building with a shingled roof and corrugated eaves of varying colours supported by what appeared to be painted tree branch cuttings. The rolled steel shutter was open, and along the roofline, boldly painted on a white sign surrounded by pictures of hammers and paintbrushes, were the words "Ferreteria El Campion." The Hardware store of the Champion was how I interpreted the signage.

"A hardware store behind a statue!" Maria exclaimed, pointing to where we were already looking.

Mateo nodded. He walked across to a concrete bench seat that was shaded by a palm. "I will wait for you here."

Robin looked at me, then the store, then the bench seat. He had worked out what Mateo had said in Spanish. "I think I'll hang out here too."

Maria looked up at me and took my hand. "I'll come with you if you like. Just in case anyone gets a little lost in translation."

Chapter 14

I looked at Maria's tiny hand in mine. "Sure," I said, and we wandered across the square toward the store.

As we approached, the wire screen door of the entrance creaked open, and a woman who looked like a forty-something version of Ruby walked through the entrance to the porch. She stood under the eaves and waited for us to get to her. She was wearing a bright yellow top with short sleeves and a white apron that she undid as we approached. Behind the apron was a full-length skirt painted in thick horizontal stripes of green and orange. Photos that Ruby had shown me of her mother flickered through my mind. She tossed the apron to let it fall across the back of a green plastic chair that sat alone on the porch beside her.

"You must be Leonard," she said in Spanish with an outstretched hand.

"Yes," I replied, taking her hand to shake in mine. "This is Maria."

She turned to Maria and leaned forward to give her an energetic hug over her protruding belly. "Ah, the shining one," she declared with a broad smile, revealing her brilliant white teeth. "It's an honour to meet you."

"You too," Maria replied.

"I'm not the father," I contributed nervously in Spanish, then wished I hadn't.

"I know. So what can I do for you, Leonard?" she asked in a direct tone.

I wasn't really sure, and I knew I was going to struggle to articulate whatever I had to say. The idea of translating emotional sentences into Spanish made me nervous.

"Thank you for seeing me unannounced, Mrs. Reyes," I continued.

"You can call me Julia. I'm sorry that Moe isn't here today. He would have appreciated meeting you."

"Yes, Julia. And yes, I would have liked to have met him too." I searched for the words in Spanish. "I think I'm here to say sorry."

"What for?"

"For disappointing your daughter, and perhaps you."

"How?"

"Your granddaughter." I wavered as the word *nieta* left my lips.

"Where is my granddaughter?" Julia asked calmly.

"Excuse me?" I replied, not sure how to interpret the question.

"Where does she lie?" she clarified.

"Oh. We had investigated the possibility of the child being brought here. But it was just impossible to arrange. I hope you understand. I offered they bury her with my departed family. Ruby accepted this. I thought she would have told you."

"My darling girl does not reveal much to her family. She's in a dark place. Why aren't you with her?"

"She didn't want me to be," I said, hoping to exonerate my absence.

"Why?"

I took a deep breath. "I believe it was because my family was not supportive of her, our relationship, or our child, and I did not champion her in a way she would have hoped for."

"And that's what you're sorry for?"

"I think so, yes."

"Well then, it sounds that God has served you what you deserved," she stated with calm assuredness. The words stung me. "If you failed to defend your relationship and your child, why should she stay with you?"

"You're right. I failed her," I admitted, surrendering to the deposition.

"No," Maria declared defiantly. "You're not right. I'm sorry, Mrs. Reyes, but you do not know Leo as I do. I depend on him more than anyone, and he has shown to me I can trust him and depend on him, even when he doesn't fully agree with or understand what is going on." She placed her open palms on her belly. "I couldn't do this without Leo. He is not a failure. I am here to support him because he is my lion." She gathered her thoughts. "Your daughter has lost a child. She is grieving."

Emphatic emotion poured from her mouth. "Leo is not responsible for her loss, and he is respecting her choice. He just drove five hours to meet you. He wouldn't be here if he didn't care."

Julia looked at me and sighed. She took a moment to appraise what she wanted to do next.

"I can't speak for my daughter's heart. That is for her to repair or leave broken. Thank you for visiting, Leonard." She leaned forward, as she had with Maria, and hugged me. The trembling in my chest was more obvious as we embraced. "I don't know what God has planned for you, young man. But he only challenges the ones he believes can handle the pressure. Don't be sorry for what happens in your life. Learn from it."

I translated her words from Spanish to English in my head with some difficulty. My mind was spinning from my hyperventilating. Maria's beaming smile reassured me we were parting on good terms.

"Thank you for your time, too," I replied as she stepped back toward the screen door.

"Safe travels," she added as she scooped up her apron and disappeared inside the building.

I turned to look at Mateo and Robin, who were both on their feet, looking to us for a sign of my task being complete. We headed back to join them.

"Thank you," I said to Maria as we crossed the square.

"For what?"

"For saying those kind words."

"They're true." She smiled warmly as she took my hand in hers again.

The drive back to Buritaca was more subdued, as we were all tired. Robin was probably just as lost in processing his experience as I was. Maria looked out the window like a tourist in a theme park. Despite the common surroundings, it was a long way from home for her.

Back in Buritaca, we dropped Robin off, and I left the car at Maria's house. I parked it next to Gustavo's shiny new truck for her cousin to retrieve. We had filled the tank on the way, and I left him extra pesos in the ashtray to say thank you.

The sun had already sunk from sight an hour earlier. We weren't too far off from the hour of our predicted return. The light was low as I walked Maria to her door. Her followers, who had set up camp around the front of the house, respected her privacy and restrained themselves from pouncing toward her.

"I know today was a big day for you," Maria said. "It's a big day to-morrow for me. I'd really like you to be there if you can. You probably want a rest, though."

"What time? I'll be in my lion suit." I smiled supportively.

"Probably around nine. Thank you, Leo." She kissed me on the cheek and pushed the door open to disappear inside.

I slept soundly that night.

Chapter 15

I escorted Maria, heavily laden with floral arrangements, decorative cotton wraps, amulets, and beads, onto the stage. We had started the morning at her house, in the backyard, where Gabrielle stood silently on her perch. Maria, wearing a simple green floral dress, sat on her haunches before the parrot. She gently rocked backward and forward, mumbling her familiar "today will be a good day" just loud enough for me to hear her as I stood at the door of the house across the yard. I noted that none of the anxiety I had previously witnessed seemed apparent in her body language. Her motion and words seemed more like a rhythmic meditation.

Gabrielle squawked so abruptly it made me jump. "Today will be a good day!" The sounds of the words in Spanish launched from her lungs with a guttural twang.

Maria took this as her cue to stand and return to the house. Gustavo was clearly waiting for this as he pushed past me to stride across the yard toward Gabrielle. He carried a wooden pedestal in his hand that was shaped like a T-bar at the top. I recognised this as the perch Gabrielle used on the stage. The macaw flapped her wings and snapped her beak menacingly at Gustavo, who ducked and weaved the attack to grab the length of chain attached to the bird's ankle. He removed the chain from the yard perch and attached it to the pedestal in his hand. He dragged a protesting Gabrielle toward the pedestal so that she had little choice but to perch on the timber staff in his hand.

Maria had her back to the commotion the whole time, her head bowed low. She raised her chin only high enough to offer me a meek smile as she made her way into the kitchen. She poured a glass of water and gulped it down.

"Ready?" she asked me in a nonchalant tone.

I shrugged. "Sure."

She walked confidently toward the front door, collecting me on the way by wrapping her arm in the crook of my arm.

"Here we go," she said with a reassuring smile.

The next hour was a slow amble of laps around the village, where Maria warmly greeted everyone who sought her attention. She graciously accepted all gifts offered to her and even asked me to carry some of the tiny statuettes of parrots, goddesses, and ecclesial virgins that made their way into her slender palms.

I had to dump most of the gifts on the ground beside the stage floor to help Maria up the short flight of stairs. The displacement of her belly from the pregnancy would have been enough to challenge her balance even without the extra load of the gifts. I also removed a few shrouds that were draped across her shoulders as I didn't want her collapsing from heatstroke under the weight of the glittering garb.

Daniela waved enthusiastically to Maria from the sentinel row of travesti guards standing on the sandy terrain before the face of the stage. Maria waved back as I helped her to sit. Gustavo appeared from the other side of the stage, proudly displaying Gabrielle, who stood on the pedestal in his hand. It would take someone as strong as Gustavo to single-handedly carry Gabrielle's imposing frame on a stand. He placed the stand beside Maria, bowed somewhat theatrically to her, and turned to leave the stage.

"Now what?" I asked Maria as I noted the hundreds of eyes watching us eagerly from the dunes.

"I just sit here and call Gabrielle in my head."

Her words gave me a distraction from the sense of vulnerability bubbling up in my stomach. I noted that Gabrielle, on her perch, with her tail almost touching the ground was taller than I was. I instinctively took a few steps to the side to remove myself from the attention directed at the stage.

Maria closed her eyes and started rocking backward and forward, whispering, "Loro Santo, Loro Santo."

The crowd chanted in harmonic unison with Maria. "Loro Santo! Loro Santo!"

Gabrielle started shifting her weight from foot to foot in the way parrots often respond to music. Maria suddenly stopped rocking. The crowd knew this signal. A hushed silence fell like a feather. Gabrielle also stood motionless.

Maria opened her eyes abruptly. "My name is Gabrielle. I have a message from God..."

As Maria drew a deep breath to continue, a woman's voice from the crowd abruptly interrupted.

"Liar! She is a liar!" the woman called out in Spanish with a shrill, condemning tone.

I recognised the woman as Pablo's mother. The crowd turned in unison to the source of the declaration as Pablo's mother pushed her way to the front, followed by a small group from her church congregation and the local priest dressed in his black Christian robe with a white sash draped across his shoulders. He held a staff adorned with a Christian cross before him and took a stance that commanded authority.

"You killed my son," she continued.

The audience moved away from the angry posse. Pablo's mother saw opportunity in the bare earth revealed before her. She spat on the ground defiantly. The congregation all spat on the ground as well.

"You are a liar," she said with confidence as anger welled up in her ample bosom.

I looked at Maria, who appeared to be in a trance. I approached her and gently shook her shoulder.

"Maria!"

She jolted the way people often do when disturbed from a deep slumber.

"What's going on?" she asked, clearly puzzled and unaware of the current happenings.

The priest pushed his way to the area in front of the stage.

"This blasphemy must stop. You are not a messenger from God." He pointed at Maria with the tip of the cross in his hand. "You are just a greedy liar!"

"Greedy? Liar? Why would you say that?" Maria asked with obvious bewilderment.

"The church, the house of God, has storm damage. It needs a new roof. The donations to rebuild the church are now being given to you and your stupid parrot."

"I'm not asking for money! I'm not asking for any of this!" Maria defended herself earnestly. "It is you that is greedy if you only care about your money!"

"How dare you!" the priest challenged.

"Yes, I dare if all you care about is your money and your roof."

Gustavo lumbered across the sand past the row of travesti guards, who all looked at him earnestly for direction. He started pushing the church congregation away from the stage, likely swearing, but my Spanish vocabulary didn't include any of what he was aggressively blurting out. The irate congregation looked at Maria and continued to spit on the ground as Gustavo shoved them backwards. Pablo's mother broke away from Gustavo's reach and tried to climb the stage.

"You killed my son! Devil girl!"

Daniela, although dressed like a girl, had the strength of a strong young man. She sprung up onto the stage in an agile leap and rushed Pablo's mother, muscling her off the stage.

"Leave her alone!" Daniela commanded fiercely.

They virtually rolled off the stage together and continued wrestling on the ground. I jumped off the stage to break up the fight. A riot suddenly ensued between the congregation and Maria's devotees, with me caught in the middle. I glanced at the stage to see Maria sitting frozen in wide-eyed fear.

"Maria! Do something! Say something!" I yelled to her as the vexed mob converged on me from both sides. "They will listen to you!"

I didn't see it coming, but I felt the impact of a clenched fist thrust aggressively against my temple. My knees buckled without warning, and I likely lost consciousness before I hit the ground.

Chapter 16

It's a surreal feeling when your last memory is in one location with its unique whirlwind of events, and then your next conscious moment is in a completely different environment under drastically different circumstances. I was lying in a hospital bed wearing a spotted, pale blue gown under a stiffly woven sheet with a tube connected intravenously to my arm. I assumed it was isotonic saline, but I didn't know for sure as my eyes failed to focus in my stupor. My bed was beside a window, and the streaming light forced me to squint as I regained my sense of presence. As I lifted my arm to check that all my limbs were intact and working, I read *Santa Marta Hospital* on the label of the plastic bracelet that identified me and the date of my admission. A silhouetted figure appeared under the window and approached my bed. My eyes played tricks on me as the streaming light haloed around the figure, making it appear that the person was arriving at my bedside from the surrounding radiance. I rubbed my eyes with the palm of my hands, hoping to speed up their return to focus. As I removed my hands, Maria's beaming smile greeted me. I could then see she had been sitting in a chair below the window.

"Leo, my Leo. I'm so sorry," she said, taking my hand and pressing it to her cheek.

"How long have I been here?"

"Only a day."

"A day?" Memories of the riot flooded back to me. "Why didn't you say anything? You could have stopped them."

"I didn't know what to do."

"They could have killed me."

"No! That could never happen. You are my lion. No one could ever hurt you."

I lifted the arm that attached me to the drip.

"Look at me. I'm clearly not invincible."

"You have to be. I can't do this without you," she declared earnestly as she climbed on the bed next to me and wrapped her arms around me.

I was so accustomed to Maria seeking protection from me in this way that I didn't even think to protest. I placed my free arm across her back and noted thankfully that nothing hurt as she had jumped onto me with no concern for my comfort. To ensure they were still part of the team, I wiggled my toes while we held each other.

"Maria."

"Just hold me."

"Maria..." I repeated more insistently.

I can't remember exactly what I was going to say, but she quickly interjected.

"Can't you see that I'm just a stupid, scared girl? Everyone is putting me on this crazy pedestal, and all I am doing is falling. Can't you just hold me? Stop me from falling."

"Okay."

I allowed myself to relax into the moment, like I had all those months ago when she guided me to her secret pool. The grogginess going on in my head made it easier to separate myself from the often noisy analytical part of my brain. The silence of the moment, lying there with Maria hugging me tightly as her bulbous belly pushed into my ribs, was peaceful. As I allowed myself to relax, I became conscious that our breathing slowed and synchronised like a tender dance. Sadly, I didn't allow the moment to extend very long. My failing was an inability to live in stillness.

"I need you to be honest with me," I pressed as my thoughts found their foothold.

"I have been."

"Did you have anything to do with Pablo's disappearance?"

"No, I swear."

****

Once the doctors checked my vitals and all my scans were clear, I was free to leave the hospital. Someone had packed up and stored my clothes in the hospital room closet. I later discovered that Maria had stayed with me the whole time I was an inpatient at the Santa Marta Hospital from the moment I arrived. She likely managed my wardrobe. I never asked. I dressed, and we jumped into a taxi together for the hour-long drive back to Buritaca.

We drove straight to my research facility as Maria said that a couple of Daniela's travesti friends were waiting for us there. Gustavo had Daniela running errands, so she had arranged for her friends to greet us on our return. I thought it was just a friendly gesture, but when we arrived, a small gathering of the church congregation, including Pablo's mother, was also waiting for us.

As Maria stepped out of the taxi, Pablo's mother led the gathering to call out abuse to Maria. I hadn't learned how to insult someone in Spanish, so I couldn't understand most of their taunts. They spat on the ground again but kept their distance as Maria's travesti friends barricaded her from harm whilst exchanging threatening gestures with the congregation. We entered the lab, and the travesti stayed outside to guard the entrance.

"That went well" was all I could offer for encouragement.

"Sorry."

"Don't be. It's not your fault."

Carlos was tending to botanicals and checking on the tissue samples in the agar plates as we walked in.

He greeted us cheerfully with a broad smile. "Hola, amigas. Welcome back, my friend. How are you feeling?"

"I'm fine, thanks. No concussion, apparently."

"We will have to teach you how to fight better, I think."

"Hopefully that won't be necessary."

Maria helped herself to the corner of the room that served as a kitchen and put on the kettle to make me a cup of coffee. One thing was for sure, the coffee was excellent in Buritaca, particularly when you have easy access to the freshest grind of the premium quality beans. I had a mild headache, so the coffee was a welcome gesture as she placed the aromatic serving in my hands.

"Can I get you anything else?" she offered supportively.

"No. But thanks for the coffee."

The sound of voices unified in rhythmic chanting drifted toward our ears like a tide finding higher ground. The noise became steadily louder, and the words became clearer.

"Loro Santo! Loro Santo!"

The volume of the chanting grew steadily until it was right outside the lab.

"Loro Santo! Loro Santo!" was all we could hear.

You would have had to yell to speak over the din.

I opened the door. The chanting crowd cheered when they spied Maria standing inside.

A young man stepped forward. I didn't recognise him, but he looked local with his tanned skin and sea-blown fringe.

"Come with us! It's a miracle!" he beckoned to Maria.

Maria immediately looked at me for guidance.

"What should I do?"

"Go with them, I guess. It's okay. I'll come with you."

"Are you sure?"

"Yes, I'm fine. I need the exercise, and I'm your lion, remember?"

We stepped outside, and the crowd enthusiastically surrounded Maria and lifted her to their shoulders.

"Loro Santo! Loro Santo!" they resumed as Maria sat atop their shoulders like a buoy bobbing on a wake of exultation.

They walked all the way back to Maria's home in an excited procession. Maria's feet never got to touch the ground. I followed closely with Daniela's travesti friends. They lowered Maria as we approached the house together. A large, framed, antiquated painting of a woman standing on the shoulders of what may have been a child sat against the wall of the porch that was cleared of the mound of gifts and offerings. The texture of the art was so darkened with age, it was difficult to make out the detail. The shrouded lady, like many Christian images, had her hands placed together in prayer. Perhaps it was light beams painted around her, emanating from her or from behind her. Although tanned and dull, they were likely originally golden and bright. Dozens of flickering candles on the wooden porch surrounded the painting. Robin approached us from across the road.

"They found it here on the wall this morning. No one knows how it got here. It's Our Lady of Guadalupe."

"So, who put it there?" I asked openly to anyone within earshot. Someone must have seen how such a large painting had made its way onto the porch.

"It's a miracle. Maria is the blessed mother of Christ. Loro Santo!" a female voice hailed, breaking the extended silence that had been the response to my query of the tightly packed crowd that surrounded us. I looked at Maria, whose dumbfounded expression matched my thoughts.

"Holy parrot," I offered with a hint of skepticism.

The front door opened, and Daniela poked her head out to see what was going on. She squealed excitedly when she spotted Maria and raced into her arms for an exuberant hug.

"What about Sylvia and Gustavo? What do they know about this?" I asked Robin, wondering if there might be a less miraculous explanation for the painting's sudden appearance.

Daniela turned to me. She must have understood my question, but she answered my question in Spanish because her English wasn't good enough.

"I was with them all day yesterday as we had to sort through the church assets that have been accumulating. Gustavo wanted secure storage, so he had a warehouse built just down the road. We finished late, and when I returned this morning, the painting, it was just there."

"Church assets?" What sort of assets were being accumulated that required a warehouse was a thought that instantly crossed my mind.

"By the way, that's the Manichaean," Robin added as he pointed across the crowd to an old, long-bearded, Chinese-looking man in a pale linen robe surrounded by an entourage of similarly dressed Asian attendees.

"Did he tell you why he's here?"

"It's bizarre. He says nothing. I think the way it works is that his people take a guess at what he's thinking, and then he just nods or shakes his head. How that got him to Colombia, I do not know."

"So you don't know what he wants."

"No idea."

The gathering of devotees peeled away to allow the Manichaean to approach Maria. He bowed respectfully. I couldn't determine how old he was. He could have been fifty or a hundred and fifty. He held his hand out in a way that suggested he wanted to touch Maria's pregnant belly. Maria looked at me. Again, I could only shrug. She nodded approval, and the Manichaean gently placed his palm to Maria's belly.

"Hm" was the only noise he made.

He nodded to one of his assistants. The attaché approached diligently with a small, ornately decorated box covered in silver and gold symbols that I didn't recognise. He opened it to reveal a bright green gemstone that was the shape of a football and the size of an orange. It had a carving in the middle that appeared to be an "M" inside a circle. The Manichaean took the opened box and offered it to Maria.

She accepted the gift politely, saying "gracias" as she stooped awkwardly in a move that resembled a curtsy.

"Try bowing," I offered encouragingly and gave her a demonstration.

Maria followed my lead, and the Manichaean smiled warmly. He placed his palms together in much the same way as the lady in the painting and bowed respectfully. He and his entourage then simply walked away. Maria looked at the box containing the glistening gemstone in her hands and then at me.

"What just happened?"

"It's a gift of acknowledgement of you and who your child is," Robin answered. He looked like he was about to burst into tears. "It's perfect!"

I looked at the gemstone more closely. It had a marking inscribed about a millimetre deep.

"I like the inscription. It looks like an 'M' for 'Maria.'" I also wondered if the letter somehow represented Manichaeism? Every other devotion seemed to have its own iconography. Perhaps this was his brand?

I turned to Robin to ask if my hunch was correct, but he looked like he was deep in thought, so I let it pass. He turned to Maria.

"Maria, are you up to speaking to your followers today? They'll want to hear from you."

I didn't know who was more nervous about the idea, me or Maria, considering the ordeal we had just been through the previous day.

"I see you have bodyguards now," Robin added, referring to Daniela and her friends. "Gustavo instructed them to protect you."

"And we will," Daniela added confidently.

"Gabrielle is already waiting for you on the stage. Your father arranged everything earlier in anticipation of your return," Robin continued eagerly.

Maria looked at me, but it wasn't my decision.

"It's up to you," was all I could say.

Maria just nodded. Robin took that as a yes.

We headed into town together with frocked bodyguards protectively surrounding Maria. Gustavo joined us when we met him along the way. He clearly would not tolerate any harassment of his daughter today. Robin and I followed closely. Behind us was the loudest and most exuberant cacophony of singing, dancing, and chanting that I had encountered so far. We arrived at the stage. Maria looked up to see the wooden pedestal beside her chair conspicuously missing something.

"Where's Gabrielle?"

Robin gasped as he raised his hands to his cheeks. "Holy shit."

Someone had stolen the parrot.

Chapter 17

Daniela looked back and forth between us and the vacant stage. Perhaps hoping for another miracle? One that would return Gabrielle to us.

"Maria, I'm so sorry. We came to protect you. We should have left someone with Gabrielle. It's all my fault," Daniela blurted out in Spanish.

"So now we have a missing parrot?" I felt obliged to state the obvious.

The crowd that had followed us from Maria's house amassed around us.

"We have to tell the police," Robin said.

"To file a missing parrot report?" I replied.

I surveyed the surrounding crowd, looking for a sign of suspicious behaviour.

"Do you think it was the spitters?"

"Who?" asked Robin.

I clearly hadn't shared the nickname I had given to Maria's detractors, who were now habitually shooting saliva from their mouths to the ground in their display of indignation and defiance toward Maria and her Church of the Holy Parrot. They always seemed to be lurking somewhere on the periphery. Could they have been so bold and despicable to sabotage events by stealing or harming Gabrielle? I pointed to Pablo's mother and the congregation, who were making their disassociation with the large, supportive crowd obvious.

"It could be anyone," he replied, turning to Maria and giving her explicit instructions. "Ask the crowd what they saw."

Maria immediately responded and scooted to the stage as best she could with her expanding belly. She quickly scaled the stairs, faced the crowd, and addressed them, calling out as loud as she could in Spanish to be heard over the rumble of confusion ramping up in the crowd.

"Did anyone see who took Gabrielle?" she asked.

Heads jerked back and forth in the crowd as everyone looked for someone who might speak up. No one did. She took a deep breath and tried again in English.

"Has anyone seen Gabrielle?"

A hushed silence was her only reply from the disturbed collective.

A lady with an Indian accent called out from the crowd, "Perhaps it was another miracle? Has he returned to heaven?"

"She..." I mumbled as I contemplated the idea.

Another woman's voice piped up. She sounded American. "Speak to Gabriel. Ask him where he is."

"Ask her..." I muttered as I tried to focus my mind on solutions beyond the esoteric options being offered.

Robin shot me a glance that I read as "enough of the gender correction." I concurred we had a bigger problem to attend to than Gabrielle's gender identity. We needed to work out her location, and the sooner, the better.

Maria appeared to like the suggestion of the American woman. She plonked herself down in her usual seat beside Gabrielle's now empty perch. She was clearly scared and confused about the loss of her valued companion as she began rocking backward and forward in the manner that was now familiar to us all. The crowd instantly responded to her signal and chanted along with her.

"Loro Santo! Loro Santo!"

Maria's movements were far more focused than I had ever seen before. She looked like she was pushing out a gym session of abdominal crunches as she lunged her body forward rapidly, only to push herself back again with the same gusto.

"Loro Santo. Loro Santo." I couldn't hear her over the bellowing crowd, but I could see the words forming on her lips with fierce intensity.

Then Maria became suddenly silent. Her body stilled, and she remained poised as though listening for a distant voice. The crowd hushed, countenances filled with eager anticipation. Maria's eyes shot open, and with a voice of bold confidence, she addressed the crowd.

"My name is Gabrielle. My physical presence is of no consequence. I am with you in spirit."

The crowd cheered. I gave Robin a look of desperation that told him I really needed him to explain what was going on in a way that my brain could fathom. Robin just shrugged off what he was witnessing and hearing with a casual sense of acceptance.

"When channeling, the messenger does not need to be physically present. Some channeled entities are allegedly alien, and have never even existed in our world. Who knows the boundaries of consciousness? Maria can receive images or ideas from anywhere that her physical form can verbalise."

"So why doesn't Gabrielle speak in everyone's mind instead? That would make the message more reliable, and comparable for consistency?"

"Perhaps one day we will all have a greater connection with the divine. But for now, look at all the phones and cameras that are popping up in the crowd. She is the voice for a broadening audience who will learn how to switch on their spiritual potential via her instruction."

"Whose instructions? Maria's or Gabrielle's?"

"That's a good question." He nodded with no effort to answer it.

"What if she's wrong?" I replied with enough skepticism in my tone to prompt Robin to try a little harder to answer my question.

His silence left me seeking answers in the sea of faces, all looking eagerly toward Maria. Even at a glance, there were far more foreigners than locals present, confirming Robin's assertion that her audience was indeed broadening to an international level.

"So, are we now not worried about the whereabouts of Gabrielle?"

"Yes, but we have a work-around until we find her."

I felt immediately uncomfortable with the suggestion of a work-around. It was like this whole Loro Santo thing was a steam train that simply would not derail due to any event or circumstance, including a disappearing parrot.

Maria was still in her state of trance. Although her eyes were open, you could actually tell that her "energy" was different. It was the only way I could relate to what I was witnessing. And when she spoke in this state, it definitely wasn't the Maria I knew that was speaking.

"We must prepare ourselves for the Christ. Only the strong will survive. The weak will perish, and the strong are not the ones with bodies of might. The strong are the ones with hearts filled with light, and the weak are those who have succumbed to fear and greed. These feed anger and selfishness. This leads to hateful behaviour, which ends in suffering and death. It will not be the Christ that destroys these people. It will be their own darkness that drags them down into the abyss. Right now, we are in the river of change. We are all treading water. Our legs kick and our arms flail to keep our heads above the murky depths. Those who clutch to fear and greed, as though these values offer a life support, will slowly sink away from the light. They will die hanging desperately onto the heavy values that weigh them down."

Powerful words emanated from Maria's mouth with unwavering confidence.

"For those who remain, we find salvation in working together. It is their connection with others, their ability to create solutions and harness compassion in their heart that will allow them to survive and thrive. We will only survive with connection to our environment and all of God's children."

I was expecting Maria to announce a crisis because of Gabrielle's unexplained disappearance. But she seemed to focus only on what sounded like a collective existential crisis. She drew attention to her hands by spreading them in a wide circular action over her head as though gathering something in toward herself with her open palms. Her hands then came together in front of her belly. The tips of her thumbs joined, creating a straight line across her belly. Her hands pointed downward toward her navel, with her fingertips touching, to complete the triangular formation she was relating with her story.

"The time of suffering as a path to God is over. Suffering in the mind enslaves you to fear and despair. Be prepared for the new Christ! There are three essential values of the new era he will demand of you: connection, creativity, and compassion," she said confidently in a voice of calm sanctitude. "Your new task will be workship, as opposed to worship. The Christ is like a flame that can light other flames, losing no radiance. You are the candles, and the Christ will light the fire within you." Her hands held their position, forming an inverted triangle over her protruding belly. "Channel these three values into all your thoughts and deeds, and you will find your flame."

I felt a distinct chill run up my spine. I'm sure I was not alone in this response to Maria's profound instructional oration. The voracity and certainty of her speech whilst referring to herself in the third person definitely gave the impression that someone or something was speaking through her. Maria's head dropped to her chest, and her hands fell away to dangle by her sides. She sighed heavily and then lifted her head again with a far more familiar look in her eyes. She turned to me and smiled with gentle assuredness to let me know she was okay. The crowd cheered ecstatically. Connection, creativity, and compassion. We had our instructions. How were her followers going to interpret this? Robin jumped up to the stage to assist Maria. He would look after her. I took this as an opening to remove myself from the jubilant crowd. I headed back to the lab.

Carlos was dividing and labelling samples of plants strewn across the bench in the lab. He had white earbuds protruding from his ears, and his rhythmic movements suggested that the music was to his liking. We nodded an understated greeting to each other as I entered. This encouraged me to consider that we were becoming comfortable working together.

"So, what do you think of all this?" Carlos asked as he pulled out the earbuds.

"I'm happy with the results we're seeing with these new samples."

Carlos chuckled to himself. "I meant with Maria and the holy parrot."

"Oh, all *that*? I don't know what to think. I don't know a single test that could verify anything that's going on there. It's such an expression of faith. I'm not used to that."

"Faith?"

"I like to see and measure things for real."

Carlos looked at the earbuds in his hands. "To play my music, my phone is signalling my tiny speakers, is it not?"

"So?"

"My tiny speakers are interpreting the signal to play the music, are they not? So my tiny speakers are a receiver and an interpreter of the signal, are they not?"

"And if you streamed that music, we wouldn't know exactly where you are streaming the music from?" I added, in an effort to work with his analogy.

He nonchalantly put the earbuds back in his ears and picked up his secateurs to continue cutting plant samples. His head bobbed to the music that he was enjoying again. I wanted to object by arguing that Maria was not the same "tiny speaker" as his earbuds. But then I thought about what Robin said about the sunset. What signals did I have available to me that I couldn't understand or interpret? I relied on manmade technology to do my work. Was there a hidden technology or signal in all things to receive and interpret? What technology would test such a theory? It wasn't my field of expertise. So much of what was going on in Buritaca at that moment wasn't my field of expertise, and I was becoming uncomfortable with how very little I knew about this phenomenon of Maria. Just about everyone else around me seemed to have a comfortable understanding of it, and I was like the dumbest kid in town who just couldn't get it.

"Are you going to the beach party tonight?" Carlos asked loudly, without removing his earbuds. "That should be a sight."

"What beach party?"

Carlos removed his earbuds. "What?"

"What beach party?" I repeated now that he could hear the response he had asked for.

"The Manichaean is hosting a beach party in honour of Maria and her child."

"How does a guy who doesn't speak host a party?"

"I guess we'll have to turn up and find out."

He put his earbuds back in and resumed bopping along as he returned to his work.

Chapter 18

The undulating sandy dunes of the Buritaca beach were a hive of activity. The entourage of the Manichaean had used large staffs carved from bamboo shafts to dig long pits. They had then filled these with firewood and lit their timber assemblages. By the time I arrived with Carlos, the sun had retired for the day, and the fiery red coals the attendants were spreading out in the pits illuminated the twilight. The locals and tourists were taking part with gusto. They presented the fire-pit attendants with platters of raw fish laid on banana leaves. They buried the offerings wrapped in leaves in the coals for cooking. The event made me realise how many people were now in Buritaca in response to Maria's divine providence. I estimated at least a thousand people were on the beach that night.

"Feeding of the five thousand?" Carlos commented.

He was obviously just as astounded by the number of attendees as I was.

"A party of biblical proportions," I replied.

Although I wasn't religious, I knew he was making a Bible reference.

"I wonder if they'll part the ocean as an encore," I added to suggest I knew some of the Christian mythology.

Robin joined us.

"Did you bring your fish?"

"I didn't know I should have."

"The ceremony is to signify the sacrificing of the old 'Piscean' era. So they cook fish."

"How long was the Piscean era?"

"Around 2000 years," he replied in a matter-of-fact tone.

As I let the gravity of the time frames involved sink in, I realised they did not etch the pits in the sand in a straight line. They had clearly arranged the luminescent coals in an angular formation that resembled the letter M.

"The pits are in the same shape as the inscription on the stone. Is the new era the 'Maria' era?"

Robin gave me a puzzled look, and then he laughed cheerfully.

"That's not an M. It's the astrological symbol of waves for Aquarius. The Manichaean is celebrating that Maria is birthing the age of Aquarius."

"Does she know that?" I enquired as I suddenly noticed the itch of my eczema.

Robin ignored my query and continued his explanation of the symbolism unfolding before us.

"The gemstone he gave Maria is a Demantoid Garnet, an Aquarian stone. It's a very spiritual gemstone. Considering its size and origin, it's a good thing Maria's father doesn't know of its true value."

"How much?" I couldn't help but ask.

"I'm estimating around priceless."

"Holy..."

"Gemstone," he completed for me.

Robin held up a bag of fish that I had failed to notice he was carrying when he arrived.

"How does fish for dinner sound?" he asked with cheerful jocularity.

"Great. But does Maria know about all this?"

"The Manichaean probably forgot to tell her. I guess that happens when you don't speak at all."

"I think she needs to see how far this is going."

"She might want some fish, too," Carlos added.

"I'll go see where she is," I said as I turned to head back into town.

Robin turned to Carlos. "Can I leave this fish with you to give to the Manichaean?"

"Sure." Carlos shrugged.

"I'll come with you," Robin said.

I think Robin was keen to be included in anything that involved Maria and her new ecclesiastic responsibilities.

The most likely place to find Maria was at her house. As we approached, we could hear that she was home, and so was Gustavo. Things were not going so well in the Santos family's home. A loud argument in Spanish bellowed through the thin walls of the dwelling.

We overheard Maria's furious tone. Robin looked at me with concern. He likely couldn't understand the Spanish being exchanged inside the house.

"This wouldn't have happened if you had not made me capture Gabrielle!" Maria yelled with exasperation.

"You should have taken better care of him. Why did you leave him alone?" Gustavo answered defiantly as we approached the open front door.

Maria and Gustavo were engaged in a standoff in the middle of the main room. Sylvia was in the background, closer to the kitchen, watching the confrontation with trepidation.

"I was in the hospital because they beat Leonard unconscious in the fight that you started!" Maria blurted out, her face flushed.

Impulsively, Gustavo slapped Maria harshly. Maria reeled on the spot from the blow. Sylvia screamed. Just as impulsively, Robin and I rushed in through the open front door to stop Maria from falling as she teetered backwards toward us. We caught Maria, a shoulder each, and helped her back to a steadier stance. Thankfully, Gustavo likely realised that his behaviour was not fitting for an audience. He retreated out through the side door into the yard as though he had somewhere else to be. The assault badly bruised Maria's cheek.

Maria turned to us and pleaded, "Please take me away from here."

I looked to Sylvia for guidance, who nodded sympathetically as she wiped tears from her face. The commotion had clearly drawn attention as Daniela and Maria's travesti guards were rushing to the house as we escorted her across the porch. They flanked us as we made our way down the street. Despite the calamity, onlookers, oblivious to her trauma, tried to touch Maria and sought her blessings. She was overtly trembling in a mix of shock and fear under my arm. I wasn't sure where exactly we were taking her. We hadn't the chance to tell her about the Manichaean's event on the beach. As we turned onto the main road that led to the centre of town, a new entourage confronted us, heading our way. Although the light was poor in the dimly lit street, I could see the man heading the group was someone of importance in religious circles. He was a portly, balding man, perhaps in his sixties, wearing a black suit and a black shirt with a Roman collar depicting his clerical role. It was the ornately decorated purple and gold stole draped across his shoulders that suggested he was a big gun in his clergy. He looked at us curiously and appeared to recognise Maria.

With one of the thickest Italian accents I believe I have ever heard, he addressed us in English. "My name is Cardinal Antonio Vecci, a representative of the Vatican. Can you please explain this?"

He held out what appeared to be a document in the vacant space that separated us. I wasn't sure who exactly he was talking to as his tone reflected general indignation that wasn't directed anywhere or to any-one specifically. As Maria looked up at me quizzically, Robin stepped forward and took the document on behalf of her. He flicked through the pages.

"Holy cow," he uttered, and his jaw dropped in awe in response to what he was reading.

"What is it?"

"I think it's a transcript, translated into Italian, of everything that Gabrielle has been saying through Maria. How would the Vatican have this?"

"I bet it was the priest," I surmised. "He's sending in the muscle to shut this down."

Assuming that the document had its own gravitational field of incrimination, Cardinal Vecci continued, "I would like to speak to Signorina Maria."

"Bugger that. Not now."

That's all I could think of saying as I pushed past him and his little ensemble of priests. I'd had enough for one day, and I was sure Maria had too. We left the perturbed posse standing in the middle of the road and headed straight for the research facility. I still nestled Maria under my arm, considering what she had just been through. As we entered the facility, Daniela instructed her travesti friends to remain outside to guard the door. I don't think anyone was going to disturb Maria any more that night. We clearly would not make it to the Manichaean's party. The bruise on Maria's cheek was distinct and familiar.

Chapter 19

I wondered how I was going to deal with the fact that Maria was now very comfortable spending the night with me in my tiny cot at my lab. She slept well but restlessly, as usual. I don't think I slept at all, as usual. Her constant tossing and turning signalled her vivid dreams of distressing events or reflections of conflict occurring in her mind as she slumbered. This was a stark contrast to her cool delivery of Gabrielle's messages on the stage. I was becoming inextricable to this girl who was either struggling with the weight of being the divinely inspired emissary of a new epoch or suffering a schizophrenic breakdown. Perhaps it was both?

I had spent much of the night awake, trying to make sense of these possibilities. So much of my life had become focused on asking questions that had no conceivable answer. My futile efforts eventually slid toward slumbering exhaustion. My mind wanted to solve the mysteries encircling Maria. But, as I held her, my heart wanted to entertain recollection of the beautiful moment we shared at her secret pool. Maria was clearly unaware of my conflicted emotions as she wrestled with the demons of her sleep.

Robin joined us for coffee in the morning. It was a good idea that he brought freshly cooked arepas, as Maria's appetite and her ability to scarf down whatever was put in front of her was still impressive. Robin had the manuscript that the cardinal had given him, and his appetite was more attuned to the material he was attempting to interpret.

"This is wonderful. My understanding of Italian is pretty average, but I think this is when Gabrielle described the new baptismal rituals required to prepare for the new Christ."

I hadn't been present for all of Gabrielle's revelations revealed through Maria. This was the first I'd heard of a new baptism ritual. I had a dozen questions that immediately popped up in my head, but Robin eagerly continued.

"The water baptism is a belief in divine power. Gabrielle has added the air baptism: to know thyself."

"So how do you baptise someone with air?" I asked, eager to get a question in before Robin continued.

"I have no idea, to tell you the truth. She's only mentioned that it is necessary to prepare for the Christ."

"Does Gustavo know about this? I imagine he would plan a hefty baptism fee if he did."

"I don't think Gustavo fully understands the details of Gabrielle and Maria's connection and insights."

"He probably doesn't care. If it pays well, that's all he needs to know."

"And she declared that the new Christ will offer the fire baptism: to forge destiny," Robin added enthusiastically.

"No wonder the Vatican is nervous. This could quickly escalate into a turf war," I said.

Maria just sat and ate her arepas, as though the conversation had nothing to do with her.

"Where's all this going?" I asked her. "Do you know how these new baptisms will proceed?"

Maria just shrugged and smiled at me as her cheeks billowed from the shovelled maize and fried plantains.

"You know, if you name the father, all this goes away."

Maria just glared at me as she continued to fill any remaining void in her mouth with food.

Robin responded to my frustration with an attempted diversion from the topic. "Perhaps she's tapping into a fundamental truth? These ideas are not new. Faith has always been a path to personal empowerment—the original intention of what we call the spiritual movement."

"I see the opposite," I had to interject. "Religion seems to suppress people with fear-based dogma."

"I think you're referring to the current era of 'literalism,'" Robin defended. "In literalism, followers just believe what they're told. That's a more recent phenomenon, as the world has seen a massive expansion of inclusion of the masses into what were historically spiritual practices of select groups and their initiates. They did not intend the process to include fear."

"So what happened?"

"I guess that by bringing spirituality to the masses, the ideas had to be simplified for mass consumption. Fear is often used to motivate people until they understand how to transcend that fear. It's the same reason fairy tales and folklore stories are often scary."

"Aren't you offending billions of people by saying their faith is just a simplified version of a bigger picture?"

"Not at all. Look at learning to play the piano. You can't start with a sonata. It's too much. You start with simple melodies. Literalism is the simplest form of spiritualism. A god on a cloud is an idea even children can grasp. This is the purpose of the water baptism—to get started on the path."

I had to stop and contemplate Robin's opinion. My work had to do with known facts and hypotheses related to these known elements. For me, the sharing of science had always respected the facts, but it had never been my job to relate science to the masses. I imagined that, when simplified for the sake of introduction, scientific concepts might include inaccuracies that would be a consequence of the simplification.

Robin watched me like someone waiting for a penny to drop from a precarious ledge. "Now there are billions on the path," he added, eager for me to see his point of view. "Not just a selected few. What Gabrielle is doing, through Maria, is showing us the sonata. Collectively, we are graduating from the piano scales, and Gabrielle is the conductor."

"Do you really believe that?"

"I've researched all kinds of spiritual movements in my career. None of them come close to what's happening here."

"What about the guy from the Vatican?" I asked, hoping to focus on more practical matters.

"The Vatican has a choice to make, like everyone else. Either you join the movement, or you join the spitters."

I immediately felt a pang of concern for Maria as I'd already had a painful experience with the conflict the spitters could bring to the table.

"If this continues to escalate, it's in their interest to be a part of it and claim ownership," Robin continued. "If it dies out, they'll distance themselves." He lifted his wallet from his pocket. "I think I know what to do."

He shuffled through the battered leather pouch and pulled out what appeared to be an ID card. The laminated print showed a picture of Robin looking particularly cheerful, his dazzling teeth dominating the image. In a font that appeared hand-drawn in Old-World calligraphy resembling a biblical script, the embossed letters C.M. stood out prominently. A watermarked logo of a tower with the inscription "University of Louisiana" encircling it covered the entire card. I assumed this was to lend authenticity to the title granted.

"This is my free pass into the Vatican and all religious sites. The university issued it to me, and it identifies me as a comparative mythologist—a C.M. I'll speak to the cardinal."

"What are you going to say?"

"I don't know. I'll get a sense of where they're at and move forward to a solution if I can."

It didn't sound like an ironclad plan, but it was the only one we had. We had to find out what the Vatican wanted and whether they intended to assist or were yet another source of threat to Maria and her still-missing prophetic parrot.

Robin held up the manuscript he had been reading. "In the meantime, we need to get this out there and translated into as many languages as we can."

Maria had the day off from addressing the horde of eager followers, as Robin was using the time to establish what the Vatican representatives were going to contribute or impede. I had my work to do with Carlos, who was doing a stellar job providing exotic botanicals for us to test as potential life-extending elixirs. Maria was happy to hang about with us. She spent most of the day arranging the botanicals into colourful bouquets that made the lab look like it could double as a wedding photo studio. She decorated every bench top and shelf with dazzling blooms. I almost had to fight to keep some workspace that Maria otherwise would have gladly decorated with a delightful floral display. I imagined that the simple act of arranging flowers was a welcome relief for Maria, who had otherwise had unrelenting commitments during what would have to be the most tumultuous period of her life. Maria never complained about her commitments to the church that had arisen around her, and she didn't ask me to take her away from her mob of eager adorers. I had a momentary flashback to the day I met her, when she seemed eager to leave. What was it about her previous life that made the holy parrot commitments so easy for her to accept without complaint?

Long shadows extended across the floorboards below the light streaming through the lab window. That was my sign that it was getting late and time to wrap up for the day. What was I to do with Maria? If I asked her to stay, I think she would interpret the invitation as being permanent. As much as part of me was comfortable holding Maria through the night in my little cot at the expense of any reasonable sleep, I had to set boundaries somewhere. I opened the front door and looked at Maria.

"Maria, it's time for you to go home."

She looked at me with the moment of hesitancy, where protest was likely to follow in her next breath. Instead, she approached me, kissed my cheek, and headed out the door without a word. Daniela and her travesti friends had been waiting outside the lab. They quietly surrounded Maria as supportive escorts, and together they headed up the road toward Maria's home. I closed the door and turned to view my blossom-laden room. I had to smile. "Boundaries" was the name of the horse that had already bolted through and was now miles away from my little corner of Buritaca. Sending Maria home was not likely going to tame the galloping events.

✳✳

I was eager to find out what the outcomes were in the discussions between Robin and the cardinal. Robin's idea had worked. He had convinced the cardinal to be Maria's spiritual guide, neither accepting nor rejecting the divine nature of her pregnancy. It apparently visibly relieved the cardinal to be given a way out. It was, perhaps, wise of Robin, in his discussions with the cardinal, to leave out the part that the winds of whispers were strong in Buritaca this day, as word had quickly spread about the manuscript being labelled as *The Book of Gabrielle*. The cardinal had brandished the document detailing the communication between Gabrielle and Maria as a raging indictment against Maria. The townsfolk hailed it, though, and translated it into multiple languages. I preferred the title *The Book of Parrot*.

As much as I felt I should have stayed in my lab the following day, I couldn't help but head to Maria's home to catch up with the latest developments. Our walk to the stadium in the morning looked more like a celebrity parade compared to previous efforts. Maria and I led the group, and her travesti guards were close behind. Gustavo had found a position in the parade just behind the travesti. He didn't appear at all comfortable, as immediately following him was a parade of religious regality. The cardinal, dressed in an ornately decorated red robe and finished with a matching tall, peaked hat, kept as close to the front as he could. Robin told me his hat was a biretta. The red colour was apparently symbolic of the cardinal's willingness to spill his blood for the church. I imagined that if he upset Gustavo's investment in Maria's church at all, his willingness to spill blood would be tested. An embellished green stole finished the cardinal's attire. Six men surrounded him, all dressed in black, identifiable as priests by their collars. If they had added sunglasses and a few extra pounds of muscle, they could have doubled as mafia bodyguards. The parade participants continued, with the Manichaean and his entourage close behind. The Manichaean's humble hooded cotton robe, matching that of his enclave, was a stark contrast to the cardinal's. I assumed they hadn't arm wrestled for their relative positions in our makeshift procession and that the Manichaean had perhaps exercised gracious discretion in allowing the cardinal to precede him.

By the time we reached the stage, Maria was once again looking like a life-sized doll covered in an assortment of gifted scarves, flowers, and glittering adornments.

Maria, Robin, and I walked up onto the stage as the travesti assumed their guard positions on the ground in front of the waist-high rostrum. The cardinal and his crew had followed us toward the podium, but the Manichaean and his entourage politely blocked the stairs so that the cardinal could not proceed any further. I was grateful, not only for Maria's sake, in that the additional company clearly made her nervous, but also because the stage was not likely strong enough for the added weight. The cardinal probably didn't know that they had only made its foundations out of coffee pallets and reed mats.

Maria began her ritual amidst the loud chanting of "Loro Santo" around her. This would have likely been the first viewing of the ritual for the cardinal. I watched him somewhat intently, looking for any reaction that may signal imminent concern for Maria.

Once Maria entered her state of trance, she immediately lifted her head and instructed the tightly packed audience in Spanish.

"My name is Gabrielle. I am a messenger from God. Everyone, breathe in deeply and exhale. Again, breathe in deeply and exhale. Now as you breathe in, prepare the words, 'I am' in your breath as though the words are the very air you breathe."

The crowd of participants continued the rhythm of Maria's breathing instructions. As they collectively drew in a long breath, the eeriest sound ensued. I could hear the whispered word *soy*, the Spanish word for "I am," resonating from their throats. Some participants had translated the instruction for themselves, and the sound of "I am" vociferated as they inhaled. Before this moment, I didn't know that we could talk whilst breathing in. I'd simply never tried. Their communal sigh of gentle exhalation followed the softly swallowed words.

"Soon, as you breathe out," Maria continued, "you will finish this statement silently in your mind's eye. I will instruct every one of you with what you need to hear. I will teach you who you really are. What I tell you is for you, for your ears only. Only share your silent breath as you focus on your identity. Keep your identity secret and secure in your mind. Allow your breath alone to deliver your identity to the world."

A distinct chill rippled down my spine. I looked across to Robin, who clearly knew exactly what was going on. He had mentioned the air baptism, "to know thyself." Was this what he was referring to? Was Maria about to share revelations with each one of us about our personal identities that we may have never contemplated previously?

Maria continued speaking with a calm certainty that continued to rattle my understanding of her and of what was going on.

"Bring forward your sick and ailing brothers and sisters."

"What?" The word blurted out from my mouth, betraying my immediately distraught reaction. What did she intend to do?

A line of hopeful initiates quickly emerged at the base of the stairs. Amid all the commotion of the crowd, I saw the Manichaean nod to his entourage. They responded to the gesture with almost military precision as they flanked the line of people on either side to make it clear to all where the line was. Their position created the appearance of a funnel for others to join the line. How they had known to create such a precise formation in response to nothing more than a nod was beyond me. A middle-aged Colombian lady who looked like a local was the first in line. A Manichaean assistant guided her up the stairs and escorted her across the floor to Maria. I had been standing about six feet behind and to the side of Maria until this point. Instinctively, I felt the urge to step back and give space for whatever was about to occur. The lady immediately dropped to her knees in front of Maria and bowed her head in the most overt offering of reverence. Maria placed her hand on the lady's head. The hushed silence was so profound that I could hear only my heart thumping in my chest. Maria leaned forward and appeared to whisper into the ear of the eager participant. The lady nodded, and an appreciative smile gently emerged at the corners of her mouth. Maria then drew the woman forward into a warm and lingering hug.

She then held her arms out in a gesture that the woman should address the crowd of enthralled onlookers behind her.

"Breathe in 'I am,'" Maria instructed the lady in Spanish. "Then breathe out your truth without saying a word."

The lady stood and turned to the crowd. She shot a nervous glance at Maria, who simply nodded. The woman opened her arms to the audience and breathed in deeply as the word for "I am" resonated from her throat in Spanish.

"Soy..."

She then breathed out in a way that I can only describe as an exhalation of all the tension from her body. It appeared to be more of a release of intention than air.

"Own your true identity, and it will heal you," Maria declared with a tone of serene assuredness.

The roar of approval, clapping and cheering, was thunderous as the Manichaean's man escorted the lady off the stage. The next initiate copied the actions of the first and knelt before Maria with a bowed head. This time, a young man who looked like he was European and perhaps thinner than you would expect for his height. Again, Maria whispered briefly in his ear. He nodded, and then they embraced tenderly. The man knew that he then was to stand, face the audience, and breathe out his new identity to the world for the first time. He breathed in with such gusto that he looked like he was trying to draw all the air surrounding the audience into his mouth. The guttural rumble of the words "I am" emanated from his throat. Then, with all the voracity of the inhalation, he appeared to push every inch of his body toward his expired breath. Maria then addressed the man in English.

"Know your true identity and heal yourself!"

The combined relief and exuberance in the man's expression was enough to motivate even the most skeptical to want to take part in whatever Maria had just offered this man. They escorted yet another happy participant from the podium. I clutched at the eczema in the crook of my arm as a swarm of hopefuls joined the line at the base of the stairs. I hadn't noticed that Robin had moved across toward me. He whispered in my ear as a third hopeful knelt before Maria.

"We're going to need a second set of stairs. They can then exit on the other side of the stage."

I don't know what I was expecting him to say or ask, but I hadn't imagined his concern to be such a simple, pragmatic issue. Once again, his comfort with the proceedings was just as surprising as the nature of the unfolding events. I returned my attention to Maria, who was now touching the head of the third participant, an overweight middle-aged man with a pale Anglo-Saxon complexion. Maria touched his bowed head. Oddly, she did not lean forward to whisper in his ear.

She simply stated, loud enough for me to hear, "You do not believe enough yet. Return when you are ready."

The puzzled participant stood and hugged Maria. He left the stage without performing a breathing ritual for the audience. This procession of hopeful participants continued for at least two hours. Maria whispered a word, or she didn't. She declared a healing, or she didn't, for hundreds of participants. I had no idea what selection process she was using to determine whether someone was ready for this faith healing exercise. I also noticed that some members of the audience appeared to question or doubt their own capacity to take part before approaching Maria. The odd one or two were walking away from the queue of hopefuls.

Robin seemed delighted. He had resumed taking a ledger of participants. I wasn't sure what details he was recording regarding each candidate, but I assumed he would share the information with me at some stage down the track. The cardinal appeared uncomfortable with the proceedings. The Manichaean maintained a broad smile reminiscent of the wonderment of a child.

Over the next few days, Maria continued her new routine, which began with her usual rocking and "Loro Santo" chanting. Her audience continued to grow, particularly now that the word had spread that "healings" were part of the show. Once she awakened in her

Gabrielle-linked trance, she invited the audience to participate in the "I am" mantra that accompanied collective, deep, accentuated breathing. I continued to be enthralled by the sound of hundreds, if not thousands, of people simultaneously chanting "I am" as they inhaled. The sound had its own presence and power that made the ritual even more captivating. Part of me wanted to join in, but my sense of education, like a heavy chain in my mind, dragged me back. I noticed that the only other non-participants were the cardinal, his platoon of priests, and the spitters. They stood motionless, perhaps in silent protest to the participants who drew breath in writhing rapture around them. Once again, Maria had pressed my buttons of self-consciousness that embarrassed me to feel like I was an aloof child, avoiding an opportunity to grow up.

They had constructed a second set of stairs overnight to accommodate Robin's suggestion that Maria's devotees enter one side and then exit the other side of the stage. Each day, hundreds of new people lined up before Maria's podium, hoping for a blessing and healing. Robin had set up at a collapsible card table next to the first set of stairs, where he continued to record the name and details of every participant in a ledger. I was on the stage with Maria, mainly because I was now so fascinated with what was developing. I watched intently as Maria placed her hand on the head of each person presented before her by one of the Manichaean's team members. We all waited with bated breath as she somehow determined whether the person was to hear their "identity" from Maria or whether they must return at an unspecified later date when their ears were "ready" to hear the utterance of their profound truth. No one that I was aware of had shared their given "identity," so it remained Buritaca's greatest secret amongst the inducted faithful.

Word was spreading fast that Maria, speaking as Gabrielle, was offering healings. Oddly enough, claims of miraculous cures were spreading like wildfire. I couldn't hear what she was whispering into the ears of her delighted disciples, and I wondered what my "true identity" would be. I found myself undeniably questioning the identity I had given my-self. Then the oddest thing happened. Three police officers walked onto the stage and approached Maria.

The first policeman approached her as she was finishing her hug with a tear-drenched lady whose beaming smile divulged her recent epiphany, whispered in her ear by Maria. The officer ignored the sub-lime interaction.

"Miss Santos," he declared authoritatively in Spanish, "we are plac-ing you under arrest."

I stepped forward with my hands raised, palms facing the police-men, to show I meant no harm.

"Is there a problem?" I asked in their language.

"We have orders to place Miss Santos under arrest," the second officer answered with just as much authority as the first.

"What for?"

"For practicing medicine without a licence," the third policeman answered, justifying their presence on the stage.

"What? That's ridiculous."

They didn't budge. Maria hadn't moved the entire time this dispute was playing out. The first officer noticed she seemed to be a bit out of it, and he roughly grabbed her arm to demand her attention.

"Whoa!" I insisted as I moved behind Maria, placing my hands protectively on her shoulders.

The audience reacted poorly to the police officers' actions and started calling out for the officers to leave Maria alone. They had already caught me in the middle of one riot, so a second involving the police was something I hoped to avoid. I gestured for the officer to give me a moment. Thankfully, he let go of Maria's arm, and I tried to rouse her from her state. She slowly woke from her trance and looked at the policemen with astonishment. She turned back to me.

"What's going on?"

"We have to go with the policemen. There's been a misunderstanding."

The crowd booed and protested vociferously as the law enforcement escorted Maria off the stage.

Chapter 20

I stood outside the Santa Marta police station. As much as I was there out of concern for Maria, I couldn't help but notice that the police had the best office space in all of Santa Marta. They were at the entrance to the stunning Santa Marta Marina. Their view was the Caribbean Sea over a squadron of luxury yachts moored inside a commanding concrete breakwater. They had issued Maria a fine for practicing medicine without a licence, and a processing procedure was necessary at the station before we could move on to the courthouse, locally known as the Palacio de Justicia. As I wasn't officially a next of kin, they ushered me outside to wait as they completed their formalities inside. I had elected to escort Maria in the police car on the to drive to Santa Marta. I was told that she had been with me in the ambulance when I was unconscious after my blow to the head as they transported me to the hospital just down the road. So a return of the favour seemed appropriate, particularly since Gustavo was not keen to get involved. Despite her best intentions, Sylvia was essentially too hysterical to be of support to anyone. So we collectively suggested that she stay behind for now. We explained to her that the drive to Santa Marta was a formality. The prosecution was seeking to ratify the allegation, and a judge would preside over whether Maria had actually committed an offence.

A taxi pulled up in front of the Tayrona monument that was on the esplanade, a stone's throw from the station. I saw Robin getting out. I waved to get his attention, and he jogged across the stretch of ground to my side.

"I probably won't understand anything that's going to happen today. But if you're happy to translate, I can at least offer support."

"Thanks, mate."

I had sometimes wondered whether Robin had Maria's best interests at heart or simply a plan to use her to fulfil a living myth strategy he had envisioned. His eagerness to help had me leaning toward the possibility that he genuinely cared, despite whatever global denomination of religion fantasy he was concocting.

His timing was perfect as Maria eagerly pushed through the police station doors. She hurried across the pavement in our direction. Her bulbous pregnancy made it look like she was rolling toward us. She punched me in the pelvis with her belly button as she failed to decelerate before wrapping her arms around me.

"Don't let them put me in jail!" she demanded as she clung to me as best she could over her swollen pregnancy.

"No one is going to put you in jail," I promised, although I hadn't convinced myself against the possibility.

I recognised the police officer who approached us from the station as one of the issuing officers who had confronted Maria back in Buritaca. He looked annoyed, perhaps because, despite her incapacitated status, she had run away from him.

"I am to escort Ms. Santos to the Palacio de Justicia now," he grumbled in Spanish as he caught up.

"¡No me toques!" Maria roared, vexed fury in her eyes.

Even Robin would have understood that Maria was not about to be handled by the police officer, who quickly dropped his arm. I thought we would have taken the police car to the courthouse, but walking was the offered option, so we silently paved our way to the Palacio.

It was perhaps a five-minute walk. The word "palacio" was apt as the stark white building was huge. Its grand entrance was adorned with towering ionic columns, and the polished marble of the expansive staircase continued through the giant, heavy oak doorway into the building's antrum. Our escort left us to speak to a receptionist, who pointed toward our final destination.

We sat on a long wooden bench with our unnamed police officer, like children waiting outside a school principal's office. I imagined Maria was thinking something similar, where both scenarios often end with the declaration of a wrongdoing and a punishment is imposed. A clerk of the court popped her head out from the interior and ushered us in. I did not know what was about to transpire, and my concern immediately heightened, making me wonder whether we should have arranged legal representation for Maria, despite the short notice of the disclosure. I had no experience in court procedure. It wasn't my area of expertise. Considering this was in Colombia and in Spanish, it added to any fish-out-of-water anxiety that might be in my immediate future.

They showed us to another long wooden stall at the front right, facing the adjudication bench. Maria sat, flanked by me on one side and Robin on the other, before the magistrate. He was a greying man, perhaps in his seventies. He looked tired. A suited gentleman, who I assumed was the prosecutor, sat in the adjoining stalls to the left. His attention to reams of paperwork in his hands had me concerned—if the paperwork applied to Maria's case, shouldn't we have seen it? Another man, who just stared forward, sat beside him. His slim, stooped posture and thick bottle-rimmed glasses gave the impression that he may be someone academic.

"That's Dr. Martinez. He's my family doctor," Maria declared.

At least we knew who had made the complaint against her.

"Perhaps you and Gabrielle are bad for business?"

The prosecutor stepped forward and handed the documents he had been sifting through to the magistrate. He perused the paperwork and then looked across at Maria. He addressed her directly in Spanish.

"This is not a trial. It's a hearing to determine whether you have committed a crime."

"Your honour, my client has filed a formal complaint against Ms. Santos for practicing medicine without a license. This is an offence that is unlawful, and the court should punish her accordingly," said the prosecutor.

"Ms. Santos, how do you respond to these allegations?" asked the magistrate.

Maria looked across the room at the prosecutor and then back to me with the most pleading look. She trembled uncontrollably, as I had witnessed of her far too many times. She turned to the magistrate and replied in Spanish.

"I have done nothing wrong."

I really didn't know whether anything I could say would help or hinder Maria's defence. But I thought that the poor girl was going to rattle herself apart into a wreck on the floor if I didn't do something. She turned to me and repeated herself in English.

"I haven't done anything wrong."

I squeezed her hand gently in a gesture of support and stood up. My Spanish diction was about to undergo a formal hearing.

"Your honour, I am a scientist and an associate of Ms. Santos. If I may explain? There has been a misunderstanding."

"Please do."

I cleared my throat, more to stall in order to gather my thoughts. Preparing a statement of defence for Maria was another oversight that would have been handy.

"Miss Santos is not offering any diagnosis or cure for any disease. What she is offering is her opinion. She believes that faith can help heal physical and emotional ailments. She's sharing this belief publicly and offers no guarantees and takes no payment. Everyone has the right to their beliefs, and Miss Santos is merely expressing hers. She believes that faith can heal."

I hoped that was what I said. Maria seemed pleased. Robin was clueless, but smiled supportively.

"But members of the public are claiming to be cured by her," the prosecutor interposed.

"They are, in fact, claiming healing in response to their faith in her. That is different."

"Do you have any evidence of medicines being administered by Ms. Santos or any guarantee of a cure being offered by her?" the magistrate asked the prosecutor.

He turned to Dr. Martinez, who had continued to stare straight forward into space until this moment. In response to the quizzical look from his legal representative, he simply dropped his head and appeared to look at his shoes.

"No, we do not, your honour. But this evidence will be easily obtainable."

"Do you have any evidence of harm from Miss Santos's actions?"

"No, your honour," the lawyer replied sheepishly.

The magistrate peered at the prosecutor and then at Maria. With a sigh that betrayed his ennui, he picked up his gavel and looked at it as a fortune teller looks at a crystal ball, hoping for an insightful vision.

"An accusation of practicing medicine without a licence is a serious offence, Miss Santos. I defer this case for one month. If, Dr. Martinez, you do not provide evidence substantiating your claim in that time, I will dismiss any continuing proceedings regarding the matter."

He laid the gavel back on its plate and then wearily pushed himself up to his feet, using the felt-clad armrests of his chair. Unceremoniously, he proceeded out through a side door close to his bench.

I sat back down next to Maria. I took her hand again.

"Let's get you back to Buritaca."

"So that's it? It's over?" she asked.

"Well, not exactly." I turned to Dr. Martinez and resorted to speaking to Maria in Spanish for his benefit. "He won't find any evidence that you are practicing medicine without a licence because that is not what you're doing. He simply doesn't understand, and he's feeling threatened."

She squeezed my hand affectionately. The gratitude expressed in her eyes was endearingly clear. We all stood and headed out of the courtroom.

"Is the officer going to give us a lift back home?" Robin asked as he held open the door for Maria.

We looked around the room and then down the adjoining corridor. Our escort had clearly vacated the premises.

"I guess not."

As we descended the marble stairs to the pavement, Maria turned to me as she continued to clutch my hand.

"Your Spanish is still terrible."

"Thanks. But good enough to keep you out of jail."

"Do you believe that faith can heal?" she challenged.

"I'll hail a taxi," I quickly said.

Perhaps I wasn't quite ready to answer such a big question. Maria smiled. I think she enjoyed finding my buttons to press. She stumbled slightly, holding her belly.

"Are you okay?" Robin asked as he stepped toward her to assist.

"It's the baby. I think he just did a jump in my belly. Maybe he just fell over laughing at Leo?"

Maria's joke clearly pleased Robin immensely as he fought back his own laughter.

"How far along are you?" he asked, perhaps to save me from more teasing by changing the topic.

"I think about seven months. Not long now."

Sylvia was beside herself when we returned with the news that they had suspended all charges against her daughter. Maria was so exhausted by the ordeal that she retreated to her bedroom as soon as her feet touched the dusty road outside her house. I asked Robin to make an announcement to Maria's followers. Although he couldn't speak Spanish, I was confident they'd be able to work out what was going on in every language represented in the rapidly expanding cultural diversity of the enclave.

Sylvia's response to the news was the same as to every event she encountered. She disappeared into the kitchen to prepare food. I sat at the dinner table with Gustavo, whose grumpy demeanour wasn't about to be disrupted by any sunshine. We sat there awkwardly, and I inwardly wished that Maria or Robin would join us to save me from Gustavo's accusing stares. I wasn't sure whether he actually blamed me for something or whether that was just his resting fractious face.

Sylvia returned to the table with a plate of some delicious cake portions she had made, known locally as torta de plátano maduro, a popular plantain cake prepared from ripe plantains, guava paste, cinnamon, mozzarella cheese, and eggs. I liked it so much that I made a mental note to look up the recipe after the meal.

"Thank you for taking such good care of my daughter. I cannot thank you enough," she stated in Spanish as she touched my shoulder tenderly.

She looked across to Gustavo with provocative intent.

"Yes, thank you," Gustavo said.

"You are welcome. But I will need to get some of my work done eventually," I replied politely in Spanish, although I was now tiring of my declarations of needing to get work done without actually taking the steps to achieve the goal.

I think I was becoming comfortable with the distraction. I was actually feeling quite proud of myself for how I had assisted Maria at her court hearing. It was a more fulfilling sense of achievement than anything I had experienced to date in my scientific pursuits. Robin knocked on the front door to let us know he had returned, and he joined us at the dinner table, taking a seat. I offered him one of Sylvia's delicious cakes.

"Do you know about the bonfire?" Gustavo piped up as he filled his mouth with the cake.

"Bonfire?"

"On the beach. The escupitajos are burning the books of Gabrielle," he continued in his native tongue.

It intrigued me that the word *escupitajos*, which effectively means "spitters," had clearly become a colloquial expression to refer to Maria's detractors.

"The spitters and the local priest have constructed a large fire," he continued. "They are spitting on copies of *The Book of Gabrielle*, and then they throw the copies into the fire. They're chanting, 'God save us from this devil girl and her child.' It's okay. We'll just print more copies. I'm going to put up the price."

My translation of Gustavo's revelation made Robin squirm uneasily in his chair. Gustavo responded to his obvious disquiet.

"Nadie lastima a mi hija," he reassured Robin, who clearly didn't understand what was being said. "Mi familia lo es todo para mi."

I explained to Robin that Gustavo was reminding us he was not going to let anyone hurt his daughter.

Despite the reassurance offered by Gustavo, Robin remained agitated. "There's something we need to discuss. If the legend is to be fulfilled, the haters—spitters included—will probably play a major role in this child's life."

"What are you saying?" I asked.

"Historically, in every story from Osiris to Dionysus, or Serapis Christos to Jesus, the Christ has been born, sacrificed, and then resurrected. People like the spitters are a potential threat to the child."

The back door to the house slammed shut with a loud thud. Sylvia went to the back of the house to investigate. When she returned, she was quite distraught.

"Maria is gone," she blurted out in Spanish.

What happened next I can only relate based on the hearsay of onlookers who witnessed the events. There were so many people in Buritaca by this stage that it was virtually impossible for anything to occur without someone seeing it.

Maria was wearing only her sleeping nightgown as she strode toward the spitters and their massive funeral pyre of books. Despite her diminutive stature, she confronted the spitters with all the confidence of a raging bull.

"Do you want to be saved?" she roared at them in Spanish. "Do you think spitting on books and cursing me will save you? Are you so pathetic that you fear an unborn child? You want my baby dead? Here I am. Cast me on the fire and destroy us both. But you won't—because you are cowards." She walked defiantly amongst the spitters, who moved away from her in fear. "Your hearts are full of fear and selfish hate. You pray to God to save you! But why should he? Why would he save your pathetic souls? What do you bring to the world to make it a better place? Why do you deserve special treatment? Your wailing and crying is just for you and no one else."

Maria approached the smouldering fire. She dropped to her knees and drove her palms into the ash. She wiped the ash over her face.

"Look at me." She faced off with the spitters, who were now wailing with fear more than ever. "Yes. Be scared. Be terrified. I am showing you the blackness in your own hearts. It is your reflection that you hate and despise. Not me and my child, but your own selfish darkness."

Maria began walking in the ash around the fire's periphery.

"Gabrielle's message is clear—it is people like you, with your spitting and cursing, who will burn in the light of the new Christ. Spit on me now as I walk in the fire of my child's light. I dare you!"

Maria scooped up some embers and threw them at the spitters. She singled out the spitters and tormented them further.

"You? Do you dare?"

She picked up more embers and threw them. The spitters screamed and crossed themselves, hoping to save themselves from the devilish exhibition they were experiencing. Maria continued to single them out with smoking embers clutched in her tiny fists.

"You?"

The spitter in front of Maria retreated so quickly that she fell over backward and covered her face desperately in case Maria was about to breathe fire over her.

"This is your first and final warning," Maria commanded. "Try to harm my child, and your souls will burn in flames a thousand times hotter than any hell you can imagine."

From seemingly out of nowhere, the Manichaean and his entourage appeared. With heads bowed under monastic hoods, they silently formed a circle around the fire, facing outward, deftly creating an effective barrier between Maria and the spitters. Maria continued to scream her fury at the spitters, who scrambled to disperse and escape the girl possessed by a raging spirit.

By the time I arrived with Robin, the spitters had dispersed and Maria had taken off by herself somewhere. We saw only the Manichaean and his people standing as silent sentinels around the fire.

"Why would they have done this?" I asked as I looked at the piles of charred papers, not really expecting an answer.

"This is what people do when they feel scared and helpless. The idea of Maria's child frightens them. For the spitters, the only Christ of value is a dead Christ. A dead Christ is silent. A living Christ may hold them accountable for their dark thoughts and selfish deeds."

I had to contemplate the gravity of the threat to Maria and her child that Robin was proposing.

"Could they be after her now?"

"Possibly, yes. If they regroup, we've got a potential lynch mob."

"How do we prevent that?"

"We won't be able to placate their fears right now. They'll be too wound up."

"That's a worry."

"So, we have no choice but to give them something greater to fear—Gustavo."

"So much for love will conquer fear," I muttered to myself.

"Oh, it will," Robin assured. "But we have to allow for two opposing world views. The first is where someone else is responsible for your outcomes, and your pain and suffering is a consequence of forces outside of you, including other people's actions. That's where the spitters are right now. Gustavo's rage will be of greater consequence right now than Maria's pregnancy."

"And the second?"

"The second is where you are responsible for your outcomes. Any pain and suffering is yours to transcend by taking responsibility for your thoughts and actions."

"Which I assume the spitters aren't ready to do," I concurred.

"Not tonight, at least."

"It seems like your expertise is psychology, not spirituality," I said, intended as a compliment.

"Our psychology is the filter for our spirituality," he replied as he continued to assess the situation. "Gustavo can mobilise the travesti as well."

"Good idea. They'll help us find Maria," I added as I surveyed the remains of the tumultuous scene. "She often retreats to my lab when she's distraught. I should head there."

"Perhaps I can wait at the lab while you rally Gustavo into action? I don't think I'd be any good trying to explain to him what needs to be done."

I agreed and jogged toward Maria's house. I ran into Carlos on the way, so I told him what had happened. We decided he could go around the village asking if anyone had seen Maria while I unleashed Gustavo on the spitters. I wasn't sure exactly what kind of hell was heading their way, but if they needed a new level of scared to back off their plans against Maria, they were about to experience it.

It was possibly about two hours that we allowed for Maria to turn up somewhere. I regrouped with Carlos and Robin at the lab. It would have been around midnight by then.

"No one knows where she is." Carlos shrugged.

A dim streetlight muted by layers of dust poorly illuminated a lumbering shadow on the road. Gustavo. As he approached, we saw a small posse of travesti following him.

He called out to us in Spanish as he passed. "The escupitajos won't be a problem anymore."

We didn't have the time or energy to explore exactly what he meant by that, but his confidence was reassuring. I imagined Gustavo being defined as a weapon of mass destruction in a newspaper somewhere in the coming days.

As I watched Gustavo and his crew disappear into the engulfing darkness, a deductive thought found its way into my head. "I think I know where to find Maria," I declared. "We need to meet back here in five hours, so get as much rest as you can until then. It could be a long day ahead of us."

Chapter 21

I spent most of that night worrying about Maria. I was confident that my reasoning as to her whereabouts was sound, but there was nothing I could do about it for at least five hours. Maria must have overheard Robin's predictions of future events, and they rattled her enough for her to take on the spitters at their book barbecue whilst barefoot in a nightgown. It scared me to know I couldn't vouch for her whereabouts. I wasn't even certain she was alive. Frightened people do stupid things, and they were very frightened around that fire last night. If the spitters had found her or cornered her, what would they do to her? Religious people have a well-known history of seeking to destroy anything that scares them. How far were the spitters prepared to go in silencing or eliminating this girl and her child? If she was where I suspected, what would we need to have with us as precautionary measures? So, rather than sleep, my already overactive mind created a multitude of scenarios regarding Maria's whereabouts, including a short list of items including torches, blankets, matches, a first aid kit, and drinking water. The intensity of my restlessness only reminded me of the impact Maria had had on my life, and how much I cared about her.

When my alarm sounded at five in the morning, I sprang out of my bed, adrenalised and ready to go. I turned on my lights and began rummaging around for the list of necessary items for the day. Robin and Carlos had arrived together. One of them knocked on the door to announce their presence, and then they joined me inside the lab. I showed them the supplies I was gathering.

"Where are we going?" Robin asked with trepidation.

"I should have asked you to bring a rucksack," I chastised myself audibly.

"I have one in my car." Carlos nodded and disappeared outside again.

I quickly threw most of the supplies in my rucksack and gathered up the rest, including the blanket to take to Carlos. Robin and I met him at his Jeep, where he was dusting off a canvas duffel bag that had padded shoulder straps woven into the thick fabric.

"Perfect," I commented as I stuffed the blanket into the large sack. "There it is," I said as I pointed to the solitary star hanging low on the horizon. As much as I had wanted to take off in the middle of the night to find Maria, I had to wait for that star to rise. It was the only way I knew where to go. "It's this way."

I led Carlos and Robin into the jungle, following the star the same way that Maria had shown me when I first met her. I explained along the way where we were going and why I hoped to find Maria there. It was a long shot, and we had a lengthy journey ahead of us. We walked for hours as the sun brightened above the horizon, shrouding our guiding light. We trudged silently together and found the valley that led to Maria's pool just as the star was completely expunged by the sun's dominant luminosity. It was difficult enough for us to make the journey in hiking shoes with water and supplies. If Maria had made this journey ahead of us in the dark, in her state, would she have even made it? If she had collapsed at any point along the way, we could have easily walked right past her if the lush growth concealed her.

We followed the noise of running water. I hoped it would be the waterfall that cascaded into Maria's secret pool. Pushing forward, we found the opening. It was clearly the oasis that Maria had shown me as the details of the environs had lived on vividly in my mind's eye. I dropped my rucksack and ran to the cave, desperate to discover if my punt was accurate. Maria was lying on her side just inside the cavernous opening. Her feet appeared badly burned, blistered, and bleeding from the fire and long walk.

"She's over here!" I yelled to the others so they would join us quickly.

I crouched over her.

"Maria?"

I was about to check her pulse, but the sound of my voice created a ripple of movement within her. She turned toward me and weakly held her arms out for me to hug her. I leaned forward on my knees and cradled her in my arms. I was so relieved that she was alive, and I knew she was just as happy that I had found her.

"They want to hurt my baby. Don't let them hurt my baby."

"I won't. I promise."

Robin and Carlos entered the cave. Maria looked down at her night-dress. It was becoming soaked from her loins.

"What's happening?" Maria asked.

"I think your water just broke," I replied. "You're about to have this child."

If I was right, we were about to be propelled into a situation that none of us felt capable of dealing with. I had a gut-wrenching flashback of the traumatic experience my ex, Ruby, had endured and the tragic outcome that ensued. I shot Robin a nervous look. He turned to Carlos, who appeared more stupefied than anyone by the suggestion.

"Carlos, start a fire. Boil some water," he commanded frantically. "Bring the blanket over here. I'll see if I can get a signal and call for help."

"I can feel it. It hurts. Leo, I'm scared."

Maria's declaration stopped us dead in our tracks like deer stunned by headlights. Was she confirming what I had just surmised? We were all genuinely scared.

"Guys! Get on with it!" I urged Robin and Carlos, hoping my feigned confidence would snap us all out of our panicked imaginations to get on with our respective tasks. They shook off their whispering demons, and they left me with mine as I watched Maria agonise in response to her body that had kick-started its birthing autopilot. I couldn't calculate the likelihood of a child surviving a premature birth in such primordial conditions, but I guessed the odds were against us. Carlos had headed back to the supplies we had left at the other end of the pool, while Robin swirled around in circles outside the cave, his phone held aloft. His persistence revealed the futility of his efforts.

"It's okay. I'm here," I reassured Maria as I continued to hold her. My words reminded me of the desperate sense of uselessness that was washing over me.

"There's no signal," Robin called back to us. He returned with a blanket from the supplies that Carlos had thrown to him as he rummaged through the rucksacks.

"I don't suppose you've ever delivered a baby before," he asked me frankly as he opened the blanket to lay it on the ground. Maria looked at me hopefully, as though I was likely to say yes. Carlos returned with provisions for a fire and a small metal container not much larger than a cup for us to boil water in. I didn't answer Robin, as I didn't want my answer to cause any alarm, particularly to myself. Carlos started sorting the small pile of wood to begin a fire. Thankfully, Robin didn't press for an answer.

"Now what?" Carlos asked, wanting to be helpful.

I wanted to answer, "Who knows?" But I thought I should at least look as though I knew what I was doing. I was about to make a random suggestion, but Robin piped up as he lit a match for the miniature bonfire.

"You know, the early Christ myths often had the child being born in a cave. Just saying."

"Well, this should be fine, then," Carlos replied supportively. He was clearly trying to be encouraging in a situation that exuded extreme duress. "But Maria is two months premature, is she not?" he continued. "A cave is perhaps not a good idea."

"Carlos?" I chastised as gently as I could so as not to alarm Maria.

He just shrugged to say that he was just drawing attention to facts.

"Well, these stories had Jesus, like the legend of Dionysus before him, born at seven months." He looked at me, giving his best expression of reassurance under the circumstances. "So I'm sure everything will go well." He turned back to his task, perhaps not entirely convinced by his own encouragement.

"Fire's going. I'll get some water," Carlos added, breaking our focus on weak attempts to predict success and wishes for divine appropriateness.

He took the cup to the pool and scooped up as much water as his tiny pot would hold. Maria screamed in response to the contractions that were strengthening. Robin and I collected Maria's tiny frame between us and lifted her from her dusty and now soaked position onto the blanket.

"Maria, I have to look to see if the child is coming out correctly," I said, knowing that I didn't really know what correct looked like. I assumed I should see the crown of a child's head, at least.

Maria nodded. Carlos and Robin both froze again, betraying their discomfort and bewilderment.

"How's that water coming along?" I asked Carlos.

"I'll check," he responded and spun on his heel so his back would be to us.

I looked at Robin, waiting for him to move.

"I'll go help Carlos," he said.

Robin turned away and gave his attention to the fire starting efforts a few metres away, just outside the entrance to the cave. I lifted Maria's nightgown to check on her progress.

"Okay, this is definitely happening," I declared, as I was confronted by the sight of the child's presenting crown and the muddy mess of blood-stained bodily fluids saturating the ground below Maria's thighs.

"It hurts!" Maria screamed.

I dropped the hem of her gown and reeled backwards, my head spinning with an anguished sense of déjà vu. "I can't do this," I blurted.

"What?" Maria replied, tilting up her head to me.

Her head dropped to the ground. She clutched at her loins and roared out a shrill scream that reverberated off the cave walls. Suddenly feeling claustrophobic, I scrambled to my feet and rushed to the entrance of the cave. I couldn't breathe. My heart was pounding furiously, and my chest felt like it was crumbling from crushing anxiety. I dropped to my knees as the pressure inside my guts forced vomit from my mouth.

"Leo!" Maria screamed from the cave as her torso jerked in strengthening contractions.

Robin rushed over and squatted next to me, placing his hand between my shoulder blades. I desperately tried to draw a breath as every muscle in my torso spontaneously contracted to expel any air I had left in my lungs. I rolled onto my side in a foetal position, clutching at my chest.

Robin turned to Carlos. "He's having a panic attack."

Carlos grabbed the pot he had just placed over the fire and rushed over to us. Without warning, he launched the contents of the container at my face. The liquid, still chilled from the mountain-fed lagoon, snapped me out of my delirious stupor. I drew an enormous breath and filled my depleted lungs with air.

"All good?" Carlos enquired as the empty pot continued to swing under its handle in the grip of his hand.

"Yeah, I think so," I replied, sitting up. I continued to test the working capacity of my lungs with slow, deep ventilations.

Robin looked at me earnestly. "Leo, I know what you've been through. We all know what's at risk here. You need to find that place in you where your courage resides and let it out."

I understood immediately how Robin could motivate Maria to step up to what they had both accepted as her calling. It was in that moment that I finally took the idea of being Maria's lion seriously. The spitters had shown that fear was an enemy for Maria and her child, and I couldn't let the stampede of frightened horses in my head take precedence over the lion that needed to be awakened in my heart. I got back to my feet and marched back into the cave.

"What the hell, Leo?" Maria demanded, sweat pouring from her grimacing countenance.

"I had a few demons to shake off," was all I could offer to defend my actions. "They're gone now. And I'm here for you. I'll get you through this." I looked toward Robin and Carlos. "We all will."

Robin and Carlos nodded reassuringly.

I took Maria's hand. "I think I say breathe and push."

She tried to follow my instructions. "I can't, really. I'm too tired."

I believed her. She was barely conscious, and I couldn't imagine how she could have any energy left. I don't know what I was thinking, but the words came out of my mouth.

"Maria, call Gabrielle."

Either I thought we needed all the help we could get, or I was still suffering hypoxic psychosis from my panic attack. Nevertheless, the idea seemed perfectly reasonable to Maria. She began gently rocking her body backward and forward while on her back by pushing with her feet through her bent knees. She was barely moving, but the undulations seemed to calm her and give her confidence.

"Loro Santo. Loro Santo," she whispered to herself as she closed her eyes to focus on wherever she found Gabrielle in her inner world.

"Yes. Use the breathing," I encouraged.

"Loro Santo. Loro Santo," Maria continued.

Her voice was becoming thin and inaudible. A horrified chill ran down my spine.

"Maria? No. You have to stay with me."

I looked to Robin and Carlos, desperately hoping that they would know what to do. My panicked expression choked away any valuable suggestion they may have provided. Maria had passed out. I couldn't get her to respond to me, no matter what I did.

"I don't know what to do," I confessed.

"I could fill this and throw cold water on her face," Carlos offered, holding forward the small pot in his hand.

"No!" Robin and I replied in unison.

He shrugged. "It worked last time."

Robin dropped to his knees beside Maria's head.

"Gabrielle!" he yelled. "Push!"

Maria sprung to life, and she cried out what sounded like a roar from her lungs. Her abdomen flexed and contracted strongly, and her body expelled the tiny child into my arms. The action was so powerful and focused that I barely reacted in time to assist the miniature man's entry into the outer world. Maria collapsed again. Robin was closest to her face.

"Maria?" he asked as he stroked her sweat-drenched hair. "Gabrielle?" he said, hoping for a response. "I think she's completely unconscious."

Maria continued to lie still, but she was clearly breathing, albeit weakly. I lifted the tiny, premature child from under her nightgown. A pulsing lifeline still attached him to Maria, and I wasn't eager to disturb it. I looked at the tiny child cradled in my blood-soaked hands. The fragile nature of what was in my hands astounded me. It was like holding a small bird. I realised the reason I asked Robin to boil water was so that I could wash my hands before this moment occurred. Carlos went to collect more water, perhaps thinking the same thing. He returned with his pot of water.

"It's still cold. But I think it'll do."

Robin poured small amounts of the water into his hand and dribbled the liquid offering over the child in my hands to wash off the remains of the blood and birthing fluids. Carlos checked Maria's pulse and lowered his ear to Maria's face.

"She's still breathing. Can she feed the child while she's unconscious?"

"I have no idea. Will she be expressing milk after seven months of pregnancy?" I asked with an alarmed awareness that this was all occurring extremely early.

Carlos raised his palms defensively. "Well, I'm not gonna take out her boob and squeeze it to find out."

"Don't look at me," Robin said. "So much for three wise men." He chortled.

"What?"

"You know, birth of Christ, three wise men. We followed a star to get here."

I didn't find Robin's tendency to draw analogies all that helpful or encouraging.

I delicately handed the infant to Robin. "Sorry, Maria," I mumbled as I reached through the V-neck opening of her nightgown and squeezed her breast in a drawing action that I imagined would express milk from the compressed glands. Nothing happened.

"I don't think she's expressing. I think it's too early."

"You've given me an idea," Carlos declared as he slapped Robin on the back. "Unless you need me immediately, I'll be back in a minute."

Robin and I shrugged, and he headed out of the cave into the forest. Robin continued to clean the child with the remaining water. He placed the child in the cradle of Maria's limp arm that was resting beside her on the blanket. I was becoming concerned that the child didn't appear to be moving. His colour looked ruddy, but on the verge of blue. There didn't seem to be a lot going on regarding life signs. Robin continued his task, and he lifted the edge of the blanket to sponge away any remaining moisture. The massaging motion must have stimulated the tiny tot, who gasped a deep breath and gurgled a few coughs as the new lungs took their first breaths. The child's complexion improved instantaneously to a healthy pink hue. Robin smiled at me reassuringly. He pulled out his pocketknife, exposed the blade, and lifted the umbilical cord with his other hand.

"Are we doing this?"

"I guess so?"

He cut the cord and did his best to tie a knot in the child's oozing thread.

I grabbed the small pot that was now empty. It was an effort to get to my legs. Somewhere between physical fatigue and adrenal exhaustion, they had lost their power. I shook them back to life and went to the pool to wash my hands and collect more water.

While I was at the pond, Robin continued his efforts with his pocketknife by cutting a small strip off the blanket. He then loosely wrapped the child in a swaddle and returned him to Maria's side. Carlos returned as I was heading back to the cave. Immediately, I noticed his face and arms covered in raised welts.

"What on earth happened to you?"

"I got you these."

He opened his pack and pulled out a large dripping chunk of honeycomb, loosely wrapped in a palm leaf.

"I remember we passed a hive on the way here. I had to fight for it." He held out his prize proudly. "It was Robin who gave me the idea. Gold, frankincense, and myrrh."

I looked at him blankly.

"As close as I can get here, anyway," he said as he walked past me to the cave. "When you grow up in the jungle, with no western medicines, you learn that the Bible story wasn't about random gifts from three kings. We know these as midwifery resources."

Carlos swung his rucksack off his shoulder, and it landed on the soft earth with a thud. He pulled out another palm leaf, put it on the ground, and placed the honeycomb on the open leaf. He reached into the bag again and retrieved a fistful of tree bark scrapings.

"This is the closest I could find to frankincense. It's a bark we burn to ward off insects and mosquitos."

He aimed at the fire and tossed the specimen into the flames. Aromatic white smoke began drifting up from the smouldering herb. With the amount of blood and fluid spilled in the birthing, I imagined that keeping away bugs wasn't such a bad idea. He reached into his bag again and drew out what looked like crystalline beads of sap that oozed out from tree knots. They looked familiar because eucalyptus trees in Australia often have these features.

"It's not myrrh either. But if we boil it, it has astringent and anti-bacterial properties to wash Maria and the child. It's good for bleeding wounds."

He dropped the beads into the tin of water in my hand. I guessed my job was to place the tin over the fire. As I positioned the tin on some of the more solid coals, Robin ran his finger through the seeping honeycomb and examined the thick amber offering that clung to it.

"Liquid gold," he said with a grin. "Of course!" he continued delightedly. "He's right. These were said to be the birthing tools of ancient Egypt. They would also anoint newborn kings by ceremoniously placing honey on the tongue of the child."

"In the mountains, they use honey to feed infants to supplement milk," Carlos added.

Robin looked at the infant squirming in the blanket beside Maria.

"What do you think?" asked Robin.

He took my lack of protest in a moment of uncertainty as agreement and lowered his finger to the infant's mouth, touching his upper lip with the honey. The child responded by jutting his tongue out toward the amber offering. Encouraged, Robin continued and lowered his finger to the child's mouth again, and the infant eagerly began sucking.

"It's working!" Carlos declared triumphantly.

Robin seemed mesmerised by the child's eagerness to accept his offering. "A new king is born." The child continued feeding from his finger.

I checked the temperature of the water that now had the myrrh droplets dissolving in it. It wasn't too warm. I was eager to get to helping Maria now that we felt the child was being reasonably cared for despite the bizarre maternity setting. I took the cup across to Maria, swirled the contents, and poured some of the myrrh water over Maria's nightgown to wash away the blood. She stirred.

"Maria! Your child is born. It's a boy," Robin piped in.

Maria was conscious enough to be aware that something was moving in the crook of her arm. She looked at the child and smiled.

"Maria! What's the child's name? Tell us," Robin encouraged enthusiastically.

I remembered how important it was for Robin to learn the child's name.

Maria made a single sound. "J—"

She passed out again before completing whatever she was about to say.

"Maria?" Robin could see that she was not capable of continuing. "Did you hear that? Was it a J?" he asked.

"It could have been a G. It's the same sound," Carlos said.

"Holy shit. It could be."

"She could have been saying, 'just give me a second,'" I added, knowing that would likely confuse Robin even further.

"No! We need a name," he pleaded to the roof of the cave.

I looked at Maria, who now looked like a slumbering angel with her little gift from God huddled beside her. "Well, for now, we need to get Maria and her unnamed child to a hospital."

Chapter 22

We filled our water bottles from the pool. The agreement was that I would carry Maria for the first half hour. Robin carried the swaddled child while watching for a signal on his phone. Carlos carried my rucksack on his chest and his own on his back. He couldn't see his feet because of the extra load, and we frequently heard him say "ouch" as he kicked or bumped something protruding from the forest floor. We planned that if any of us fatigued, we would rest and rotate the respective loads. At the end of a half hour, I had to admit I was struggling with carrying Maria's limp weight, despite her diminutive stature. I checked both the child and Maria for life signs. Both were seemingly okay. We rotated, and Carlos took over carrying Maria as he was probably the strongest out of the three of us, and I carried the two rucksacks. Robin used the opportunity to place the child on the ground and take off his long-sleeve shirt, leaving only his collection of necklaces on his bare chest.

"I thought you'd have a tattoo for every religious icon in the world," I commented.

"There'd be too many. Every time I consider getting a tattoo, I can never decide which symbol is more important to me. So I haven't even started."

He lifted the bundle of amulets sitting against his chest with his palm. "What you see here isn't even a fraction of my collection of symbols. You should see my apartment back in Louisiana. It's a shrine dedicated to every faith in history." He tied the shirt around his waist and lifted the child again.

We continued on, and it was my turn to yelp every time I kicked something solid that I couldn't see, which I did frequently.

It was about an hour later that Robin declared he had a signal on his phone. We called the police in Buritaca. They gave us the number for the hospital in Santa Marta. The phone was on loudspeaker, and Carlos, the most fluent in Spanish, described the situation to the emergency department nurse, whose name was also Maria. Her reply was difficult to comprehend because of the staccato effect of poor reception. She had to repeat herself at least a dozen times so we could put together different words from the multiple exchange efforts. The gist was that they were going to send a helicopter. But to where? We were somewhere in the thick Colombian jungle. We agreed that the best thing for us to do would be to press on to the main road outside Buritaca. At least there was a decent opening there, and the signal would be stronger to communicate further. We estimated we had another hour of walking ahead of us. It was likely how long it would take to get a chopper to the area, anyway. Carlos believed that the support would come from Bogotá or Medellín, and they were hundreds of miles away.

Carlos elected to keep carrying Maria. He was clearly a lot stronger than I was. I urged Robin to carry the bags, and I took the child and phone. I was happy to save my toes, which were now fairly beaten up. Robin was lighter on his feet than Carlos and I were. He didn't stumble or bump into anything once on the remaining journey. Growing up in the wetlands and having to jump tree roots and rocks probably had something to do with his inherent agility, despite not being able to see the ground at his feet. I felt as though I was the weak link in the trio with my underdeveloped aching limbs and city-boy stubbed toes.

Carlos's phone in my hand pinged with a message. It was instructions on how to send our location using the phone GPS to the hospital emergency team. Once we were close to the road, a helicopter landed in a tussock beside the Troncal del Caribe, only fifty metres from where we entered the forest. A man in a hospital first-aid outfit jumped out of the helicopter. He unbuckled a stretcher that was strapped to the fuselage and ran with it toward us. After brief introductions that none of us could quite hear because of the sound of the thrusting rotors, Carlos lowered Maria, still unconscious, onto the stretcher. He took one end of the stretcher, and the first-aider took the other as he beckoned for Robin and me to join them. We huddled together around the stretcher, crouched down as instructed to protect Maria and her child from the helicopter wind. Carlos elected to stay behind. He took the rucksacks and moved out of the spinning rotor range. Once we were all securely in our seats, and they fixed the stretcher to its cradle, with Maria strapped to it, we lifted rapidly. I held Maria's tiny child in my arms as we headed out high above the waves folding over the Caribbean coastline to the Ernesto Cortissoz Airport in Barranquilla.

The chopper ride was short and fast, and the airport was a twenty-minute drive from the General Hospital of Barranquilla. The risks being taken by the ambulance transfer driver to combat traffic were hair-raising, likely adding further life-threatening risk to Maria and her child. A team of doctors and nurses met us at the emergency entrance, and they quickly wheeled Maria and her tiny child out of sight behind the flapping doors of the emergency wing corridor. There wasn't much more for us to do except find a room in Barranquilla where we could get some rest and await the outcome. I left my mobile number with the receptionist and walked with Robin down Calle 30 toward the Plaza Del Pescado, where we were told we could find suitable accommodation.

We found a twin share on Carrera 38 that was close to the hospital. We both crashed early that night once we'd had a feed at the KFC up the road. I was expecting to be happy to tuck into some familiar flavours, but I found the opposite. The experience left me keen to return to Buritaca where I had been discovering where to find the best fresh local food. I received a call from the hospital the next morning. Maria and her child were stable, and we could visit.

They permitted hospital visitors at nine, so that's when Robin and I returned. We sat silently beside Maria's bed as she slept. I felt so relieved that she had survived the ordeal of birthing her child in a cave. The nurse reassured us she was encouragingly well, with no concerns beyond exhaustion and mild dehydration. She had a saline drip attached to her arm. I felt a sense of déjà vu from when Maria had sat beside my bed in similar circumstances, waiting for me to wake up after my donk to the head. Maria stirred, and we both jumped out of our chairs to her bedside. I took her hand.

"Maria?"

"Where's my baby?"

"He's in a humidicrib just down the hall."

"What's that?"

I didn't know the Spanish translation. "It's a neonatal intensive care unit."

"A what?"

"A special bed for delicate babies."

"Oh."

"You're both lucky to be alive," I said.

"Because of you, my lion."

Robin rolled his eyes and then pressed Maria for what he desperately wanted to know.

"Maria, we need to know the name of the child. You began telling us in the cave."

"I did? I don't remember."

"That's quite okay," he reassured her, although his agitated body language didn't match the sentiment. "What's the name of the child?"

Maria paused for a moment, clearly struggling to remain cognisant.

"I don't know."

"What do you mean, you don't know?" Robin asked.

I was about to tell him to settle down, but he reined in his own horses.

"I don't know. Gabrielle didn't tell me."

"Would you like to name your baby?" I asked, trying to be helpful.

"It's not my choice. None of this is my choice," she reminded us. "Gabrielle must name the child."

"Well, could you ask him?" Robin asked, a little too eagerly.

"Her," I corrected, "but I think you need to back off, Robin. She's been through a lot. She might remember with some time and rest."

"I'll try to remember, I guess," she told Robin supportively.

"Get your strength back first," I said. I took her hand in mine. "There's a little man you need to meet."

I pressed the buzzer that the nurse had shown me earlier for when Maria awoke. She popped her head into the room and saw Maria attempting to sit up in the bed. I smiled and nodded to the nurse. She reappeared less than five minutes later, pushing a humidicrib. The child was within.

"My baby! Can I hold him?" Maria exclaimed in Spanish, tears filling the creases at the corners of her eyes.

"Soon. Very soon," the nurse said, also in Spanish. "He just needs to be in a special environment for a little while longer."

Maria shot a nervous glance my way.

"He'll be fine. He's a strong little one, they tell me."

Maria's nervous expression persisted, so I attempted distraction.

"You missed Christmas by four days, though. Your little Christ was early."

"Actually, now that you mention it, he was exactly on time," Robin corrected.

"How do you figure that?"

"The twenty-fifth of December was the solstice date two thousand years ago, the longest day of the year. That date was a pre-Christian recognition of the birth of the new season, celebrating the sun god. The literalist Christians turned it into the birth of the son of God. December 21 is the solstice now. Our little unnamed Sun God, or son of God, was right on time."

Maria turned to me and beamed the brightest smile, which charmed my heart. Sun God or son of God were points of discussion that were not for me to worry about. Seeing Maria happy and healthy was all I needed.

"By the way, I finally have a sample of the water from your secret pool."

Robin looked at me quizzically.

"We filled our water bottles below the waterfall. Now I can find out if your spring of life is something in the water."

Maria smiled warmly again. That smile remained etched in my brain.

Chapter 23

They kept Maria and her unnamed child in the hospital for the next month as she and her child both gained strength. Her little boy was putting on weight nicely. There was a moment of alarm regarding his lung function that seemed to sort itself out. Maria was expressing milk, and she was eager to feed and bond with her new son. The doctors were still cautious about the child's premature birth, and so they adopted a mix of assisted feeding and nursing from Maria.

Despite all her efforts, Maria could not seem to communicate with Gabrielle. She suggested that maybe she could only speak with Gabrielle telepathically while the child was inside her. Now that the child was out, the communication would only be between the child and Gabrielle. This frustrated Robin immensely, as he was desperate to learn the child's name to give him a mythological context. Maria refused to name the child, saying it was Gabrielle's choice. This meant that the child would likely remain nameless until he could speak and name himself.

I hadn't seen Maria for a week. As I walked down the corridor of the hospital, I heard raised voices coming from Maria's room. From what I could tell, Maria was arguing with her father, Gustavo, in Spanish.

"Come back to Buritaca. Our church is not collecting donations from the people here," Gustavo roared. "And this hospital room, all to yourself, is costing us money."

"I don't want to! And the baby is not ready to leave!" I heard Maria counter vociferously.

I knocked on the closed door, and the cacophony from within halted instantly.

"Come in!" Maria called out.

I opened the door to see Sylvia standing beside Maria's bed, holding a plate adorned with a bright green birthday cake. She had mastered the art of smiling cheerfully to hide underlying discomfort. Robin was sitting on a chair in the room's corner. Obviously, he hadn't understood whatever kerfuffle had been transpiring before I entered, as his chair was the furthest point away from the bed that was possible in the small room. Gustavo stood at the foot of the bed. His face was still ruddy from yelling. Cards, flowers, and gifts, likely from her village friends and adoring followers, cluttered the room. Maria was sitting up in the bed, nursing her unnamed child.

"Maria, I can't afford to keep paying for this hospital bed. You must come home," Gustavo insisted.

"There's plenty of money in the Church of Gabrielle now," Maria challenged with an uncommon softness that was probably to avoid disquieting her child.

Gustavo must have felt outgunned in the current battle once I was in the room to support his daughter. He barely acknowledged my presence as he manoeuvred around me to leave the scene he had just created. Silvia lingered awkwardly for a moment and then put the cake on Maria's bedside table and followed her husband. She gave me a kiss on the cheek as she walked past me to the door. Her eyes held a lingering gratitude that her lips could not utter.

"How is everyone?" is all I could think of to say to disrupt the heavy veil of conflict.

"I'm good," Robin said.

I was sure he was still stewing about the absence of child-naming, though.

"Fine. How are you?" Maria said.

Her spirit was clearly elevating with every second since her father left the room.

"It's nice to get some work done again," I said. "I'm a lot closer to discovering what's causing the telomere elongation in the cell samples of the locals."

"What?"

Maria had a cute way of scrunching up her nose when she wanted to convey that I wasn't making any sense to her.

"I think I may be closer to working out what's helping people live longer here."

"Something in the water." She winked confidently.

"Yes, in fact, it's potentially something in the water. I worked it out, thanks to Robin, actually."

"Really?" Robin chirped, breaking out from his sulkiness.

"I was looking for an isolated botanical. You talked of bringing people together. You gave me the idea to do the same with the botanicals I'm studying. On their own, they have minimal influence, but when working together, it magnified the benefits. It's known as a compounding effect. And it's an effect that can occur when botanicals mix naturally in the local water."

"So Maria bringing people together may have the same compounding benefit?" Robin added, showing no interest in the biological value of my findings.

"Yes, perhaps."

"So what now?" Maria asked, making more of an effort to appear interested or impressed.

"I need to confirm my test results and then give them to the drug company, Pravus."

"And then they patent the formula, harvest every plant needed in the Sierra Nevada, and then sell the plants back to the people who already get the compounds for free," Robin chided.

"This way, more people, not only the locals, can benefit from the compounds."

"At a price," he challenged.

"I heard about Gustavo being concerned about his church's income," I said.

I thought changing the topic was necessary before I started feeling guilty about the impact of my research.

"He won't let the people see me for free."

"You know, the people have been waiting a month to see this child. Maria is stronger now. The child will cope. Have you seen the number of people camped out there?"

Robin pointed to the curtained window. Maria jumped out of the bed and walked across to the window, still cradling her child. I couldn't help but notice how completely Maria's body had recovered from her pregnancy. Through her flimsy hospital gown, I could see that her petite and nimble frame had returned, and she no longer looked like she had swallowed an inflated beach ball. She peeped through the curtain. Truly thousands of people were outside. I was already aware of Robin's revelation, as I'd had to drive past them to visit Maria.

"There are so many." She looked at me. "There's more and more every day."

"Robin, can I speak to Maria alone for a moment?"

"Sure."

He smiled at Maria to reassure her that the crowds of adoring people were perfectly okay. He headed out the door as I sat on the edge of the bed.

"Maria, I need your permission to take a tissue sample from your child. It will show if there is anything special in his genetics."

"You're always so serious. You know it's my birthday today."

"Yes, I know."

I reached into my pocket and pulled out a little red vinyl gift box. Maria trotted across the room toward me to see what I offered. She eagerly snatched the box from my hand.

"Happy birthday." I smiled as she popped the lid open.

She squealed with joy as she held up the gold pendant attached to a golden linked necklace. She looked at the embossed symbol in the centre of the ornament. "Is that an M for Maria?"

"Great minds think alike. It's actually the symbol for Aquarius. I'm doing my best to go with the flow."

"It's beautiful. I'll wear it forever!" she said as she fumbled with the necklace clasp.

"Here, let me help you."

I held out my hand, and she dropped the necklace into it. She spun around and lifted her hair to reveal her slender neck. I reached around and clasped the necklace latch, and the pendant dropped to sit in its new home on her chest.

I was sitting on the edge of her bed that was lowered to allow for little legs, so I wasn't towering over her as usual. Our faces were almost level, so I leaned forward to kiss her cheek. She turned back toward me, and our lips met. Our kiss lingered. Her lips tasted sweet. It was a moment in time that left a monument in my heart. But as usual, I withdrew, awkwardly conflicted.

"Maria."

"Yes, Leo?" she whispered, perhaps hoping for a sweet suggestion.

"The day you were to meet Pablo. You had a bruise on your face. I have seen you with a similar bruise on your face. Did you really just fall that day?"

Maria made no mistake of showing her disappointment as she looked at the floor.

"No."

"What happened?"

"I was on my way to meet Pablo." She continued to gaze at the pale beige tiles below her bare feet. "My father stopped me and asked where I was going. I told him where and that Pablo was seeking money from me."

"Did your father hit you?"

Maria nodded.

"My father was furious. Perhaps about the money. I'm not sure. He told me to go home and that he would deal with Pablo. I did as he said. I don't know what happened after that, I swear."

"Is that why you asked me to take you away from here?"

Maria cried in soft sobs that built as she tried to find the courage to continue.

"He hurts Mamma too."

"Is that why you say you need to take care of your mother? Do you feel you need to protect her?"

Maria nodded. Her tears began falling to the tiles before her toes. I pulled her in close to me and hugged her as she buried her face into my shoulder and wept. She held her little boy between us, the eyes in his upturned face observing his anguished mother. Before this moment, I had been preoccupied with worrying about what I had gotten myself into. From then on, I could only concern myself with Maria's safety and wellbeing. If she had asked me if I loved her at that moment, the answer would have been on my lips in a heartbeat.

I held her for what was probably a lot longer than what I remember the moment to be. Holding Maria in that hospital room might be the most cherished memory of my entire time in Colombia. I could feel her heartbeat calming and slowing as she recovered from the painful testimony. Her breathing became less and less disrupted by her gulping back her sobbing.

I reached into the other pocket of my jacket and pulled out one of the swab kits I stored in my lab.

"May I?"

"Of course."

I took a tissue sample from the child's gums. He didn't seem perturbed in the slightest by the gentle massaging of his gums with the swab. I sealed the sample in a small plastic vial that was just over the length of the swab stick.

"I have to go," I said, because staying any longer would probably have invited trouble.

"Okay. But before you go, I have a birthday cake I want to share with you."

She pointed to Sylvia's cake on the table. I smiled as I wondered how Sylvia had created such an iridescent green icing for Maria's cake. It was the same colour as the bums of all the ants you see in the area, which had me jumping to conclusions that we were about to hook into an ant-bum flavoured dessert.

"Sure."

Maria placed her child on the bed and picked up the knife that came with her lunch tray. She cut two hefty slices, revealing a double sponge cake with a generous layer of cream in the middle. She propped herself on the bed beside me, and like two naughty kids, we ate excessive portions of birthday cake together. The cake was delicious, and it didn't taste of ants.

"You know how Robin talks about the birth of the Age of Aquarius?" Maria asked through a mouthful of cake. "Did you know that my star sign is Aquarius?"

"Of course it is." I smiled.

"There's more."

"Why am I not surprised?"

"Robin told me that our star signs have an opposite. One that helps us to stay balanced. For Aquarius, it's Leo."

"You know this all could just be just coincidence?"

"You're really struggling with all this, aren't you, my lion?"

"Shut up and eat your cake."

Chapter 24

Buritaca was looking a lot more like the village I first encountered when I arrived in Colombia. Maria's oration stage was possibly the only distinguishing new feature. It had seen no action since that day Maria had taken off into the jungle. She was still in the hospital with her unnamed baby boy, and most of her followers camped there in the available surrounds. The Barranquilla municipality was likely overwhelmed by becoming the sudden campground of thousands that came to their city overnight.

I wasn't sure if the Vatican representatives were still in the village or in Barranquilla to be close to the action. There were no visitors allowed for Maria and her holy offspring beyond those who were authorised. I believe her guest list only included her family, Robin, and me. I'm not sure how the cardinal would have appreciated not making the VIP list to visit the new Christ.

The Manichaean approached me with his entourage on the street outside my lab.

"Hello," I said and greeted him with a respectful bow, my palms meeting in front of my chest.

The Manichaean and his followers all bowed their greeting. I wasn't expecting much conversation in accordance with the Manichaean's reputation for being a man of few words.

"Hello, Leo," the Manichaean said quietly with a thick Chinese accent.

His entourage looked at each other with unabashed astonishment.

"I hear you don't say much," I said, just as surprised that he had said anything at all.

"No words. Thirty years," he whispered.

It was obvious that his vocal cords had had little practice over that time. He spoke like someone testing out a new skill, slowly, deliberately, and with concerted concentration.

"You clearly have something you want to say to me."

The Manichaean looked at me squarely. "Boy dead."

"Pablo?"

The Manichaean nodded.

"How do you know?"

The Manichaean turned his attention to the lush Sierra Nevada slopes that towered in the distance.
"Birds tell," he said.

I followed the Manichaean's gaze. I could see birds circling in a valley that divided the mountain range.

"Okay," I replied, taking a moment to register what the Manichaean was pointing out to me. "Can I ask you a question?"

The Manichaean nodded.

"Do you believe the boy is the new Christ?"

I thought I would make the most of the fact that he was speaking with me.

"Hmm." He brought his palms together in the same manner as our greeting. "Boy in deep water."

It wasn't the answer I was reaching for.

"Drowns or learns to swim," he continued.

I had to think about the Manichaean's cryptic answer for a moment.

"It's up to him?" I asked, seeking clarification. "It has to be more than that, though, doesn't it? You and I don't need to decide whether we are the new Christ."

"We not in deep water." This is all he said regarding the matter.

"One more thing," I added, now that we were chatting so candidly. "How did you find out about Maria? Was it in a dream or meditation? Something that would help me understand all this?"

The Manichaean reached through the gaping sleeve of his gown to a hidden pocket and pulled out a cell phone.

"Internet."

"Huh." Again, not what I was expecting.

The Manichaean smiled warmly and bowed again. He walked away with his team, who also bowed respectfully as they walked past me.

Carlos's Jeep was outside the lab. I figured there was no time to waste following up on the Manichaean's shared insight. I entered the lab. Carlos was mixing botanical preparations and dripping the solutions onto agar plates.

He nodded. "Hola."

"Hola, Carlos. I need you to come with me. I think I know where Pablo is."

"Really? Okay."

"Can we take your Jeep?"

"Sure."

We jumped into his 4X4 and headed into the jungle. We followed a dirt road that led to the coffee plantations, high in the mountain's escarpment. It didn't take long until we were traversing the road cut out of the steep incline of the valley. As we pressed on, I caught glimpses of the birds circling high above the dense forest canopy. When they appeared to be as close to directly above us as possible on the narrow track, I asked Carlos to stop. He cut the engine, and without the engine's diesel roar, we heard the birds squawking.

"This way." I pointed down into the valley where the calling was the loudest.

The steep ravine was tough to traverse, and we had to climb down using tree trunks and rocks as anchor points. Some birds that had made their way down through the woodland scattered noisily as we approached. It wasn't too long before we came across what appeared to be the body of a young boy. The boy's clothes were haggardly ripped and his flesh torn away in chunks. It was a horrific sight. Large black vultures had been feeding on the unfortunate lad. If the boy had jumped from the road, he could have landed where we found him. The same if someone had thrown him this way from the road. Carlos rushed at the remaining birds menacingly to shoo them away.

"Loro Santo," he whispered as he took in the macabre scene.

I pulled out my phone and approached the body just close enough to take a photo whilst fending off the birds. I thought it would be a good idea to send it to the police to show what we had discovered. We were deep in the forest gully, and unfortunately, there was no signal.

"I'll stay here. You go get the police," I offered as a solution to the situation.

I guess it was about an hour that I spent waving my arms and bashing sticks against tree trunks to keep the vultures at bay. The more eager birds perched just outside my swing range and screeched their disapproval at me by opening their sharp beaks widely, distorting their already ugly wrinkled faces that were completely devoid of feathers. They flapped their long black wings and stomped their feet on the branches in defiance of my efforts. The stench of the decay was choking, and I felt as though the odour was sticking to my skin, which was damp with sweat from the hanging humidity in the valley.

When Carlos arrived back with the police, the two officers shimmied down the hillside just as we had, and Carlos remained on the road. I stepped back, and they examined the body as they shielded their nose and mouth from the malodour. The first policeman put on a set of latex gloves and inspected the hands of the boy, still intact. The other police officer turned to me and addressed me in Spanish.

"So you think it's the missing boy?"

I had only seen Pablo twice. The ravages of the vultures and the fall had left his face terribly mutilated. Only deep blackened sockets, stained by congealed blood, remained where his eyes had once resided. The dimensions of the body were correct, however, and the hair looked the same.

"Sí." I nodded.

Chapter 25

The police asked me to run DNA tests on the tissue samples they found under Pablo's fingernails at the crime scene. I probably had the only genetics analyser in the entire Magdalena Department, and as I was using Sanger sequencing, it was probably the best quality equipment in the area. The samples matched Gustavo's swab sample. He had offered a sample willingly to the police, perhaps not fully aware that the samples might be incriminating.

I didn't discuss with Carlos the details of what the police suspected, but we stood together and watched at a distance as they led Gustavo in handcuffs from his family home into a police car. The genetics test suggested only that Pablo likely had a fight or incident with Gustavo. The tissue under Pablo's fingernails could have just resulted from a scuffle between them. It wasn't helpful for Gustavo's case that we found the body on the road between the coffee farms and the village. If Gustavo had killed Pablo and then dumped the boy's body in the jungle on the way to work, that wasn't a well-thought-out plan. I couldn't help but think of Gustavo's often repeated assertion that he would do anything for his family. Pablo could never have imagined that the consequence of Gustavo's commitment would leave him dead and ravaged in a gully. I wondered if the Manichaean's insightfulness included an understanding of events that had led to the poor boy's demise.

"Does Pablo's mother know about this?" Carlos pondered as he watched Gustavo being shoved into the back seat of the white police ute.

If not for the distinct green stripe and the word Policia written on the doors and windscreen, the vehicle looked more like a farmer's battered work vehicle.

"I don't know," I answered honestly, which worried me.

I approached the police officer, who was heading toward the driver's seat of the vehicle. I recognised these policemen, and I knew they did not speak English, so I worked out how to phrase my question in Spanish on the way.

"Excuse me, constable. Has anyone contacted Pablo's mother?"

"Yes, but she is in the Barranquilla hospital."

"The same hospital as Maria? Why?"

"A car hit her daughter," he answered matter-of-factly. "She is in a coma."

I had to process the information for a moment. What on earth was going on in Buritaca? Was it an accident or a deliberate attack against Pablo's family? Was the incident attached to Pablo's death in any way?

"Oh, no! Can you call your people in Barranquilla?"

What if Pablo's mother also linked the incidents? If she knew Gustavo was the primary suspect, she might have been considering vengeance.

"Maria may be in danger."

The officer didn't seem too concerned about Maria's potential predicament. He jumped in his seat, started the engine, and simply nodded as he drove off. I ran back to Carlos and repeated my concerns. He reached into his pocket, pulled out his car keys, and threw them to me.

"You had better get there as soon as you can," he said. "The police were probably not interested. Everybody's life is in danger living in Colombia."

That wasn't reassuring, but I took the offer of driving his truck to Barranquilla. I had a three-hour drive ahead of me and didn't want to waste any time.

By the time I arrived at the hospital, more had occurred than I could have possibly anticipated. I signed in and raced to Maria's room. I pushed open the door without announcing my arrival and stood in the doorway, heaving to catch my breath. Maria was sitting in an armchair beside her bed, breastfeeding her child. My entrance alarmed them both, and the boy cried.

"What the hell, Leo?" Maria exclaimed as she consoled her child, who was happy to return to feeding.

"You're okay?"

"Of course."

"I told the police to put a guard at your door."

"Yes, that was stupid, and I told them to leave."

"But you could be in danger. Pablo's mother is here. We found—"

"Leo," Maria interrupted, "I know what happened. It's okay. I am in no danger. Let me explain..."

She opened her mouth, but before she could utter a word, Mrs. Sanchez, Pablo's mother, entered the room and pushed past me. She stood in the space between Maria and me. I didn't know what to do. I would have tackled her if she made a move to hurt Maria, as adrenalised blood was still pumping furiously through my veins.

Oddly, Maria smiled warmly at Mrs. Sanchez, as though she had expected her. Mrs. Sanchez did not spit on the floor, which was my second hint that something odd was going on.

Mrs. Sanchez turned to me, which is when I saw she had tears streaming down her face. Her expression was soft and gracious. She turned back to Maria and approached her submissively. As she reached Maria's armchair, she dropped to her knees and took Maria's hand, pressing it solemnly to her lips.

"It's a miracle," she said in Spanish, as her tears escalated to outright crying.

Maria withdrew her hand from Mrs. Sanchez's embrace and reached forward to touch her face, drawing her forward to her chest in much the same way that she had embraced her followers at her air-baptism events.

Mrs. Sanchez kissed the back of Maria's child's head, who was still feeding, and whispered, "Loro Santo."

I was completely dumbfounded.

I looked at Maria. "What have I missed?"

"Leo, could you please get Mrs. Sanchez a chair so she can sit with us for a moment?" Maria asked.

I shrugged. "Okay."

I picked up the other chair in the room and offered it to Mrs. Sanchez, who accepted it with a grateful smile. I sat on the edge of the bed, bridging the space between them.

Maria explained to me in English what had transpired in the time it had taken me to drive to Barranquilla. Mrs. Sanchez clearly couldn't speak English, despite her nodding in agreement with everything Maria had to say.

According to Maria, the events unfolded as follows.

Mrs. Sanchez was sitting beside the bed of her daughter, who was in a coma. Maria entered, carrying her child. Mrs. Sanchez stood abruptly at the sight of Maria, shaken and alarmed. She started to spit on the ground, but stopped. Perhaps the habit wasn't fitting for a hospital setting? Maria addressed the distressed mother in Spanish.

"Mrs. Sanchez, I heard you were here with your daughter, Angela. I just wanted to see if there is anything I can do to help."

"How dare you come here? My son is dead, and now my daughter is in a coma because of you and that child."

"We don't know that your son is dead," Maria said.

"They found his body in a gully beside the road that leads to the coffee plantations."

Maria gasped.

"They have charged your father with murder," Mrs. Sanchez continued, eager to share her grief with Maria.

Maria shuddered at the news.

"Oh, Mrs. Sanchez. I am so sorry. I didn't know..."

"Get out, you witch!"

Maria turned to leave. Her child reached his arm out toward the bed. Maria turned back to Mrs. Sanchez with an idea.

"Mrs. Sanchez, believe what you want about me, but you cannot deny the miracles occurring around my child. You need a miracle right now."

Maria approached the bed with her child.

"Don't you dare touch my girl," Mrs. Sanchez threatened.

"I promise you, I will not."

Maria lowered her baby boy toward the bed. The child continued to reach out, and he touched the hand of the comatose girl. Maria then left the room.

I was now up to speed with events. The story should have offered me comfort, but it only disquieted me.

"Is this what you want? Thousands of people expecting miracles from you?" I blurted out without really thinking about tactfulness.

"What does it matter what I want? It is what it is."

"Then taking you away from all this simply won't be an option anymore," I said out of my untamed need to protect Maria and her child
from a future of bizarre and anachronous attention. "Choose what you
want for you and your child."

Mrs. Sanchez may not have understood our conversation, but she
detected the tension. She stood and took my hand.

"Ven conmigo," she said and beckoned me to follow her. She held
my hand all the way down the hallway. We entered the lift, continued
along another corridor on a different floor, and arrived at a room where
we found her daughter sitting up in bed, smiling at the sight of her
mother's return.

I thought it best to leave the hospital. My mind was so full of conflict regarding the future of Maria and her child. Did she realise what
she was getting herself and her child into? People wake up from comas
every day. Mrs. Sanchez's daughter waking from her coma minutes after
Maria's child touched her could have been a coincidence. But I was
quickly losing faith in any skepticism I held regarding the possibility
of miracles.

Chapter 26

The town of Buritaca seemed to transform again overnight into a holy child information centre. Every business in town, including the science lab, was inundated with public and press enquiries about Maria and her child. Most businesses deferred the interest toward Barranquilla. I was more inclined to shrug off the enquiries as the last thing Barranquilla needed was more influx of curious onlookers and devotees.

Another person who was quick to dismiss any questions about Maria and her child was Mr. Sanchez, Pablo's father. I had never met him, but Carlos pointed him out to me as he walked down the Via Buritaca like a man drained of life. I heard it had been his responsibility to identify Pablo's mutilated body.

I explained to Carlos what had happened regarding Mrs. Sanchez. It was to her credit for not blaming Maria and her child for the heinous acts of her father. Irreconcilable loss brings out the best and the worst in people. Mrs. Sanchez flipped from anger and resentment in the face of losing one child to compassion and gratitude in response to regaining the life and health of her other child. They found no ill intent regarding the car accident involving her daughter. She simply stepped out onto the Troncal del Caribe from behind a parked lorry that had obstructed her view of the road. The truck couldn't brake quickly enough to avoid the unfortunate accident. The spontaneous resolution of the trapped inflammation in the girl's cranial vault, which had caused the pressure on her brain and the coma, had the hospital staff baffled.

As expected, news of the Sanchez recovery spread through the hospital like wildfire. Her coma was as good as dead, according to the highly infectious narrative, and stories of Maria's child being able to raise the dead were rampant. The campground of followers grew louder with their chanting of Loro Santo. The miraculous event and all the associated circumstances even made international news. Our little snowball of events had become an avalanche. The airlines had flights to Colombia booked solid for the month. Ships carrying passengers across the Caribbean were wait-listed at the docks between Santa Marta, Barranquilla, and Cartagena, unable to find space to unload the hordes of people wanting to meet Maria and her holy child. Robin had arranged a holy room or healing room in the hospital for the hospital residents, who were eager for a miraculous recovery from their ailments. He was taking bookings for individual and group healing sessions. I heard of all this while I was in Buritaca. Gabrielle was still missing, and the lack of communication with Maria only added to the speculation as to the clandestine whereabouts of the parrot. I could only imagine the frenzy occurring in and around the hospital in Barranquilla.

I'd left the hospital on an uncomfortable note with Maria. I figured the exponential international interest in her escapades was likely resulting in her needing proportionate additional support, although I couldn't imagine how things could escalate beyond the already extraordinary circumstances.

The drive to Barranquilla took twice as long as usual due to all the traffic heading the same way. They had decorated their cars with flags, scarves, stickers, and banners, all declaring devotion to Gabrielle, Maria, and her holy child. The honking of horns and cheering and chanting from cars, motorcycles, trucks, and buses loaded with people removed any doubt as to the destination of the passengers.

I arrived in Barranquilla in the late afternoon. I had to show ID to a policeman at a barricade on the outskirts of town to gain access to the hospital. The arriving masses of vehicles were parking wherever they could, and the tsunami of alighting people continued toward the hospital on foot.

Inside the hospital, I found Maria in the holy room or healing room. There was no sign on the door, but I knew they referenced the room as both. It was much larger than her hospital bedroom and even had a small balcony that offered a view of the city. Maria was sitting in an armchair in the middle of the room. She was wearing a sleeveless white cotton dress embroidered with religious iconography, including images of a girl with a child and a parrot. I assumed it was a gift from one of her devotees who was talented in stitchwork. Her child, wrapped in an ornate and colourful handmade swaddling cloth, lay across her lap. There were several chairs lined against each wall. Robin appeared to be ushering people to particular chairs. Perhaps this was the queue for audiences with Maria? Maria was facing the door and noticed me arriving. She waved eagerly, beckoning me to join her, then stood and strained on her toes to kiss my cheek.

"Thanks for coming, Leo. I know you don't totally agree with this."

"It's up to you, really. I have no say in the choices you make for yourself and your child," I replied, feeling that the words I chose made me sound aloof.

"That's not true. Your opinion means the world to me. You know I rely on you."

Her emotional maturity only made me feel even more stupid for trying to distance myself from the events of her life. When scientists feel awkward, they retreat into the safe zone of scientific discussion.

"You know, I now have a tissue sample of the child. Through a process of elimination, I can determine who the father is," I suggested, likely making the situation worse. "We need to know," I added with an air of self-justification. Perhaps the drive had been longer than I thought, or I was too tired to consider being more civil?

Maria's face became ashen. "Protect me and my baby," she said with an edge of urgency. "I'll give you what you want."

I felt a rush of discombobulation. What *I* want? What did she think it was that I wanted from her? The truth? Affection? Her love? I no longer knew what I wanted from this beautiful young woman who was being hailed by thousands locally and possibly hundreds of thousands globally as the mother of the new Christ. Her statement stumped me and left me too embarrassed by my considered options to ask her what she meant. I realised that, in my mind, I hadn't articulated that question or a viable answer to it. So much of my effort was simply responding to what appeared before me. I hadn't asked myself why I was doing as I did. All the events involving Maria—feeding her, supporting her, sleeping in the same bed as her, saving her, and even kissing her—were just submissions to her will. What did I want from being so involved? I was making myself giddy overthinking her simple offer. I diverted again to my safe territory of denial of tricky emotions through a focus on scientific discussion.

"Maria, you have to be honest with me, because I will find out. Do you know who the father is?"

Robin approached, perhaps saving me from whatever hole of confrontation I was digging with Maria. He nodded to acknowledge my presence and then turned his attention to Maria.

"Are you ready?" he asked eagerly. "There are thousands of people out there looking forward to their first glimpse of your child. They've waited a long time for this."

"What if I disappoint them?"

"You won't. I promise. Just do as I instructed, and you'll be fine." He headed toward the balcony.

"I'll test the microphones."

I hadn't noticed that there was a microphone stand perched in readiness on the balcony. I quickly surmised that the room served two purposes. It presented as a space for devotees to meet with Maria and her child, and it also offered an oration platform where Maria could address the adoring masses who eagerly anticipated the first glimpse of their new Christ. Robin's last phrase caught my attention. When Robin was effectively out of earshot on the balcony, I squatted before Maria, taking her hand.

"Maria, did Robin teach you how to channel Gabrielle?"

Maria dropped her head, and without uttering a word, she nodded.

"Did he teach you the breathing baptism technique?"

Maria nodded again.

"And the healing technique?"

"Yes, that too. He was only trying to help," she added in a defensive tone. "I was so scared. I didn't know what to do."

I pressed on with my questions. If Maria wanted my advice or opinion, I needed to know exactly what was going on.

"How did you choose who would likely heal themself or not? It seemed so random. Or did Gabrielle decide?"

"I think I am part of the choosing. Robin taught me to assign a number to each person. A one or a two. A one was a healing, a two was no healing."

"So how did you choose who was a one and who was a two?"

"I would look for a sign. One bird flying past, two people sitting together, one person wearing a hat."

"Really?" I asked her, clearly flabbergasted by the simplicity of the method.

She nodded again. I thought for a moment about what else may need some explaining.

"What about the insights you shared with the audiences? You've offered very precise instructions for spiritual development."

"That's all Gabrielle."

"What do you mean?"

"It's like I get out of the way, and Gabrielle speaks through me."

I thought a moment about Carlos telling me about the radio receiver analogy. Perhaps it was a similar concept?

"Do you know how the painting of Our Lady of Guadalupe appeared on your front porch?"

"Honestly, I don't know how that happened."

The more questions I asked, the more it showed Maria was doing her best to keep up with people, forces, and events that had evolved from her declaration to her parents of Gabrielle's alleged prophecy. I knew I hadn't started the conversation well, and Maria appeared to be attempting to be completely honest with me regarding every detail that had transpired since her declaration. It was the declaration itself that still had me stumped. What was the truth? Who was the father? Was it really divine intervention? The international attention that had descended on the situation and the extraordinarily enormous crowd gathered below her balcony that extended possibly to the fringe of the city beckoned a celestial solution to the question.

I held her hand in both my hands and looked at her squarely. "Maria, what you say and do today will influence your life and the life of your child forever. It will be like the biggest "one versus two" decision of your life. If you choose One, you go along with everything Robin is setting you up for. If you choose Two, you tell the people that this has all gone too far and you want a normal life for you and your child. Please think long and hard before you go out there. If you go along with this, your life and the life of your child can never return to normal. Do you understand?"

"Yes."

I could see that the discussion of responsibility was making her anxious. She rocked backward and forward in the familiar manner she would do when she used to feed Gabrielle, and it was also the behaviour that preceded her dialogues with Gabrielle.

"Are you okay?"

"Yes," she mumbled, perhaps preferring to find comfort in her ritual than in speaking.

"I need to speak to Robin for a minute."

Maria just nodded and continued her rocking as she looked at the child in her lap. I looked to the balcony, and Robin was heading back inside from whatever he was checking out there. I headed across to him.

"Can I speak to you in private?"

"Sure."

I walked with Robin out of the room, and we stood in the hallway together. I decided I should just cut to the chase regarding what I wanted to discuss with him.

"It turns out that someone likely stole the painting of Our Lady of Guadalupe from the Santa Marta Cathedral," I said.

"Yes, I heard. And returned safely too."

"Why'd you do it?"

"Do what?"

"Do I have to spell it out? You're the only person who has what you called your comparative mythologist VIP pass. You said that with it, you could get into any church. So one last time, why?"

Robin looked like he was about to continue acting out, but then he clearly changed his mind.
"Because the people needed a miracle to seal the deal. With Maria in the middle of a scandal regarding the disappearance of Pablo, and with Pablo's mother and the spitters, it could have gone either way."

"So you fabricated a miracle?"

"No! I just borrowed a painting. It turns out that in doing so, it reinforced the belief in miracles."

"So you just approached the priest with your pass and asked him if you could borrow his painting?"

"Don't be silly. The Cathedral's sacerdote leaves the key to the church under a paver behind the enclave. There's no alarm system. It was just too easy."

"I don't get it. Why do you need this so much that you would do something as stupid as that?"

"You wouldn't understand."

"Try me."

Robin shifted uneasily. He clearly hadn't prepared for the possibility of having to explain his motives and actions. "Millions believe the last Christ walked the earth two thousand years ago. Historians keep adding challenges to the authenticity of some writings regarding the life and events of this Christ as they collate more insight into the period." Robin paced the floor before me as he gathered his thoughts on the topic. "People are losing faith or are creating random offshoot religions that they believe literally, and then everyone just argues over their supposed version of 'facts.' Do you know there are now over 450 different translations of the Bible? It divides Christianity into hundreds of sects and cults. Islam is becoming more divided and regimented with time. There are so many gods and goddesses in Hinduism, and the literal-minded followers just bicker over which one to venerate the most. Maria and her child are bringing all these people together. All of them."

"I know you taught Maria the channeling and the rituals."

"Yes! And there's so much more I have to teach her. With her absolute innocence, her child believed to be the new Christ, and me as their guide, we can bring peace to the world. We are harming no one. It is purely a matter of intention to unite the world with an understanding of transcendent consciousness."

I struggled to get my head around the impact of Robin's method and ideology. "It's more than that." I pointed to the room that was now dedicated to Maria and her child. "It's Maria's life and the life of her child that your fantasy is affecting."

"This isn't a fantasy. It's a reality you are uncomfortable with simply because it doesn't conform to your scientific methods. Your work may help people by selling longevity botanicals in bottled water. The owners will be rich, and you will have to consider the fame your discovery will attract to you." He paused for a moment to let that sink in. "This is free. It's for everyone, and you cannot put it in a bottle."

"But you're making it all up!"

"No, we're not," he retorted. "You're just uncomfortable because you can't measure what's going on here using a microscope, and you can't bottle it into standardised doses."

I didn't know how to react to his accusation. Maria had already caught me off guard by suggesting I could have "what I want." Perhaps Robin was hitting the same buttons. What *did* I want from my work? Did I want to classify everything that affects us using scientific method? The method they taught me was reductionism, where you keep isolating everything to measure effect. What Robin was suggesting was entirely the opposite.

"I'm sorry," Robin continued. "I don't mean to belittle you or your work. Everything and everyone has their place. What you are doing is important. But so is this." He thought for a moment. "This is qualia."

"What?" I had never heard the term.

"Qualia. It's the effect of directed consciousness. In this case, on a massive level. It's the power of subjective consciousness, faith, and intention. Something a scientist cannot measure or perhaps even understand. It is what you dismiss as 'placebo.' Yet no drug on the planet has greater therapy than what your methods dismiss as a scientific nuisance."

"So now you're admitting to deception by using a placebo that has no actual effect?"

"No, Leo, you're not listening. You call it placebo, and you believe it has no effect. I am calling it qualia, and I am assuring you it has a phenomenal effect."

"How can you know that?"

"I have documented evidence of hundreds of people who have experienced genuine healing from this experience with Maria and her child. And these are only the ones I know about. There are likely many more."

I knew the stories, and I had witnessed many of the transformations. There were far too many to be coincidental. Oddly, I felt a little threatened by my lack of comfort with the possibility of this effect being real. I knew well that what scientists call placebo often outperformed drugs and therapies for measurable benefit in trials, even when the drugs were the best available to treat a condition. I continued to feel uncomfortable with the phenomenon Robin was asking me to embrace.

"You said it yourself. There will be those who will want to hurt the child if they feel threatened by all of this."

"I'll take care of her. I promise. Most of the spitters have jumped ship now, following Mrs. Sanchez's lead."

"Yes, but if the one story in the Bible that concerns me is true, you need only one person to betray the Christ."

"Fair point." He slapped my shoulder encouragingly. "Don't be that person."

"I didn't mean—"

"I know."

Robin headed back toward the room. I wanted to call after him and remind him I didn't think he understood the full extent of what he was doing. But I stopped myself. Perhaps it was really me who didn't understand the potential value of what he was doing. I caught myself digging my nails into the crease of my elbow where my eczema lingered.

I followed Robin back into the room, as I genuinely wanted to see what was about to occur. I did my best to promise myself to keep an open-minded perspective. What was it that Maria was going to say to the crowd? What had Robin prepared for her? Maria, as usual, greeted my return with all the warmth and appreciation she could muster.

"I want you to be out there with me. Is that okay?"

"Of course." I smiled reassuringly.

I offered her the crook of my arm, and she jumped from her chair and wrapped her free arm in with mine. Robin winked at me with an encouraging smile. I guess he knew how I was feeling and that I was doing my best to keep up and be supportive, despite my concerns for Maria and her child.

As we approached the balcony, I saw they had set it up with multiple microphones. Some sported international news branding that I recognised. The closer we moved toward the balustrade, the more apparent it became how packed the square below was, with thousands of people all looking up in the same direction at us. Across the highway and into the streets behind, the sea of heads continued far into the distance. Onlookers billowed out of balconies on the adjoining buildings. They crowded the rooftops too. Maria caught her breath as she moved forward to see over the balustrade. It must have been an extremely daunting moment for her. Just as she could see the populace, they saw her. The crowd reacted with cheering and thunderous applause. Maria appeared completely overwhelmed. I could feel her trembling return. I put my hand on her arm that was interlocked with mine and gave a gentle, reassuring squeeze. She looked at me with the wide-eyed anxiety that I had seen so many times as we had confronted whatever challenge lay before us. This was going to be yet another. She then looked at Robin, who nodded with a gleam of determination in his eye. Maria took this as a signal. What had he instructed her to do? Whatever it was, it was about to happen. Maria smiled at me with a hint of rising confidence as she withdrew her arm from mine. She unwrapped her child. I instinctively stepped back, like I had done at the stage back in Buritaca, when Maria was about to channel Gabrielle. As tiny as she was, these moments seemed to demand space for her to do whatever grand thing it was that she was about to do. Her child lay bare on the swaddling cloth, and she tucked her spare hand between the cloth and her child. Robin clearly expected this move, and he collected the swaddling cloth from Maria and then stepped back with it to give Maria space as I had. She looked again at me, perhaps seeking my approval. I instinctively took a deep breath and held it for Maria's sake as I had a flash of the Manichaean's comment about the child being in deep water. She raised the naked child above her head.

"Loro Santo!" she called out to the heavens above her child.

The crowd went completely wild.

In a powerful and unified voice, the people chanted, "Loro Santo! Loro Santo!" The volume was so intense that the sound of the chanting felt like it was rumbling like an earthquake through the balcony below us and reverberating through my chest.

"Holy fuck," I muttered under my breath.

Robin must have heard me. He turned to me with the most gleeful expression that you would normally expect of a child at a carnival.

"Holy Parrot!" he corrected.

Robin pointed to the crowd. "Look at the people. Can you feel it?"

Everywhere I looked, everyone was hugging, kissing, and overtly expressing sheer joy. Part of me, perhaps my conditioned mind, wanted to resist Robin's invitation to join in the joy. But I silenced that thought. I could feel it. The collective's energy was empowering, unifying, and liberating. I think, in that moment, I could finally embrace the phenomenon occurring around me. I understood what Maria's role was with her child for all those people. A wave of relief flooded through my body, and the tension in my mind ebbed away. I winked at Maria as she beamed her beautiful smile my way. She sighed deeply. I could see that my acceptance of her choice was important to her. She was radiant.

Chapter 27

Carnival in Barranquilla apparently originated as a pagan celebration to welcome the spring and celebrate fertility. As with many pagan ceremonies, when the Spanish colonised the Americas, they transformed the event into a Christian celebration that preceded Lent. When I asked about the meaning of this, the most common explanation given was that it was a time for repentance and an opportunity to seek a deeper association with God. I wasn't familiar with the act of repentance or the intention of seeking association with an invisible God and found it interesting that the festival may have been undergoing its next evolution of identity before my eyes.

Large, colourful floats rolled slowly along a wending circuit through the city. These floats were mostly trucks and cars decorated or renovated to create moving extravaganzas of light, sound, dancing, and singing. The progression was paced, and thousands of dancers, band members, and acrobats paraded their way through the city. They organised the participants into groups associated with a particular piece of music, and they would play or dance to the music being performed live or broadcast via huge speakers that were part of the floating infrastructure. Choreographed dancers in traditional attire would twirl, clap, and sing as they moved forward with their troupe. The piped music was often a fusion of contemporary sounds and tribal rhythms. The performers in these performances were likely to be clad in feathers and glitter, and the dance was more vibrant, wild, and energetic.

Festive energy filled the air. They constructed grandstands to line the main carnival thoroughfares and packed them with face-painted and feather- and garland-toting revellers. They sang along with the familiar tunes as the participants paraded past their viewpoint.

Maria and her child were on a float dedicated to them. They had decorated the truck to look like a giant parrot. Enormous eyes lay over the windscreen so the hidden driver could see the road ahead. Maria was sitting in an ornately decorated armchair that looked like it was riding on the back of the parrot. There was a woven basket beside her chair that was clearly a cradle for her child. She clutched her little man to her chest, which made it easier for the crowd to see him, as she happily waved to everyone that lined the surrounding streets. The wings were open platforms where dancers dressed as macaws danced and pranced as they waved to the crowd. They could hunch down and disappear into the plumage of the fabricated wings that matched their costumes, giving their performance a peek-a-boo effect where they would surprise the crowd by magically appearing from the wings of the parrot to dance and play, only to disappear again minutes later, ready to surprise the onlookers in the next stand.

I had positioned myself in the crowd on the edge of a grandstand. I could have taken part in the parade, but being amongst the spectators satisfied my desire for cultural immersion. The other blatant reason for my reservation to participate was the size of the parade. Most years, the parade is so large that it takes about four hours for the entire procession to make the tour of the carnival circuit. This year, they estimated it to be twelve hours. Essentially, the festival participation had tripled, and I wasn't keen to walk around the steamy streets of Barranquilla behind a truck for twelve hours. But just about everyone else wanted to be in on the act. Along with the usual Colombian parade, denominations of every religion you could imagine had a float or dancers or marching musicians with banners. It would be remembered as the largest carnival parade in modern history. There was a Muslim float adorned with a large Hand of Fatima. I couldn't help but notice the very expensive-looking Vatican float with Cardinal Antonio Vecci, dressed in ornate ecclesiastical attire, commanding centre stage. I had heard that the Vatican was still not willing to commit to acknowledging the unnamed child as the new Christ. But it was good to see they were at least willing to join the party. I enjoyed watching the hundreds of colourful Hindu dancers. The whirling dervishes were mesmerising as they gracefully rotated in circles, their white robes flowing out from their hips. There were a multitude of additional religions represented in the parade that I didn't recognise.

I stood with my arms folded on the rail, watching the dazzling spectacle flow down the road before me. It was obvious when Maria's troupe was approaching as the roar of the crowd crescendoed exponentially when they spotted her and her child. Maria saw me and eagerly waved and gestured for me to jump the rail and join her on her giant floating parrot. I smiled and waved back, but shook my head to let her know I was happy to sit this one out. I was wondering where Robin was, as I knew he wouldn't be too far away from the excitement. One of the dancers surrounding the float on the road, wearing a loose cotton robe painted in the colours of a blue macaw and a parrot-faced mask, shimmied away from the rest of the dancers and headed across to me. He lifted his mask, and I was greeted by Robin's beaming smile. He was clearly in a state of euphoria as he almost leapt over the rail to embrace me. I hadn't before experienced such open affection from Robin. It suited the flavour of the day, so I threw my arms around him in return, and we danced a little jig to the music as we hugged it out. He was right. Maria and her child were having the undeniable effect of bringing people together. If it even allowed him to get an enthusiastic hug out of me, I could now appreciate what he was referring to as the essence of what he called "qualia." In this instance, the power of mass-directed consciousness toward the spirit of unity and celebration.

It was a well-timed carnival, as Maria had been discharged from the hospital a week earlier. To prevent the extraordinary horde of people from following her to Buritaca, where they would have overwhelmed the tiny village, Robin publicly announced that Maria had requested that people stay in Barranquilla to prepare for participation in the carnival.

It was a clever move, but only a temporary remedy, because after the carnival, Maria returned to Buritaca, and half the population of Latin America followed her.

It's a good thing that the land on the other side of the river, opposite Buritaca, was essentially hectares of open pasture. Overnight, it became an extraordinarily well-organised tent city. It amazed me how they could accommodate the needs of tens of thousands of people, but they somehow managed. They delegated volunteers for various tasks, which included cleaning the toilets, maintaining the water supply for drinking and showers, and rubbish removal. They performed all tasks diligently, and the place ran like clockwork.

Maria's stage was no longer in the village. The devotees reassembled it on the opposite side of the river, also on the beach. It faced the open beach and the river behind it so that the audience on the beach could literally extend for as far as the eye could see along the dunes. This new arena was next to the tent city, which took a lot of pressure off the village to house or hold such an inordinate influx of people who were eager to be near their new Christ.

Maria's procession to the stage from her home now headed out of Buritaca toward the Troncal del Caribe, where the bridge was sturdy enough for her and the massive procession that followed her to cross the river and head down to the beach on the other side. Each day, she walked through the different paths of the tent city to give the devotees the best opportunity to see her and the holy child on their way to the stage. Daniela and her travesti guards did a great job of keeping the adoration away from Maria's home, where Maria attempted to live a semblance of a normal life with her child and her mother. They also directed the movement of her devotees, the media, and curious onlookers, so they were not too imposing on Maria as she moved through her fields of fans to reach the stage.

Maria sat with her child on the stage. She no longer relied on the "Loro Santo" chant to channel Gabrielle. The chant had found a new role as an opening ritual to set the mood or energy of the event as people moved into the open arena before the podium. With everyone seated, or at least present, Maria replaced the chant with the "I am" breathwork. It continued to amaze me how eerie it was to hear so many people declare "I am," in a variety of languages, during an inhaled breath. Many of the devotees had a word, given to them by Maria, to complete their phrase on exhalation, and they did so silently, per their instructions from Maria. I began convincing myself that I could tell who had gotten their word from Maria, their expression of sublime ecstasy betraying their higher knowledge of self as compared to others. People lined up for a free opportunity to meet Maria and to touch or be touched by the child. Robin diligently recorded all the names of those seeking an audience with Maria and her child, noting the copious claims of healings.

By remaining unnamed, the child was being called "the nameless." According to Robin, this was the best possible option. He argued that our names and labels only limit us. I had to admit, he was doing a great job of guiding and supporting Maria.

As I approached Robin, he looked up from his ledger and smiled broadly. He eagerly leapt to his feet.

"Guess what?"

"What?"

He started unbuttoning his chequered shirt. He must have had quite a collection of them, as I hadn't seen this one before. As he opened his shirt, he revealed an image below the bundle of icons dangling from his neck.

"I got my first tattoo!"

He opened his shirt fully to show me that right in the middle of his chest was the image of a large circle that served as a perch for a parrot. The parrot's body filled most of the ring, and the tail trailed off to the left, below it. The large, brightly coloured bird appeared to be holding a jagged stick in its mouth. As I focused on this, I recognised it was not a stick, but the wavy lines that depict the age of Aquarius. These lines extended to the edge of the circle.

"Nice. It looks like the symbol of a superhero. Is that what you are now?" I teased.

"We all are!" he responded. "Go find out for yourself." He nodded toward the stage.

Participants continued, as previously, to kneel in front of Maria. They received their word from her, whispered in their ear. Maria said she was confident that she could continue her role this way without the guidance of Gabrielle, as she was conscious when she was receiving Gabrielle's instructions. She assured everyone she could continue the process unaided.

Maria looked up. I was the next participant. I knelt in front of her. Was I ready for my word? There was only one way to find out. The child's hand reached out to me. I took it gently in mine. Maria tenderly touched the top of my head, drawing me forward, and whispered my word into my ear. I hugged her warmly, just as every other participant had. Determined to engage in the experience, I turned to the audience, taking in a long, drawn breath.

The sound of "I am" rattled through my vocal cords.

Then, with my arms open and palms facing forward, I breathed out. In my mind's eye, I repeated the word, imagining it was a gift I was sharing with the world. Daniela then directed me off the stage, taking my arm the way close friends walk together. I looked back and saw that Robin had followed me onto the stage and was standing next to Maria. His shirt was still open, showing the impressive image of Gabrielle he had inked onto his chest. He put his hand on her shoulder and beamed. I was still close enough to hear their conversation.

"Try not to look so pleased with yourself," Maria chided him. "You have your own healing to confront."

"What are you talking about?"

"When was the last time you spoke to your father?"

Before Robin could answer—not that he appeared to be gearing up to say anything—a commotion in the crowd drew everyone's attention. A group of people, carrying something cumbersome, appeared to be making their way to the stage. People needed to move out of the way for the group to proceed, and this resulted in a cacophony of shouted instructions. I needed a moment to snap out of the moment of levity I had experienced from the ritual I had just completed. Once I felt I had regained my senses, I turned back to the stairs and quickly retraced my steps to join Maria and Robin. The elevated perspective allowed for a better view of what was happening. The group was carrying an elderly woman on a makeshift stretcher made of bamboo poles and empty coffee sacks.

I turned to Robin. "We'd better find out what this is all about," I said and then headed down the stairs on the other side of the stage, closest to the group. Robin followed.

We excused our way through the tightly packed onlookers to meet the group a few metres away from the stage.

"What's going on?" I asked a woman who looked like she was in charge.

"Señor Leo." It seemed everyone knew me as Leo. She continued in Spanish, "My name is Gloria. I am the nurse for Mrs. Martinez. She does not speak. She cannot. Sometimes she mumbles. But for three days, she has called out one name—Maria."

"Why can't she speak?" I queried.

"Demencia enfermedad," she responded.

"What are you hoping for?"

"Un milagro, Señor Leo."

The woman on the stretcher was clearly catatonic. I hadn't seen her move the entire time she was being escorted through the crowd. A cream-coloured crocheted pillow supported her head, and a brown woollen blanket buttressed her fragile frame on the coffee-sack sling. She was wearing only a simple knee-length cotton bedgown.

Robin took Mrs. Martinez's hand. There was no response to his touch. "What do they want?" he asked me.

"A miracle," I replied. A chill ran down my spine as I realised I knew the name. "Is this Doctor Martinez's wife?" I asked the nurse.

"Sí," she replied, pointing to a person who lingered at the back of the crowd. I recognised the man's slumped posture. Dr. Martinez looked at his feet, just as he had in the courtroom. He stood away from Maria's followers, but his identity was made obvious by his white coat and the role-defining stethoscope slung around his neck, the ends of which dangled over his chest. The events of the courtroom came flooding back in a deluge of doubt. I desperately tried to remember how long ago the hearing had been. I calculated it would have been just under a month ago.

"Has he authorised bringing his wife to Maria?"

"Sí, Señor Leo."

"It's a trap!" I exclaimed to Robin without attempting to restrain my angst.

"How?" Robin replied, looking for clues of my suggestion in the unresponsive lady on the stretcher.

"He's setting Maria up. He needs evidence of illegally practicing medicine or harm, and he's using his ailing wife as bait. That's why he's looking at his feet. He knows that what he's doing is wrong. I don't trust him."

Robin took a moment to contemplate my allegation. He stood on his toes to observe Dr. Martinez, who still hadn't looked up at us once. "Or perhaps he is exhausted and has a defeated spirit?" he countered.

"What kind of miracle could you possibly expect when she clearly has catatonic dementia?" I added, defending my interpretation of the unfolding events.

"I guess we'll have to find out."

"What if something goes wrong? He'll blame Maria, and she'll end up in jail."

Robin could see that I was quite distressed by the possibility of Maria ending up in jail as a result of a sly misrepresentation of her willingness to help others. He placed his hand gently on my back and ushered me back toward the stage. "Let's speak to Maria," he said.

I repeated my concerns to Maria, and Robin seemed to have gained confidence to support the opposing view in the time it took him to climb the stairs. Maria looked at Mrs. Martinez on the stretcher and then across to her husband, who continued to look only at the ground before him. The unnamed child reached up and grasped a lock of her hair. It was an innocent act, but enough to convince Maria to permit the stretcher bearing Mrs. Martinez to be brought to her. With her spare hand that wasn't cradling her child, she waved to the stretcher bearers, welcoming them and giving permission for them to come up onto the stage. The ocean of faces parted, creating a clear passage for Mrs. Martinez to be brought forward. Guided by Gloria's instructions, the six men supporting the bamboo poles carefully shifted the weight between them so that the stretcher would remain horizontal as they alighted the stairs. As they approached Maria, Robin, and I instinctively stood back to allow them as much room as possible before Maria.

The men gently laid the stretcher on the ground and stepped away toward the recesses of the stage. Mrs. Martinez's face was so drawn and withered from years of inactivity that she barely appeared to be alive. If not for the faint sign of breathing under her bedgown, I would have checked for a pulse.

Maria rose from her chair and knelt down beside the woman. She parted her knees and placed her child in a sitting position before her so that the child was within reaching distance of Mrs. Martinez's expressionless face.

She looked up and called out to the crowd, "Please, pray with me!" She breathed in deeply, uttering the single word for *I am* in Spanish, "Soy..." and then breathed out with an expression of focused attention that was typical of the ritual. Everyone in the arena, onstage and off, joined in the breathing in unison with Maria. I opened my arms just as I had when Maria had shared my word with me. I wanted to take part, and strangely enough, I felt wonderfully comfortable participating.

Once again, I felt enthralled by the impact of the sound of the harmony of the uttered prayer and the reverberation I felt within my chest as I repeated the phrase in union with possibly tens of thousands of people. Knowing how to finish the sentence was oddly empowering. It felt right.

The unnamed child giggled and squealed aloud, perhaps in response to the chanting that offered a unique vocal contribution distinct from the collective efforts around him. He clearly wanted to touch Mrs. Martinez, whose prostrate presence before him captivated his attention. Maria was holding his torso now with both hands, and she eased him forward just enough for his fingertips to brush the woman's sullen skin. The stroke of his hand across anyone's cheek would draw attention, so I watched tentatively for any reaction from Mrs. Martinez. Nothing. She just lay silently, continuing to respire with shallow consistency in stark contrast to the bellowing lungs around her offering prayer.

What happened next took us all by surprise. For the entire procession, Mrs. Martinez had lain with heavy eyelids that shielded her eyes from view. Her lids shot open, revealing milky brown eyes scarred with cataracts and encompassed by gnarled, dark crimson blood vessels. Her head fell to the side toward Maria and her child in a way that resembled the final collapse of a dying soul. The crowd fell silent in a softening wave as more people realised something had happened. I watched intently for signs of life within the frightful eyes that stared blankly toward the child, who didn't seem perturbed by the vision before him. Maria froze at the sight, and this allowed the child to break free of her grasp. The tiny boy plopped forward with arms outstretched so that his hands fell on Mrs. Martinez's face, one on her chin and the other on her forehead. Mrs. Martinez then vomited a creamy white liquid. The spontaneous projection splashed Maria's child in the face. She pulled him away, as his underdeveloped musculature would not have allowed him to do it himself. The boy took a deep breath and wailed out a startled cry that resounded loudly from the stage. Gloria leapt forward, producing a cloth from her pocket, and squatted at the head of the stretcher. She blurted out apologies in a flurry of Spanish.

"I'm so sorry! This is not unusual. I should have said something. Mrs. Martinez cannot always hold her dinner." She began wiping the liquid from Mrs. Martinez's face. Then she looked at Maria's boy and gasped as though her patient had just defiled a sacred monument. "Dear God, I am so sorry..." she continued. The cloth in her hand was now wet with vomitus and not an option to clean the boy's face. Maria lifted the frill of her own cotton dress and used it to wipe her son's face. She said nothing and just responded to the situation with pragmatic proficiency as she made cooing noises to calm her distressed child. Once her boy's face seemed reasonably clean, and his shrill cry became an ebbing sob, she reached forward to touch Gloria's arm.

"Everything happens just as it is intended," she reassured Gloria in Spanish.

Gloria ushered the stretcher bearers forward to lift the stretcher again to escort Mrs. Martinez off the stage. I looked across the sea of faces who were eagerly seeking a glimpse of the action. Despite the calamity, Dr. Martinez continued to stare at the ground before him. Under the circumstances, I found his stoicism to be extraordinary. The crowd once again opened a pathway for the entourage, led by Gloria, to leave the area. They met Dr. Martinez near the road. He took his wife's hand as they continued carrying her away from the scene. The lack of indicators of alarm in the party surrounding Mrs. Martinez reassured me she must have still been with us, despite her inanimate appearance. I dreaded to think what Dr. Martinez was planning to do with what had just transpired and been witnessed by so many people. Was he seeking evidence against Maria and her child?

I looked back to Maria, who had returned to her chair and opened the buttons of her dress to allow her child to breastfeed. She gently rocked backward and forward, reminiscent of the motion she had repeated many times before her estranged companion Gabrielle. The crowd settled, and many even copied the gentle rocking action in their own expression of connection with the moment. I never asked Maria if she missed Gabrielle. I thought it would be a stupid question. Rumours abounded, speculating whether she was alive or dead, and if alive, the likelihood of her whereabouts. None of these offered comfort or closure. Maria seemed to openly surrender to the reality of Gabrielle's disappearance as she focused with unabating grace on her role to introduce her newborn Christ to the world.

Chapter 28

"You're really doing this?" Carlos enquired as he watched me pack up my belongings in the lab.

"Yes."

"But why? We're so close to confirming the botanical mixture that can extend life. How can you walk away now?"

I was packing at five in the morning so that I had enough time to drive to Santa Marta to catch my international flight home from Bogotá. It was a very early start, and I hadn't expected Carlos to show up for a farewell chat.

"I've decided that I don't think giving a drug company the patent on these compounds is going to do the world any good," I replied as I shoved my clothing into the bottom of my rucksack. Handling the bag brought back memories of our rescue effort for Maria and the birthing of her child. "If our research is truly showing that these compounds can extend life, Pravus will send in excavators. They'll destroy the region to harvest the plants and then charge everyone who wants to buy their product to live longer a fortune. Only the rich will be able to afford it. Everyone else will probably miss out."

"Then don't give it to them. Share it with the world," Carlos challenged.

"I can't. I signed a nondisclosure agreement with the drug company. They'd sue me. It's theirs or nobody's."

"But..." Carlos started to interject but fell short of a comeback.

I could see that he was about to blow a gasket out of sheer frustration, so I tried to ease the blow.

"For Pravus's sake, it's a good thing I keep my research under lock and key so nobody else can release the results." I looked toward the antiquated safe and waited for Carlos to follow my gaze. The door was clearly unlocked, with the door wide open. The stacks of papers detailing my research findings were virtually spilling out the door.

"Imagine if someone else, someone who doesn't have a nondisclosure agreement, were to reveal my findings? We couldn't have that. Could we?" I continued, giving him a wry smile.

He looked at the safe and chuckled under his breath. His frown instantly transformed into a beaming smile. It was obvious that Carlos genuinely cared about the people—his people—in the village and the surrounds. He really wanted to find a compound that would help them be healthier and live longer. If my image of his destiny had any tenability, he was going to become quite a compassionate drug lord.

"My friend, I have to ask..."

He looked at me, and his face returned to a more concerned appearance. I stopped packing and faced him.

"Yes?"

"Did you do a genetics test of the child to see if Pablo was the father?"

"Yes, I did," I replied flatly. I had wondered if he was going to ask me about this at some stage, and this was his last chance.

"And?"

"He's not the father. Asking Pablo to marry her was a panicked attempt to find a way out of her family's shame in response to her pregnancy. Instead of helping, he attempted to extort Maria."

I was glad he didn't continue with the next obvious question: Did I know who the father was?

My rucksack was as full as it could be, so I pulled down on the straps and clipped them into their cleats to close the bulging bag. I swung it over my shoulder and headed out the door. Carlos followed me out. It must have been around six in the morning, because the crimson hue of the dawn light was hinting its arrival low on the horizon. I expected to see a single star above the gravel road ahead, like a lantern hanging in the early dawn sky, leading the way to Maria's secret oasis. I turned to look at Carlos.

"It's not there," I commented with surprise.

"What isn't there?" he replied, peering down the road, following my gaze.

"The star. The one that led us to find Maria."

"Ah, yes. The Stella Maris. It's not a star."

"It isn't?"

"No, it's a planet. Venus. It's only the morning star some of the time. It's the evening star at other times."

"Really?" I must have missed that lesson in astronomy at school. "So, if it's not there all the time, we may not have been able to use it to find Maria?"

"Then it's a good thing it was there when you needed it to be."

"I guess so. What did you call it, other than Venus?"

"The Stella Maris. I think it's Latin. It means our lady, the star of the sea."

"Which lady? Venus?"

"No. It's known as the guiding star of the Virgin Mary."

I wanted to say something, but the words choked up in my throat as it flashed through my mind that everything we had been through had begun when I said yes to Maria and followed that star. Did she know the star wasn't always there? She found her way to the cave in the middle of the night without using the star to guide her. Had she shown me how to find her oasis using the star as a guide because one day I would need to know? Could random serendipity explain all these events? Or was it divine intervention, as Robin described, "providing opportunities for growth"? I felt challenged as I identified the poignant gravity of the moment. I was about to embark on my next journey without Maria or her guiding star.

The taxi I had ordered pulled up in front of us. He must have driven from Santa Marta, as the car was a shiny canary yellow. There wasn't a single car in Buritaca that was even clean, let alone buffed and polished. The driver wound down the passenger window of the vehicle and ducked his head down toward the open window.

"Señor Lumière?"

I nodded. He popped the trunk, and I threw in my rucksack. I was short on words, but at least I had it in me to give Carlos a hug. I reached into my trouser pocket and retrieved an envelope.

"Could you please give this to Maria?"

"Sure," he assured me as he took it from my hand.

I glanced down the road to take in one last look at Buritaca and burn an image of the lovely village in my brain. Despite the dim light of the early morning, I could make out the silhouette of a man standing motionless on the curbside. I recognised the distinct pose.

"Is that Dr. Martinez?" I asked Carlos to confirm my suspicions.

He shrugged. "I think it is."

"What on earth is he doing out here so early in the morning?" I asked, not expecting an answer.

An ominous silence emerged as we watched the motionless figure. I asked the taxi driver to wait a moment and then started walking toward the doctor.

"Dr. Martinez?" I called out to let him know I was approaching. I continued in Spanish. "Is everything okay?"

He lifted his head only slightly from his habitual stance. "Is that you, Señor Leo?" he replied in Spanish in a softly spoken voice without looking up at me directly. I was about to invite him to lift his head with a snide remark that I was constructing in my head in Spanish when he continued in his native tongue, "I apologise for my appearance,

Señor Leo. I have ankylosing spondylitis. My spine is now rigid with the disease."

I was aware of the condition, often referred to as AS, and how it could fuse the spine with hunched deformity. I realised he had not been rude by looking to the ground. It was all his body had allowed him to do.

"I didn't know," I said. "How is your wife?"

"She died about an hour ago," he replied with monotone directness.

A lump leapt into my throat. I couldn't leave because Dr. Martinez now had the ammunition he needed to gun down Maria. I dreaded the thought of Maria and her child spending years in custody or being embroiled in soul-destroying court battles with a rigidly minded, despotic opponent.

He strained to look up at me again, but failed. "She had not said an understandable sentence to me for maybe three years. I just cared for her, hoping that she was aware of my love for her. In the evening, after Maria's prayers, she returned to me briefly. She looked directly at me and said, 'I love you, your powerful will, and your commitment to me keeps me alive. This disease has damaged my body beyond repair, and it will no longer support my mind. It's time for you to let me go.'" He looked at the silver-faced watch that clung loosely to his wrist by a weathered leather band. That was about seven hours ago."

"I am so sorry for your loss, Dr. Martinez," I said while at the same time forming a line of defence for Maria in my mind to translate into Spanish.

"The last thing she said to me," he continued, "was, 'I ask one thing of you, my love. Let Maria's light shine. She and her child are a gift.'"

He wept softly and lifted his sleeve to wipe tears that were shielded from me by his crippled posture.

The taxi driver honked his horn to announce his preference to get going. Feeling pressured, I was direct. "So, your case against Maria?"

He turned and started walking away, signalling his preference to distance himself from me. His spinal affliction with AS had spared his hips.

"Se acabó." He pushed out the words loudly with effort. Likely a consequence of his stiffened ribcage.

I felt such a wave of relief flush over me that my knees almost buckled. I found my feet and headed back to where I'd left Carlos standing beside the taxi.

"What was that all about?" he asked as soon as I was in earshot.

"He's dropping his case against Maria. He said it's over."

I gave Carlos a bear hug, in part to say goodbye and in part to share my relief with him. I then jumped into the back seat of the taxi and headed out of the village down the Via Buritaca toward the airport.

Three hours later, I was walking in file with the other passengers across the runway tarmac. I contemplated that the moment may be my last experience of the Colombian Magdalena Department, at least for some time. The flight from Santa Marta to Bogotá was only an hour and a half, but it was enough time for me to gather my thoughts on everything that had happened and to reassure myself that I had made the correct decision. I sat in a window seat, which offered me the opportunity for one last view of the majestic, palm-strewn Caribbean coast as the plane ascended.

I had become the one person who could have potentially hindered Maria and her child from serving thousands, if not millions, of people. I'd seen the number of views on social media showing her introducing her Christ-child to the world. It was staggering how many people had tuned in around the world for the event.

I had learned something from this experience that my university training had completely overlooked: Know thyself—and you give healing a chance. This "knowing" is simply not measurable by science. Scientific method seeks to quantify and qualify effects. It is paradoxically not a great resource for answering the fundamental questions in life like, *who am I, why am I here, and how do I feel about my choices?* Everything my training taught me seemed to lead me away rather than toward these fundamental concerns of existence. I studied science because that was what I had to do to be a scientist. I researched telomere elongation in the Department of Magdalena because that was the job description assigned to me by Pravus. Pravus determined the value of the research, not me. I did not determine the value of my contributions, either. They did. I compared my actions with Robin's. I often based choices on curiosity without really giving much consideration to the intention I brought to every situation. Robin arrived in Buritaca with a purpose and an intention. He just required a particular circumstance to fulfil his vision. Maria and her holy child were the vehicle that Robin had spent his adult career preparing himself to drive. I genuinely believed that he intended to bring people together and that he would do his best to protect Maria and her boy, come what may. Maria's initial involvement was more akin to my own. Someone else, in her case a parrot, told her what her involvement would be. She accepted the instruction with expected trepidation at first. But the young woman on the balcony holding her child aloft for the world to see had embraced a purposeful destiny that she would likely uphold with fierce determination for the rest of her mortal existence.

That's why I lined up to discover my "word." Knowing thyself—or *gnosis*—was beyond the practical skills of my training. This was a harsh reality to confront. But I did. Since receiving my word from Maria, I had done the gnosis breathing ritual every morning. In a year of practicing this technique, my eczema had definitely improved. Was it a coincidence? Who knows? The practice also made it easy for me to give up smoking. In reflection, I think the habit was attached to anxiety. I had believed smoking to be calming. The breathing ritual, with its inherent self-awareness, seemed to negate the need and even the rationale for the cigarettes.

As for the identity of the child's father, I don't think anyone was ready for that knowledge. This is where my skill set had its advantages, but I couldn't justify its value. My genetic investigations led to the conclusion that Gustavo was the likely father of Maria's child. I suspect Maria had buried the event so deep in her psyche that a miracle was the only option left available to her. No wonder she would rock backward and forward, saying, "Today will be a good day." It was her way of suppressing the terrible memories that were violent or sexually abusive. It also explains how she found the forest oasis in what was probably an attempt to run away. But she then felt obliged to return to protect her mother. I figured that was why her dreams were so restless and tortured. Whilst sleeping, she was conjuring disquieting images of the abuse that she and her mother had endured. But Gustavo was in jail now, where he could never hurt Maria or her mother again. Maria asking Pablo to marry her was a panicked attempt to find a way out of her family's shame. It also explains why she was so eager for me to take her away from Buritaca when plan A with Pablo failed and eventually backfired. She needed a miracle.

I pictured the image of Maria sitting in her yard before her majestic parrot, Gabrielle. "Today will be a good day." It was Maria's desperate prayer for a better life, as every yesterday was a tragic memory of misery. And then she got her miracle.

I wrote to the directors of Pravus and explained that my findings concluded that the reason the telomeres in the community were so long and they lived such long, healthy lives was not because of some magical elixir but because of an absence of the usual elements that cause telomere and life shortening. I explained the science of free radicals and how we create them in response to oxidative stress. These reduce telomere elongation. Our telomeres shorten, and our life expectancy shortens with elevated oxidative stress levels. By living simple agricultural lifestyles, the inhabitants of the Department of Magdalena avoided the pesticides, herbicides, heavy metals, manmade radiation, and pollution that kills millions every year in industrialised nations under the umbrella of oxidative stress. They drank coconut water and not soft drinks. They ate fruit and vegetables rather than processed, packaged, and refined foods. The forest that surrounded them cleaned their air. Their water is pure and alkalinised by the plants and minerals that made their way into the waterways as they forged down valleys through the Sierra Nevada. I was looking for a compound that elongated telomeres, but what I ultimately found was a lifestyle that simply slowed their damage and breakdown due to lack of exposure to damaging environmental effects. The promising compounds I tested did not elongate the telomeres. They simply protected them against oxidative stress damage by creating a nutrient and antioxidant-rich, slightly alkaline environment for the cell cultures I tested. I could have revealed which were more effective, but ultimately, the results pointed toward a nutrient-rich, alkaline diet being healthy for longevity. In my letter, I concluded that unless the directors of Pravus wanted to go into the business of alkaline vitamin water, there was no profit opportunity for them in the Department of Magdalena.

Using my genetics analyser, I discovered Maria's unnamed son had particularly elongated telomeres. Was he somehow superhuman? I couldn't say. Essentially, we are all born with long telomeres, and they shorten over life. I had no other infant telomere samples to which I could compare his, so I had no baseline of expected telomere length in infants. I could find out. But did I want to?

I hadn't told Maria that I was leaving. Part of me judged this as being uncaring. The other part of me knew that she would have desperately sought to talk me out of it, and she probably would have succeeded. She would likely have assured me again that she would give me what I wanted. Such a statement of commitment coming from her again would've torn a hole in my chest. Everything about my experience with Maria showed me what happens when we seek to contribute in a way that is greater than our image of ourselves. Maria had discovered how to surrender to a significant cause or purpose for her life and the life of her child, regardless of how frightening that prospect may be for her. I saw how scared she could be, as she would rock backward and forward, trembling uncontrollably. But she stepped up anyway. And in doing so, with Robin's guidance, she was going to serve the world in the most profound way. In the note I left for her, I told her I thought she was the bravest person I had ever met. I wrote how I adored her with all my heart for being such a beacon of hope for the rest of us. Her influence inspired me to seek the same courage in myself.

That's why I had to leave. I had my life at home to sort out. Julia had clearly been in contact with Ruby regarding my visit. My phone had rumbled with the first sign of a signal in the taxi. Ruby had left a message. It stated simply, "Call me when you get home."

I had to forge my path, and it was going to require a lot of unravelling of limiting beliefs and values that had been ingrained in me through my education and social conditioning. Maria couldn't give me what I wanted. I had to give it to myself. She would have likely hated or at least resented me for a long time for making that choice. I simply would not have allowed myself to stay and possibly become the one person who could betray her and her child by revealing the findings of my investigations.

Finally, were my genetic investigations conclusive regarding the paternity of the child? Essentially, they weren't. If divine intervention conceived the child, Gustavo's genetic profile would still be within the child's genetic makeup, as Gustavo was the biological grandfather of the child. So Maria's declared version of conception, guided by a macaw called Gabrielle, remained on the table, and unless she or Gustavo confessed to sexual abuse, we could never know for sure.

Epilogue

The first thing I did, when my flight landed, was put on a jacket. It surprised me how cold the Melbourne climate felt compared to Buritaca. The second thing I did was call Ruby. It went well. We both acknowledged that we had a lot of healing to do. We found our way through the maze of regrets and misunderstandings to restore our relationship. I explained to my mother how disappointed I had been in her lack of support for my relationship and its consequences, that I needed and expected my autonomy. I understood her motivation, that it was essentially the fear of the unknown that drives a parent to protect a child with controlling and sometimes condemning behaviour. Perhaps I had grown from my experience in Colombia?

Back in Colombia, the whispers in the wind finally revealed that Gabrielle was alive and had become the surreptitious trophy of the drug baron Diego Antonio Rodríguez. The extravagant ranch of the baron was on the outskirts of the city of Macao in La Guajira. Despite being within the milieu of a desert, the ranch was apparently lush with palm trees and fertile fields of grass. Its location, about two hundred kilometres east of Buritaca, served its owner well, as it was close to the Venezuelan border. It was also within an easy commute to the Caribbean Sea. Apparently, Gabrielle refused to say anything despite all the drug baron's efforts to find someone who could make the holy parrot speak. Hearing Gabrielle declare, "Today will be a good day," had become the ultimate blessing in the minds of all who knew the legend of the heaven-sent bird. Gabrielle's silence had become a serious cause for embarrassment and consternation for the highly superstitious drug baron. I heard that the Manichaean and his team were on the case. They planned a stealthy rescue mission of Gabrielle. It would delight Maria to get her companion back, unshackle her from any perch, resume their feeding rendezvous. That would be a good day, for sure.

I also calculated how long it would take for every man, woman, and child to receive their gnosis "word" from Maria. If we allowed just thirty seconds per person, where Maria whispered every minute of every day, without rest, it would take her over seven thousand years to give everyone on the planet their special word. She had insisted we keep our "self-knowledge" word to ourselves. I figured she recommended this to avoid the risk of ridicule from those who only knew fear, justifying a tragic and disharmonious world. Robin's point stuck in my mind that there would always be "spitters" who sought to sabotage or even destroy the value of Maria-as-Gabrielle's teachings. It was a reminder that we must be careful with whom we share our true identity, as some may not be ready to hear it. So I'm going to share my know-thyself mantra here at risk of ridicule and judgement from the spitters in the world. To be honest, I believe everyone was being given the same word to complete their "I am" mantra. I believe that's why Maria was confident about continuing the ritual, despite her lack of connection with Gabrielle.

Every morning when I wake up, the first thing I do is find a space where I can sit quietly. I rock backward and forward, breathe deeply, and whisper Loro Santo to myself. I do this a few times because it reminds me of Maria, as I continue to miss her with every waking breath. It also helps me to invoke her spirit so that I feel she is present with me as I complete my mantra. Once I can visualise her sweet smile vividly in my mind's eye, and I feel connected with her, I then sit still. I breathe in deeply, to the bottom of my lungs, as I vocalise the words, "I am." I hold that breath and that thought momentarily. Then I exhale completely with all the conscious attention I can to add my intention and purpose of my word to the breath.

My meditation and mantra that I begin every day with is "I am love."

THE END

Angel A is an Australian author and filmmaker who shares insights and experiences of varied cultures through narratives that are compelling, inspiring and insightful. Mary Poser is Angel's first novel. Angel's award-winning passion for writing screenplays and novels reveals a richly diverse world of conflict, love and hope.

Holy Parrot is Angel's second novel. The first novel, Mary Poser: Butterflies and white lies as Bollywood comes to Nashville, received multiple international literary awards.

2017 Foreword Reviews Indies Book of the Year Award Finalist
2018 American Fiction Awards Winner.
2018 Best Book Awards Winner
2018 NYC Big Book Award Winner
2018 International Book of the Year Finalist
2018 Paris Book Festival Runner-Up.
2018 Readers' Favorite Finalist
2018 Independent Author Network Book of the year Finalist
2018 London Book Festival Honorable Mention
2018 BookViral Millennium Book Awards Long List
2018 New Apple Book Awards Official Selection
2018 Body, Mind, Spirit Book awards winner
2019 Independent Press Award winner
2019 New York Book Festival winner

www.angelsleap.com

CPSIA information can be obtained
at www.ICGtesting.com
Printed in the USA
BVHW041231221122
652522BV00005BA/131